Praise for

JOANNA WAYNE

"Joanna Wayne masterfully weaves a story
of dark secrets and unforgettable evil."
—*USA TODAY* bestselling author Karen Young
on *Alligator Moon*

"Lose yourself and your heart in the sultry
Cajun setting Joanna Wayne brings to life
in *Alligator Moon*."
—reader favorite Judy Christenberry

"Wayne creates compelling relationships and
intricately plotted suspense that will keep readers
guessing in this page-turning, heart-pounding read."
—*Romantic Times* on Harlequin Intrigue novel
Attempted Matrimony

Dear Reader,

Welcome to the sultry world of south Louisiana. As a lifelong Louisiana resident, I've always loved the romance and mystery associated with the bayou country and have been fascinated with the lore of the Cajun people. That's why when I got the idea for *Alligator Moon,* I knew I had to write the book. It's more than a story of suspense and romance— it's a journey into a world where alligators slither through murky bayou waters and passion rules the hearts and minds of the citizens.

This is John Robicheaux and Cassie Havelin's story, but it's much more than that. It's also the story of how decent people can become so caught up in a diabolical lie that it destroys them. But mostly it's a story of suspense that entangles the hero and heroine until they are forced to open old wounds and give themselves a chance to love again.

I love to hear from readers. Please visit my Web site at www.joannawayne.com. Or drop me a line at Joanna@joannawayne.com. Let me know if you'd like to receive my electronic newsletter. If you'd like a Joanna Wayne calendar for 2004, include your snail mail address.

Happy reading,

Joanna Wayne

JOANNA WAYNE

Alligator Moon

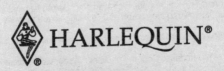

HARLEQUIN®

TORONTO • NEW YORK • LONDON
AMSTERDAM • PARIS • SYDNEY • HAMBURG
STOCKHOLM • ATHENS • TOKYO • MILAN • MADRID
PRAGUE • WARSAW • BUDAPEST • AUCKLAND

ISBN 0-373-83613-9

ALLIGATOR MOON

This edition published by arrangement with Harlequin Books S.A.

® and TM are trademarks of the publisher. Trademarks indicated with ® are registered in the United States Patent and Trademark Office, the Canadian Trade Marks Office and in other countries.

www.eHarlequin.com

Printed in U.S.A.

JOANNA WAYNE

is a multipublished, award-winning, bestselling author known for her cutting-edge romantic suspense. She lives with her husband just outside the steamy, sultry city of New Orleans, Louisiana, near the bayou country that was the inspiration and setting for *Alligator Moon*. A narrow bayou runs behind her house and most afternoons you can find her on the back patio, a glass of iced tea in hand, her fingers typing away on her laptop computer, enjoying the ducks, turtles, egrets and various other wildlife that share her domain. On rare occasions an alligator has even been spotted swimming by.

Joanna has always been an avid reader and she claims that writing her novels of romantic suspense was a natural progression from reading them. Not only is the writing exciting and rewarding, but also she loves the research. In the process of gathering material for her novels, she has rounded up cattle by helicopter, gone on trips deep into humid swamps, walked deserted beaches in the moonlight, visited morgues, looked through gritty crime-scene photos and visited FBI headquarters. And those are just a few of her research adventures.

Writing is more of a passion than a job for Joanna. She loves nothing more than taking a hero and heroine from breath-stealing danger to happily-ever-after. Who could complain about a day like that?

PROLOGUE

DENNIS ROBICHEAUX gave the propofol thirty seconds to work, then leaned over the patient. "Can you hear me, Mrs. Flanders?"

"Is she fully under?" Angela Dubuisson asked, not looking up from the instruments she was readying for the surgeon.

"Yeah. They can't resist my French kiss."

"Are we still talking about patients?"

"Now, boo, you know you can't believe all that trash they talk by Suzette's."

"That's not a problem since I don't hang out in smoky bars that smell like crawfish and grease."

"You don't know what you're missing."

"Sure I do. A bunch of drunks looking for an easy lay."

Dennis fit the endotracheal tube down the patient's throat, slowly, easing it past the relaxed muscles, the task almost second nature to him now.

Angela pulled the blanket over the patient. "How's she doing?"

"All that's left is to hook her up to Big Blue," he said, nodding toward the anesthetic machine. Dennis finished sealing the tube so that the patient wouldn't choke on her own saliva. "Down for the count. Where's our surgeon and his faithful nurse?"

As if on cue, the door to the operating room swung open and Dr. Norman Guilliot strode in, his hands still dripping from the sanitizing scrub. Angela became far more animated now that the self-proclaimed king of scalpel makeovers had appeared. She handed him a towel, then helped him into his gown and gloves. Susan Dalton was a step behind the doctor, her blue eyes dancing above her surgery mask.

"Got Ms. Ginny Lynn all ready for you, Doc," Dennis announced.

Dr. Guilliot leaned over the patient and pinched the excess skin beneath her chin, pulling it tight. "In for the works, isn't she?"

"Eyelid, face and forehead lift."

"Must have a sentimental attachment to the nose," Dennis said.

"She just wants to look her best for the glory of God," Guilliot said, mimicking the patient as he ran a finger under the delicate eye area. Ginny Lynn was the wife of the Reverend Evan Flanders, a TV evangelist who'd become a household word in the New Orleans area.

Dr. Guilliot lifted the fatty tissue above the lid, pinching and pulling it away from the eye before beginning the delicate task of marking his incision lines in blue.

Dennis monitored his machine. "Want me to make the initial incision for you, Doc, since Fellowship Freddie's off on his minivacation?"

"No, just stick to giving your Versed cocktails to the patient. The surgery has to be a work of perfection. We can't have any scars showing when she goes back under the bright glare of fame."

"I doubt Frankenstein's scars would show beneath the makeup she wears," Susan said.

"Careful," Dennis said. "You're talking about the Lord's anointed."

"What's the deal with Fellowship Freddie?" Susan

asked. "I never see him with a woman. Does he swing the other way?"

"He's got a girlfriend," Dennis said. "A real looker, way too hot for him."

"I guess you checked her out," Guilliot said.

"Me? Mess around with a friend's woman? You know me better than that."

Easy chatter, the kind you didn't get in a big city hospital. That was one of the reasons Dennis had jumped at the offer to work with Dr. Guilliot at his private clinic. Not only that, but he and the surgeon got along great. If Guilliot treated him any better, Dennis would expect to be in the will.

But the deal clincher for accepting the position had been location. The restored plantation house was practically in his backyard, and good Cajun boys like himself didn't like straying too far from home.

Angela moved in beside the doctor as he started the procedure. She'd been his tech nurse for twenty years, had come with him sixteen years ago when Dr. Guilliot had left his position as chief of reconstructive surgery at a New Orleans hospital and established the Magnolia Plantation Restorative and Therapeutic Center.

Like any good tech nurse, Angela worked like a seamless extension of the surgeon's arm. He reached, she was ready with forceps, scalpel, surgery scissors, lighted retractor or lap sponge.

"How are her vitals?" Dr. Guilliot asked.

"Blood pressure's down. Ninety systolic. I'll drop off on the gasses." Dennis turned the knobs, making small, precise adjustments. "How's the new Porsche?" he asked. "Had it full throttle yet?"

"Close. She's one sweet piece of dynamics."

"How 'bout I take her for the weekend and break her in the rest of the way for you?"

"Touch that car, and you lose an arm."

The chatter continued, from cars to fishing and back again. They were thirty minutes into the operation when Dennis felt the first pangs of apprehension. "Pulse rate is dropping," he said. "I'm going to inject a vial of ephedrine."

"What's the reading?"

"Fifty-five."

Dennis opened the vial, injected it through the IV line and watched the monitor, confident the ephedrine would kick in and do its job. The seconds ticked away.

"How we coming?" Guilliot asked without looking up from his work.

"Pulse and pressure not responding." Dennis opened another vial of ephedrine and injected it through the IV. "This should take care of it."

It didn't. The numbers continued to slide. Dennis's hands shook as he tore open the next vial and injected the drug. Still no change. Damn. There was no explanation for this. The woman was healthy. He'd read her chart.

Susan rounded the operating table, took one look at the monitor and gasped.

"What the devil's going on?" Guilliot demanded.

"Not looking good."

"Then do something, Dennis. I've got her wide open here, and I'm not losing a patient on the table."

Dennis hadn't prayed in quite a while. It came naturally now, under his breath, interspersed with curses as sweat pooled under his armpits and dripped from his brow.

Guilliot kept working. "Give me a reading."

"She's full code."

"Sonofabitch!"

Susan moved to Dennis's elbow. "Stay calm. You can do it. What else do you have?"

"Calcium gluconate." He injected the drug. Fragments of his own life flashed in front of him as if he were the one slipping away. The sound of his Puh-paw's voice singing along to his fiddle music on Saturday nights. The smell of venison frying in the big black skillet. The way Kippie Beaudreaux's tongue had felt the first time he'd kissed her.

The past collided with the present, all bucking around inside Dennis while the monitor continued to glare at him, daring him to defy it.

No easy chatter now. No reassurance. Just deadly silence. He turned to Guilliot. The usually imperturbable surgeon had backed away from the table, jaw clenched, looking totally stunned.

None of the glory. All of the blame. The role of the anesthetist. Dennis grabbed a vial of bretyllium.

Too little, too late.

"Oh, shit!" Angela shoved the instrument cart out of the way, jumped on the black footstool and started pumping on the patient's chest, hand over hand.

Finally Guilliot snapped out of his paralysis and took over for Angela, pressing the patient's heart between the sternum and the spine with quick, steady motions.

Dennis was so scared, it was all he could do to hold the long needle as he filled it with epinephrine.

Susan grabbed his arm. "Not intracardiac, Dennis. Not yet."

"Get the hell out of the way." Holding the needle in one hand, he grabbed the edge of the sterile drape with his other and ripped the fabric from the runners.

Guilliot stopped pumping as Dennis slid the point of the needle under the breast bone. The room felt small. Icy cold. Quiet, as if they'd quit breathing so that the patient could have their breaths.

They all watched the abnormal rhythm play across the face of the monitor, but Angela said the words out loud. "The tack."

Dennis snatched the paddles from the crash cart and stuck them to the patient's chest. The shock lifted her off the table, but still the monitor screen went blank.

Asystole.

Dennis administered the shock again. And again.

Finally Susan took his arm. "She's gone, Dennis."

"No one loses a cosmetic surgery patient on the table." Guilliot's voice boomed across the operating room, as if he were God issuing an eleventh commandment.

It changed nothing. Ginny Lynn Flanders was dead.

CHAPTER ONE

Six months later

CASSIE HAVELIN PIERSON stared at the sheet of paper. The divorce decree. All that was left of her marriage to Attorney Drake Pierson. She'd have expected the finality of it to be more traumatic, had thought she'd feel anger or pain or maybe even a surge of relief. Instead she felt a kind of numbness, as if the constant onslaught of emotional upheavals over the past year had anesthetized her system to the point that it was unable to respond.

She tossed the decree into a wire basket on the corner of her desk and went back to pounding keys on her computer. Almost ironic that the next word she typed was the name of her ex-husband, but he was all the news these days—him and his client's suit against Dr. Norman Guilliot.

Leave it to Drake to snare the hottest case of the year. Acclaimed plastic surgeon to the wealthy pitted against the best-known TV evangelist in the south. The locals fed on the details like starving piranhas on fresh flesh, but then New Orleanians always loved a good scandal. So did her boss. It sold magazines, and circulation numbers sold advertising.

The Flanders case had been the hottest news item going for the past six months, even beating out the young woman who'd accused one of the city's famous athletes of rape. The reverend was on TV every week, proclaiming the gospel according to Flanders and shedding tears over the wife he claimed had been lost to a case of malpractice by the famed Cajun surgeon. And somehow Drake had expedited the trial beyond belief to take advantage of the hype.

Cassie finished the article, hit the print key and picked up the phone on the corner of her desk to make another stab at reaching her dad in Houston. The president of the United States was probably easier to reach, but then the president didn't draw nearly the salary Butch Havelin did as CEO of Conner-Marsh Drilling and Exploration.

She dialed the number and waited.

"Mr. Havelin's office. May I help you?"

"It's Cassie, Dottie. Is Dad around?"

"I'm sorry. You just missed him again. Did you try his cell phone?"

"I did and left a message there, as well."

"I'm sure he'll get back to you soon, but if this is an emergency I might be able to track him down."

"No need for that, but thanks for the offer." She hung up the phone and slid her notes on the Flanders v. Guilliot case into a manila folder.

"You're looking glum for a Friday night," Janie Winston said, stopping by her desk. "Bad day?"

"No worse than usual."

"A few of us are going to Lucy's for happy hour. Why don't you join us? You can drink as much as you want and stagger home from there."

"Staggering through the warehouse district on a Friday night. Boy, does that sound exciting."

"Not only glum but sarcastic. Why do I smell a rat named Drake Pierson behind this mood? What's he want you to give up now, the sheets off the bed he shared with you?"

"Too late. I burned those after I found he'd brought the Tulane cheerleader to the townhouse to take her testimony. Besides, Drake is old news." She reached over, retrieved the decree and handed it to her co-worker.

"Over and done with. I'd think you'd be celebrating, not sulking. He really is lower than pond scum, you know?"

"Evan Flanders doesn't think so."

"Evan Flanders has visions of dollar signs dancing in his head. So, forget 'em all. Let's go get a margarita."

Cassie was tempted. She almost said yes, then spied the postcard propped against her pencil cup. "Actually I'm going shopping tonight."

"Buying something suitable for a hot divorcée?"

"Could be, or at least for a relaxing vacation far away from this humidity."

"Now that's what I call a divorce party. When are you leaving?"

"Immediately, I hope, if the airline will let me use my flight credits for the last trip I had to cancel."

"Does Ogre Olson know about these plans?"

"Not yet."

"That explains the glum. No way the guy is going to let you leave with the Flanders case going to trial in just two weeks."

"Only because he thinks the Pierson name in the byline carries some clout."

"You'll never hear him admit that. Clout might translate to an increase in salary."

"No, he'll use the usual bull. The timing couldn't be worse for *Crescent Connection*. I don't have the time blocked off on the vacation chart. I'm putting the man in a major bind, and..."

"And you'll owe him big time," Janie joined in as they quoted in unison the boss's last word on everything.

"So where are you going on this impromptu vacation?"

"The Greek Islands."

"Wow! When you play, you play first-class."

"Come with me."

"I would in a New York minute if I had a little more money in my vacation fund."

"How much do you have?"

"Somewhere under five dollars. Not even enough to buy a box of assorted condoms for the travel bag."

Cassie's cell phone rang. "Buy something really hot," Janie said, walking away as Cassie grabbed the phone. "I'll spring for the condoms."

Cassie murmured a hurried hello.

"Hi, sweetheart."

Her dad, finally. "You are one hard man to reach."

"Sorry about that. Damn merger's going to drive me nuts before it's over and done with."

"Don't you have a merger committee and a VP working on that?"

"Yeah, but when the going gets tough, I hit the front lines. Is anything wrong?"

"No, I just wanted to get Mom's itinerary from you."

"She's not due home for almost two weeks."

"I know, but I need to talk to her."

"Big news?"

"I think I might join her and her friend for the last week or so of their trip."

"That's a great idea."

"Any chance you can fax her itinerary to me tonight or just attach it to an e-mail if you have it on the computer?"

"I don't think I have it anywhere. I don't remember even seeing it."

"You must have. Mom wouldn't leave the country for six weeks and not tell you how to reach her."

"I was in London when she left. I assumed she'd given it to you."

"No."

"Sorry, baby. All I know is what she told me. She and Patsy...Patsy somebody. Anyway their plans were to spend a few days in Athens then leisurely tour the islands."

"Patsy David," Cassie said, filling in the last name for him.

"That's it. She's an old high school buddy of your mother's. Evidently they hooked up when Rhonda went back for her fortieth reunion."

"Patsy must be quite persuasive to talk Mom into a six-week vacation abroad."

"It'll be good for her, especially with me working so much. Why don't you give Moore's Travel a call? It's right here in The Woodlands. One of your mother's friends from church works there, and Rhonda always lets her book our nonbusiness flights. I'm sure they'll have a copy."

"What's the church friend's name?"

"I'm not sure. But they'll have the info in their computer system, so anyone can help you. Have them fax an itinerary to my office when they fax one to you."

They talked a few minutes more, about nothing in particular. When they hung up, Cassie picked up the postcard and stared at the picture of a small Greek village and the brilliant blue sea beyond. Beautiful beaches. Ancient ruins. Picturesque windmills. Snowy white monasteries. Living, breathing Greek gods.

Goodbye, Drake. Hello, Greece.

JOHN ROBICHEAUX stepped through the open door of Suzette's and scanned the area looking for his brother Dennis. It didn't take long to locate him. He was seated at a back table, his hands already wrapped around a cold beer.

John maneuvered through a maze of mismatched tables and chairs, nearly tripping over a couple of young boys who were playing with their plastic hot rods on the grease-stained floor. The air was stifling and filled with the smells of fried seafood, cayenne pepper and stale cigarette smoke—enough to choke a man. Worse, the jukebox was cranking out a 70s rock song at a decibel level just below that of a freight train.

A typical Saturday evening at Suzette's. Later the families would leave and the drinkers and partiers would take full charge, not staggering back to their homes until the wee hours of Sunday morning. John planned to be long gone by then.

He dropped into the rickety wooden chair across the table from his brother. A young waitress he'd never seen before appeared at his elbow.

"You want a beer?"

"I'll take a Bud."

"Draft?"

"In the bottle if you've got a real cold one."

"Icy cold."

"Bring me another while you're at it," Dennis said. "And keep 'em coming."

"You looking to have a good time tonight?" she asked, staring at Dennis through long, dark lashes so thick they had no use for mascara.

"I might be," Dennis said, giving her a once-over. "You looking to be invited to the party?"

She blushed, but smiled. "I'm just here to bring the beer."

He and Dennis both watched her walk away, her white shorts hugging her firm little ass above great thighs.

"How would you like to have those legs wrapped around you tonight?" Dennis asked.

"Not enough to do jail time."

"Those breasts look like they've been growing at least eighteen years to me. Besides, a sweet thing like that might inspire you to clean up a bit—at least use a razor once in a while. You're starting to look like a mangy dog."

John rubbed his chin and the spiky growth of half a week. "Hope you had a better reason for this visit than insulting me."

"We're brothers. We should see each other once in a while."

"I'm easy to find."

"When you're not out in the Gulf. How's the fishing business?"

"It'll do. I've got a group of guys down from New York for a week starting Monday. Long as Delilah don't come calling, we'll be fine."

"Supposed to be a bad year for hurricanes."

"Don't take but one to be bad if she hits you dead-on."

"Yeah."

The waitress returned with the beers. Dennis took a long, slow pull on his. "You ever miss your old life?"

"Mais non." John drank his beer slowly, letting the cold liquid trickle down his throat. He wasn't about to rehash the past or his mistakes. Old horror stories should not be washed up by cold beer.

"You could be rich by now," Dennis said. "Driving a Porsche, picking up high-class babes."

"High-class babes don't screw any better than poor ones, sometimes not as well. Besides, one successful Robicheaux is more than Beau Pierre ever expected to see."

Dennis cracked his knuckles, a nervous habit he'd picked up from their grandfather. "I'm thinking of leaving Beau Pierre."

The statement was the night's first surprise and the first clue as to what had really prompted Dennis's call. "I thought you and Guilliot were close as two crabs in a pot."

"Guilliot's all right. I just think it's time I move on. Beau Pierre's starting to feel more and more like one of Puh-paw's old muskrat traps."

"You didn't knock up some local *jolie fille*, huh?"

"Nothing like that." He stretched his legs under the scarred old table. "It's just time I move on. That's all."

"You didn't feel that way last time we talked."

"Things change."

"They changed real fast. This doesn't have anything to do with losing a patient on the operating table, does it?"

Dennis choked on the beer he'd just swallowed, coughed a few times into his sleeve, then slammed his almost empty bottle onto the table. "You talking about Ginny Lynn Flanders?"

"Who else?"

"That wasn't my fault. It wasn't nobody's fault. She just had a bad heart condition that had never been diagnosed. Guilliot's gonna win that lawsuit easy."

"I just asked."

"Well, I just answered."

Not honestly, John figured, judging from Dennis's reaction. But he sure as hell wasn't in a position to tell anyone how to live his life. "When will you be making the move?"

"Soon, but keep it quiet. I haven't told Dr. Guilliot yet, and I want him to hear it from me first."

"Good idea. Have you told anyone else?"

"Nobody I can't trust. You ought to think about a

change, too, John. You can't live in that old trapper's shack and avoid life forever."

"I'm not avoiding." He chased the lie with a swig of beer. "Where are you planning to go?"

"I'm thinking about Los Angeles. I got a buddy out there I went to medical school with. He says the field's wide open. Lots of job opportunities and enough sun-bronzed hotties to make me forget my Cajun *bellos*."

"Might not be as good as it sounds. The rules are different once you leave the bayou country. No buddies watching your back when the gators come after you."

"I don't think they have a lot of gators in Los Angeles."

"Oh, they got 'em all right. Only the gators out there wear high-priced suits and designer shoes from Italy."

"Maybe I won't go that far."

But he was going. John could tell the decision had been made. He'd liked to have asked more questions, but that wasn't the type of relationship they had. He didn't answer questions so he forfeited the right to ask them. Still, he hated to see Dennis leave town, especially if he was being driven out.

And that was a possibility he wouldn't put past Norman Guilliot. "It's your call, Dennis. Just make sure you're the one doing the calling."

The waitress stopped by their table again. "You want another beer?"

John looked at her again, letting his gaze take it all in, from the dark, straight hair that curved around her face and fell down the back of her neck to the perky breasts and hips that flared from the narrow waist.

She was a looker, and the way she was batting those eyes at Dennis, seemed like she might have changed her mind about wanting to party.

"Make mine a whiskey," John said. His little brother was leaving town. Reason enough to hit the hard stuff.

DENNIS KEPT both hands on the wheel as he slowed and maneuvered the sharp turn. He shouldn't be driving at all after so many beers, but it wasn't far to the old house he'd rented from Guilliot's nephew. Another mile or so and he'd be home.

His mind wandered back in time. Shrimping out in the bays with Puh-paw. And on Saturday nights Muh-maw would make the big pot of gumbo. And the stories Puh-paw would tell about trapping and hunting back in the good old days before there was such a thing as licenses and limits. They'd been terrific grandparents.

John and Dennis had different mothers; it didn't matter much since Muh-maw and Puh-paw had raised them both anyways.

Dennis didn't remember his parents at all. He'd been only two when their father had gone to jail up in Jefferson Parish. He'd never come home. He didn't know that much about his mother. Muh-maw hadn't let anyone mention her name in the house, but John had told him once that she'd run off with some guy from Lafayette.

Dennis nodded, then jerked his head backward, fighting sleep. He shouldn't have taken those two pills back at Suzette's, but he'd had a migraine the first part of the week and the thing was threatening to come back on him.

He gunned the engine, then threw on his brakes when he saw something lying across the road in front of him. The car left the pavement, skidded along the shoulder, then careened into the swamp before it finally came to a stop.

Dennis wasn't sure what was on the road, but it had looked a lot like a body. Could be some drunk passed out walking home from a neighbor's. Only there weren't any houses along this stretch of road. He loosed his seat belt and opened the door. When he stepped out, his feet sank into a good six inches of water before being sucked into the mud. His good shoes, too.

He jerked at the sound of something swishing through the water behind him. A water moccasin? A gator? He spun around. Too late.

His head exploded, but Dennis never felt the pain or the blood and bits of brain spilling over his body. Never knew when he sank to the soggy swamp now red with his blood.

CHAPTER TWO

IT WAS HALF PAST EIGHT in the morning when Cassie padded to the front door of her fourth-floor condominium, stepped into the quiet hall and snagged her morning copy of the *Times Picayune*. She skimmed the headlines as she walked back to the kitchen for her first cup of coffee.

Drake and the Flanders case were beaten out for top billing by a three-car pileup on I-10, but they made honorable mention in smaller headlines about a third of the way down the page: Pierson Accuses Beau Pierre Sheriff Of Mishandling Evidence.

And whether he had or not—whether Drake believed he had or not—he could ride that horse for days. The bigger spectacle the pretrial hoopla, the less attention anyone actually paid to testimony or evidence once the trial itself got underway. And Drake was the master of spectacle.

Dr. Norman Guilliot was in for a fight.

Cassie dropped the paper to the kitchen table and poured the dark, chicory-laden brew into an oversize mug. But instead of taking it back to the table, she took it out on the balcony to watch the morning traffic of ferries, tug boats and barges along the muddy Mississippi.

The view from the balcony had been the factor that tipped the scale for buying this condo instead of the larger and more reasonably priced one on St. Charles Avenue.

The view and the fact that she could walk the six blocks to work rather than take the streetcar.

She sipped her coffee and took in the sights. The ferry from Algiers to the foot of Canal Street passed a few yards in front of a slow-moving tanker heading downriver. A sleek cruise ship was docked at the River Walk and nearer the aquarium a much smaller boat was already loading tourists in shorts and sunglasses, their cameras around their necks and their cash stashed in fanny packs that hung under paunchy stomachs.

The activity was like a restless surge of energy, constantly moving, searching for the next bend in the river, the next port of call.

The next chapter in her life. Nothing like making an analogy personal.

She glanced at her watch. Almost nine. Moore's Travel should be opening soon. Greece might be the answer to her need to go forward with her life, and she was so ready to get out of New Orleans for a while.

Besides, the trip would give her a chance to spend some quality time with her mother. They'd drifted apart during the seven years she'd spent married to Drake. Mainly because when they'd been together her mother had always cut to the chase and asked the dreaded question.

"Are you happy?"

Well, duh? I'm married to the hottest upcoming attorney in New Orleans if not the south. No one but a mother would even think to ask such a question. And if no one ever asked, Cassie didn't have to answer.

You can ask now, Mom. The answer is not yet, but I'm getting there. Greece would be a nice step along the way. But with or without Greece, I'm taking back control of my life.

BUTCH HAVELIN rolled over in bed and stared at the ceiling of his Houston apartment. It was already late afternoon in Greece. Rhonda was probably getting ready for dinner with her friend. She liked to eat early, liked schedules and order and life that fit into neat little compartments and never got befuddled with spontaneity or excitement.

Opposites attract. The problem was the attraction wore thin over time, became frayed and faded, like an old shirt after too many washings. He and Rhonda had seen thirty years of washings.

Now they lived in the same house, slept in the same bed—at least, they did the nights he made it back to their home in The Woodlands—still saw some of the friends they'd known since the early days of their marriage. Rhonda still offered her cheek for a quick peck in the mornings when he left for work and they hugged each other when he left on business trips.

Sometimes they even went through the motions of making love. The saddest thing was that he didn't even know when it had all slipped away. The passion had just crept from their lives like heat seeping from a hot bath, leaving nothing but tepidity.

Babs stretched beside him, but didn't open her eyes. The sheet slipped down and her breasts peeked over the top, soft mounds of firm, golden flesh and pinkish nipples. Small, but all perky and perfect.

Butch never bothered with trying to convince himself that what he and Babs had now would last or even that he wanted it to. She was thirty-four, only a couple of years older than Cassie. He was sixty-one. They were a generation apart in music, memories and experiences. But none of that seemed to matter when they were together. She made him potent and alive, gave him back snatches of his youth, and made him feel as if he were some stud muffin she couldn't get enough of.

He didn't want a divorce, definitely didn't want to split up his assets at this point in life. But he was glad Rhonda was in Greece, would be happy for her to stay there a few more months. Safe. Happy. And gone.

Truth was he'd never given her itinerary a thought, but he'd phone his daughter again today and feign a little concern so that Cassie wouldn't get all upset and start bugging him about why he didn't know exactly where her mother was.

The one thing he didn't need in his personal life was complications. Not from Cassie. Not from Rhonda. Not even from Babs.

Conner-Marsh was all he could handle right now, and if he let this merger get screwed up, his ass was grass. There were plenty of younger guys waiting around to knock the old man off the top.

JOHN ROBICHEAUX pulled the pillow over his head to block the jangling ring of the telephone. The whiskey from last night was blasting away inside his head like a jackhammer. His stomach didn't feel so great, either. He reached across the bed, checking to be certain he was in it alone.

He was. Time was that would have been enough to send him back to the kitchen for a hair of the dog that was gnawing away at the base of his skull. These days it just brought a quick wave of relief.

The phone kept ringing. He reached for it, started to yank it from the wall connection, then changed his mind. It might be a guide job and he could use the business—as long as they didn't expect him to ride those choppy waves today.

"John Robicheaux. Can I help you?"

"I got some bad news for you, John."

John struggled to pull his mind from the mire. "Who is this?"

"Sheriff Babineaux."

The sheriff. Shit. John must have gotten in a fight and busted up something last night. He tried to remember but only picked up bits and pieces of the night between the shattering blows of the jackhammer. "What'd I do?"

"It's Dennis, John."

"What did he do?"

"He's dead."

The words cut through the fog, jerking John from the stupor. He threw his legs over the side of the bed, the sudden move sending the room into a tailspin.

"You gotta be mistaken, Tom. I saw Dennis last night. He was fine."

"It's no mistake. I wouldn't call you with this kind of news if I wasn't certain."

Damn. This was John's fault. He should have stayed sober. Should have seen that his little brother got home safe. Now... "Did he hit another car or just run off the road?"

"Neither. It wasn't an accident, John. Dennis ate a bullet."

"Murdered?"

"Suicide."

No! Hell no! Him, maybe, but never Dennis. Dennis had a life. Beer to drink. Women to screw. A big move all planned.

"I guess I should have come out there and told you myself, but it being Saturday and all, I thought I'd better catch you before you headed out into the Gulf on a fishing trip."

"When did you find out?"

"A few minutes ago. Must have happened sometime during the night, but no one noticed the car over in the swamp until this morning. Hank LeBlanc and a couple of his sons found it and gave me a call. I'm here now."

"Where's here?"

"Bayou Road, a couple of miles before the turnoff to Dennis's place."

"Don't move the body until I get there."

"This ain't a pretty sight, John. Why don't you wait and see the body once it's down at the funeral home and Dastague's got it cleaned up?"

"Forget Dastague. I want an autopsy and I want it done in New Orleans."

"No cause, John. There's not a sign of foul play."

"Yeah, well I call a bullet plenty sign of foul play. And the cause for the autopsy is that I said so. I want a full investigation, Tom, not some half-assed job that won't get beyond the ridicule stage with a grand jury."

"Calm down, John. I know how you felt about Dennis. Hell, we all loved him. He was good-time tonic in solid form. But he had his problems. You know that."

"Yeah, well you're the one who's got them now, Tom. Full autopsy. Full investigation. Stay put. I'm on my way over there."

"There's no use. I checked—"

"I'm on my way. Be there."

The jackhammer was still at work, pounding so that John stumbled as he went to the kitchen for drugs to kill the pain. He shook four extra-strength painkillers into his hand and chased them with a glass of water from the tap.

Images flashed through his mind, like stabs of glaring light. Dennis laughing. Dennis fishing. Dennis scared as shit the time he tipped the pirogue over when they were teasing the old gator with raw chicken wings.

Dennis shaking like an old man in detox a few hours after Ginny Lynn Flanders had died on the operating table.

Suicide, hell! This had the stench of Dr. Norman Guilliot all over it.

"I'M NOT SURE who I need to talk to," Cassie explained once she got Moore's Travel on the phone. "My mother is Mrs. Butch Havelin and my father said she books all her travel through your agency."

"Sure. Rhonda Havelin. You must be Cassie."

"Right."

"I've heard so much about you from Rhonda, I feel as if I know you. Your mother and I are members of the same church and we've worked on a couple of committees together. She's very efficient and organized, keeps us all on task."

"That would be my mother."

"So, what can I do for you?"

"I need to get in touch with Mom, but I don't have her itinerary. Can you pull it up for me?"

"Are you talking about her Greece trip?"

"That's the one."

"I'm afraid I can't help you with that. She came in and picked up some pamphlets on the islands and sites of interest in and around Athens, but the friend she was going with booked the trip."

"I don't suppose you know the name of the booking agency."

"No. Did you check with your father?"

"I talked to him last night. He probably has the itinerary somewhere but can't put his hands on it."

"I hope this isn't an emergency situation."

"Nothing serious, but I would like to talk to her. Did Mom mention any specific hotels?"

"No, only that they planned to stay in smaller, family-owned establishments so they could experience more of the authentic Greek culture."

"That doesn't sound like Mom."

"I cautioned her to be careful with that when I saw her at church before she left, but I got the feeling that her friend had traveled the area before. It's a very safe part of the world."

"Mom usually thinks anything less than a four-star hotel is roughing it."

"Nothing like hooking up with an old high school friend to make you adventuresome."

"Guess not." But Cassie suspected it would take a lot more than that to make her mother adventuresome. She was probably sitting in some air-conditioned hotel calling for room service and reading a book while her friend did all the adventuring.

Cassie thanked the woman for her trouble and broke the connection. Who'd have ever thought that locating her mother would be the hardest part of planning her own vacation?

But Patsy David sounded as if she might be just what Cassie's mother needed—bold and open to new experiences. Perhaps Cassie shouldn't join them. It might throw her mother back into her maternal mode and spoil her fun. Cassie decided she'd give that further consideration if and when she actually got to talk to Rhonda.

And she wasn't giving up on that yet. She still had her ace in the hole. If her mother's next-door neighbor didn't know the details of the Greece trip, Cassie was certain it wouldn't be from lack of prying.

She retrieved Marianne Jefferies's phone number from

information and made the call. They exchanged the perfunctory hellos and Cassie got right to the point before Marianne had a chance to start her own round of questioning.

"I'm trying to get in touch with Mom. Did she leave you a copy of her itinerary?"

"Why? Is anything wrong?"

"No. I'd just like to give her a call and see how her vacation's going."

"You'll have to talk to Butch then. As secretive as Rhonda was about this trip, I doubt anyone else would know how to find her."

"What do you mean by secretive?"

"Well, anytime I asked her about the trip, she changed the subject. Might as well have just said it was none of my business."

Imagine that. "So she didn't mention any specific plans?"

"I got the impression they didn't have any. I drove Rhonda to the airport when she left. She seemed really nervous that day, which made perfect sense to me. I mean, in this day and age, anything could happen to two women traveling alone."

A morbid thought. Cassie wasn't going to go there, but she was starting to feel a bit uneasy. "I don't guess you have her friend Patsy's home number."

"No. I'm not even sure where the woman lives. Some little town in northern Louisiana."

"Minden?"

"That sounds right."

"I may try to find her phone number. See if her husband has an itinerary."

"You're out of luck there. I asked why Patsy wanted

Rhonda to go to Greece with her instead of going with her husband and Rhonda said Patsy had never married.''

No wonder she still had energy to go on adventures.

"If you talk to Rhonda, let me know how she's doing. I swear she and Patsy sound like the senior version of Thelma and Louise. Trouble, if you know what I mean. And with all those attractive Greek guys around looking for rich American women to seduce.''

Cassie finished the phone conversation, then walked to the counter, refilled her coffee cup and flicked on the radio. She switched the dial to her favorite light jazz station, tuning in just in time for the news break.

Dennis Robicheaux, anesthetist at the Magnolia Plantation Restorative and Therapeutic Center, shot and killed himself last night less than a mile from his home on the outskirts of Beau Pierre. Robicheaux had been part of the surgery team when Ginny Flanders died during a routine cosmetic surgery operation.

A suicide. Talk about stirring a handful of complications into the pot. The situation now reeked of guilt on the part of the surgery team and gave Drake and Reverend Evan Flanders a huge advantage in public opinion if not in the trial itself.

It might add a few insurmountable hurdles to Cassie's plans, as well. Her boss would want human interest stories and some investigative articles on the new development. Olson was determined to turn the previously floundering *Crescent Connection* into a magazine no local citizen would want to be without.

He wanted in-your-face reporting on issues that mattered and up-close and personal articles on the kind of stories that the citizens just couldn't get enough of. Dennis Robicheaux's suicide would fit solidly into the latter category.

Olson would have complained about an impromptu vacation before the suicide. He'd likely veto it now.

Instead of a week in the Greek Islands, she'd be tooling around the tiny south Louisiana town of Beau Pierre. It was a disgustingly poor tradeoff.

NORMAN GUILLIOT stepped into the shower, his body still humming from the orgasm he'd reached a few minutes ago with his wife. Fifteen years of marriage, and Annabeth could still touch all the right buttons to get him off.

She wasn't as hot as she'd been when he'd first met her, but at thirty-six she still had a body that turned heads. She was smart, too, a lot smarter than most folks gave her credit for being. Her worst fault was probably her extravagance. If one fur coat was too much for a climate that never saw a real winter, buy two. But he could afford her, so what the hell.

The goal now was to stay wealthy. He'd worked damn hard to get where he was, and he wasn't letting some two-bit lawyer and a TV Bible thumper yank it away from him. He was fifty-eight, years too old to start over.

Norman adjusted the stream of water until it was as hot as he could stand it, then let it pulsate onto his shoulders and roll down his taut stomach and over his private parts, washing his and Annabeth's juices right down the drain. That was okay. They were in endless supply. He squirted some shampoo into his thinning hair and worked it into peaks of lather.

The shower door opened and Annabeth poked her head inside, looking like some blond apparition floating in the fog of vapors.

"You have a phone call."

"Get the name and number. I'll call them back when I get out of the shower."

"It's Sheriff Babineaux. He says it's important."

Norman's muscles tightened and his breath seemed to be sucked into the steamy vapor that whirled around him. "Did he say what this is about?"

"No."

He rinsed the shampoo from his hair, then left the water running when he stepped onto the wine-colored carpet to take the receiver from Annabeth.

"What's up, Tom?"

"Your anesthetist killed himself."

"Dennis?"

"Yeah."

"Are you sure?"

"Oh, I'm sure. I'm looking at the body right now."

"When did this happen?"

"Sometime during the early hours of the morning. Apparently he was driving home from somewhere. He ran his car off the road just south of the Tortue Bayou."

"But you said he shot himself."

"He did. Shot himself right in the head. The gun was still lying there in the swamp when Hank LeBlanc found him this morning. He was heading out to do some fishing and saw the car. Stopped to check it out, and there was Dennis. Dead."

"Dennis? Dead?" The words tumbled about in Norman's brain, and for a second he wasn't sure if he'd said them out loud or merely thought them.

"I know this is a shocker, Doc."

"Are you certain it was suicide?"

"No doubt. Of course, his brother John isn't buying that, but the evidence is here. It's open and shut to my mind, and my mind is the one that counts in this parish."

"Is John there with you?"

"No, but he's on his way."

"So am I. I'll be there in twenty minutes."

"I wouldn't recommend it."

"Why not?"

"Dennis blew his brains out with a .45. That ain't the best accompaniment to breakfast."

"It won't be my first sight of blood—brains either, for that matter."

Annabeth was staring at him when he broke the connection.

He'd like to spare her this, but that was the thing about fame and wealth. It set you inside this giant ball and everybody who walked by felt compelled to give it a kick. She was in the ball with him, so she'd have to prepare herself for a new onslaught of reporters' feet slamming into their ball.

"What is it now?" she asked.

"Dennis Robicheaux shot and killed himself last night."

"Oh, no! Not Dennis."

His towel slipped from his waist as he reached for her and pulled her into his arms.

"Not Dennis. Please. Not Dennis."

"I know it doesn't seem possible, but these things happen."

"He didn't kill himself. I know he didn't. He wouldn't."

"You don't know him that well, sweetheart. He had some problems."

"No. Not Dennis. He wouldn't kill himself. Why would he?"

"Who knows? Maybe it's the Robicheaux blood. Look at his brother. As soon as the first blast of adversity hit, John came running home to drown himself in whiskey and the same stinking life he'd worked to escape."

"Dennis wasn't like John."

"I'm not saying he was, but he was still a Robicheaux."

"It was the reporters who did this to him, Norman, not his Robicheaux blood. They kept hammering away at him, determined to blame Ginny Lynn Flanders's death on him." She pulled away, looked in the mirror, then dabbed her eyes with the back of her hands. "What will this do to the lawsuit?"

"Nothing. The reporters will howl and make a big show about it, but in the end, it won't have a thing to do with the legal proceedings."

"I hope you're right."

So did he. "I'm going to finish my shower and meet the sheriff out where they found the body."

"I want to go, too."

"It's no place for a woman."

She barely knew Dennis, but she had a tender heart, cried over dead goldfish. He'd like to stay here with her. He sure had no desire to see the body, but he had to be certain John didn't throw some of the stinking Robicheaux shit into the mix.

This was suicide. And a suicide it would stay.

CHAPTER THREE

JOHN HIT the brakes and steered the car to the shoulder of the narrow road. A group of about six men stood in ankle-deep water a few yards away, gathered around the body. *The body. Dennis.*

The reality of the situation hovered over him, but it hadn't struck yet. Once he walked over and stood where the sheriff and the others were, once the image got inside his head, reality would grab him by the balls and squeeze down tight.

A warning screamed and echoed in his ears as he sloshed into the bog. *Hold back the day. Hold back the stinking black day.* But the sun was already beating down on him, the fetid air already clogging his lungs. There could be no holding back.

His boots sank into the mud, stirring up the mosquitoes that hid in the low grass.

"I'm sorry about this, John, really sorry."

John nodded, acknowledging the sheriff's words but avoiding eye contact with him and the others. He didn't want to feel any bond with them, didn't need their self-serving commiseration. Pity was debilitating, and he needed his wits and strength to see him through this.

He forced himself to look at what was left of Dennis. For a second, he thought he might just collapse and evaporate in the morning heat. Somehow he held it together and his training as a defense attorney checked in, regis-

tered every contingent. The position of the body, the
bloodied and shattered remains of the brain. The splatters
of blood on the thick plants that clogged the swampland.

"It's a rotten shame," LeBlanc said. "Dennis was a
good man."

"Yeah. A rotten shame. Has the body been moved?"
John asked.

"We haven't touched it," Babineaux answered.

"I want pictures before it's moved to New Orleans for
an autopsy."

"I know this is tough, John, but you need to get a grip.
What's an autopsy going to show that we can't see for
ourselves plain as day? Dennis was shot in the head at
point-blank range with his own gun. We found the weapon
right at his fingertips."

"How do you know it was Dennis's gun?"

Babineaux held up a plastic bag containing a small blue
metal Colt .45 with a brown wooden grip. "Are you going
to tell me it isn't?"

John stared at the weapon. It was his grandfather's pistol, World War II vintage, the first weapon John had ever
shot. He'd practiced his aim by firing it at tin cans behind
the house long before he was old enough to get a driver's
license.

"I recognize it," he said, figuring it was no use to lie.
Babineaux had taken the thing away from the old man
often enough when he'd had too much to drink in Suzette's
and started waving it at anyone fool enough to argue with
him.

"I don't give a damn if you found his finger on the
trigger. Dennis didn't shoot himself."

"No sign there was anyone else with him."

"You don't have any proof there wasn't. So I suggest

you get a decent crime-scene unit out here even if it means calling one in from New Orleans.''

''I don't know what they'd do that I haven't.''

''I want every detail you can sieve out of this bloody swamp.''

''I'm sorry about your brother, John. We all liked Dennis. You know that. But the guy had problems and maybe he just couldn't deal with them.''

''Or maybe Norman Guilliot couldn't.''

''Don't go making crazy accusations.''

''Then do your job.'' John swatted at a mosquito that was feeding on his neck, then walked toward Dennis's car. It looked as if he'd just lost control and slid off into the bog. A few seconds later and he'd have hit the bridge railing or possibly plunged into the rain-swollen bayou.

Maybe that's what the killer had meant for him to do. A nice, accidental drowning. The gun might have been the insurance, plan B in case the first option didn't fly. Either way, something must have been planted to make certain Dennis left the road at the specific spot where his killer was waiting.

Possibilities swirled in the fog that filled John's mind. He looked up as a black Porsche skidded to a stop along the shoulder of the road.

Dr. Norman Guilliot crawled from the low-slung car and took a few steps toward them with the same air of authority he probably flaunted in the operating room. But a few steps were all he'd be taking. Dressed in white trousers and a light blue pullover shirt, he wasn't about to traipse through the murky water the way the rest of them had.

At least not in the hot glare of the day with witnesses all around. Last night would have been a different story. John imagined him, slinking around in the dark, startling Dennis then sticking the pistol to his head. Dennis would have been an easy target, like blinding a doe with a high-powered flashlight and taking it down at point blank range. The kind of high-stake, no-risk operation a man like Guilliot would choose.

The sheriff started toward Guilliot and the rest of the entourage followed, leaving Dennis's body to the insects and the stifling humidity.

John felt the hate swelling inside him and welcomed it. He could get his hands around hate, it was so much easier to deal with than the pain. He strode toward Guilliot, reaching him a few seconds after the others.

"I'm sorry about this, John, really sorry. I don't know what else to say. I'm still reeling with the shock of it myself."

"Shock doesn't show much on you, Guilliot."

Guilliot fixed his gaze on John, a study in faux compassion. "I'm not going to get into an argument with you at a time like this. I won't show that kind of disrespect toward Dennis."

"Your concern is underwhelming."

Dr. Guilliot shrugged his shoulders. "If blaming me helps you deal with this, go right ahead, John. But it doesn't change anything. Dennis took his own life, and I guess that means we all let him down, including you."

"Dennis didn't kill himself. He had no reason to."

"Guess you best take that up with Sheriff Babineaux."

The sheriff sidled up next to Guilliot. "I told you we don't need no trouble out here, John. Why don't you go back to your place and clean up a bit? Call you a friend to go to the funeral home in Galliano and make what arrangements need to be made."

John turned and stared at the sheriff, studied his gray eyes, his two crooked front teeth and the way his bottom lip curled downward as if it wanted to crawl away from the rest of his mouth. He'd known Babineaux all his life, but he wasn't sure he'd ever really noticed him until today. Now everything about the sheriff and the entire morning were searing their way into the lining of John's brain.

"I expect, no make that demand, an autopsy, Babineaux. You see that it's done or I see your ass in court."

Guilliot moved into John's space, his eyes narrowed and accusing. "Making a big show's not going to bring Dennis back or atone for that little girl you set the monster loose on, John. So why don't you just let your brother rest in peace?"

John fought the sudden urge to bury his fist into Guilliot's gut. Instead he turned and walked back to his truck, wondering how in hell Dennis's life had come to nothing more than a decaying body half-buried in a stinking bog on the edge of the road.

Both Babineaux and Guilliot probably thought this would blow over, that John would go home and drown his grief in a fifth of Jack Daniel's, but they were wrong. Someone had murdered Dennis and John would see that the man who had done it paid if he had to strangle him with his bare hands.

If it turned out to be Dr. Norman Guilliot, the act would be pure pleasure.

CASSIE DROVE to Beau Pierre on Sunday afternoon, more to scope out the place than to do any kind of in-depth investigating. The newspapers and TV news broadcasts would carry the facts surrounding the suicide, but sterile details were not what Olson would be looking for.

Cassie had some ideas brewing in her mind, but she wanted to get a feel for the lay of the land and the emotional climate of the setting before she met with her boss the next morning.

She'd done her homework yesterday, searched for any information she could find on the small town of Beau Pierre. It was no more than a dot on the map, a fishing village a few miles south of Galliano.

It was like dozens of other fishing villages in the area except that Beau Pierre was home to the Magnolia Plantation Restorative and Therapeutic Center, the clinic that drew the rich and famous from all over the world to have the renowned Dr. Norman Guilliot surgically restore their youth.

She'd already stopped at the café in town and asked a few questions. Mostly she'd learned that folks didn't hang out in the café on Sundays and that the waitress named Lily didn't care much for reporters.

Cassie slowed and glanced at the map she'd printed from the Internet. If her directions were accurate, she should be close to the Center now. A half mile later she saw the gate, a massive iron affair just off the road.

She pulled into the paved drive and pushed the button on the entry panel. The intercom hummed softly, followed by a female voice.

"Welcome to Magnolia Plantation. How may I help you?"

She felt a little like a predator at the home of one of the little pigs. Let me in so that I can eat you. Or she could just say she was a reporter. That would get her about the same reception.

"I'm interested in touring the Center."

"I'm sorry. The plantation and grounds are private. No one's admitted except our registered guests and our staff."

"How do I find out if I want to be a registered guest if I can't view the facilities?"

"You can make an appointment during business hours and Dr. Guilliot will meet with you personally."

"I drove all the way from New Orleans. Can't I just take a quick look around?"

"I wish I could say yes, but the rules are strictly enforced to preserve the privacy of our guests. I'm sure you can appreciate that."

And keeping out reporters was just a little lagniappe. Cassie climbed from her car, walked over to the gate and peered through the ornate pattern of iron bars. The driveway was long and winding, the extensive grounds perfectly manicured. Only glimpses of the plantation house were visible through the trees, but Cassie saw enough to tell that the place was not only massive but beautifully restored.

She was still staring when a mud-encrusted black pickup truck pulled in and stopped, blocking her car between its front bumper and the gate.

The man who stepped from behind the wheel was tall and muscular with long, straggly hair and a tanned face spiked with coarse black whiskers. He walked toward her, emanating a kind of raw animal potency that seemed more than a little menacing.

"Are you looking for Dr. Guilliot?" he asked, his hard stare never wavering.

"Not particularly."

"Then who are you looking for?"

None of his damned business. She started to fire that comment at him, but stopped herself. It wasn't smart to start fights when she was sniffing out a story. "I'm just interested in the clinic."

"Like hell you are. You're interested in digging up dirt for that magazine you work for."

"How do you know who I work for?"

"You didn't exactly sneak into town quietly. Even if you had, a stranger always gets noticed here."

"Who are you?" she demanded, wishing he wasn't standing between her and her car.

"John Robicheaux."

"Any kin to Dennis?"

"His brother."

"I see. I'm sorry. His death must have been a shock for you."

He ignored her expression of sympathy. "Did Dr. Guilliot ask you to come see him?"

"I haven't talked to Dr. Guilliot."

"So you just smelled a little dirt and came running?"

"Did you follow me out here from town to harass me, Mr. Robicheaux?"

"Is that what I'm doing? Harassing? I thought we were just having a friendly conversation."

"Then your conversational skills need to evolve past the Neanderthal stage."

"I don't plan to do a lot of conversing. Two brief statements should cover everything. One, I don't like the idea of my brother's death being made into tabloid entertainment. Two, I sure as hell don't want the details surrounding his murder being manipulated by Dr. Norman Guilliot."

"Murder? The police report indicates that your brother's death was suicide."

"Yeah, well don't go laying your money on what the cops say, Ms. Pierson."

"What makes you think Dennis was murdered?"

"Not *think. Know.*"

"What makes you *know?*" she asked, trying to sound only mildly interested.

"I was with Dennis last night. He had plans and eating a bullet wasn't one of them." John stepped closer, but the fury he'd exhibited when he first arrived seemed to have settled into a brooding pain that glazed his eyes and made them dark as night.

The mood switch tangled Cassie's emotions. Had he concocted some bizarre murder plot in his mind to keep from facing the fact that his brother had taken his own life, or did he know something he wasn't saying? Was it possible that the sleepy bayou town of Beau Pierre harbored a cache of frightening secrets?

"If I were you, Ms. Pierson, I'd get in that car and drive back to New Orleans, find some nice little story about the mayor or concentrate on the city's plague of potholes."

"What is it you want from me, Mr. Robicheaux?"

"Nothing. I'm only suggesting you not become one of Dr. Guilliot's pawns."

"You surely aren't accusing Dr. Guilliot of killing your brother."

"Look around you," he said, motioning toward the broad estate beyond the ornate gate. "The gold mine of the patron saint of the scarred and wrinkled rich. My brother was a lowly, *dispensable* anesthetist, a nice scapegoat for Ginny Flanders's death. You figure it out from there."

Finally he released her from the power of his hypnotic stare and walked back to his pickup truck. He climbed behind the wheel and drove away without a backward glance.

She stared after him, feeling as if something more than a conversation had passed between. The guy had uncanny powers, a prowess at seducing the mind that bordered on the paranormal, but that didn't mean his accusations were on target.

Still when she turned to stare once again through the massive iron gates, she felt a sense of foreboding creep into her bloodstream and raise the hairs on the back of her neck. This had nothing to do with her, but deadly secrets had a way of entangling anyone who stumbled into their path.

And if there were secrets, she was certain John Robicheaux of the dark eyes and fiery Cajun blood was part of the mystery.

Either way Cassie felt sure she hadn't seen the last of the man. She'd reserve judgment until later on, whether that was good or bad.

JOHN HAD KNOWN the reporters would start pouring into Beau Pierre before Dennis's body was good cold. That's why he'd done his homework, picked out the best one to pull into his murder theory. He knew the sheriff would try to downplay it, and Guilliot's lawyers in the Flanders's trial definitely would, but John had no intention of letting that happen.

He'd decided the *Crescent Connection* was the way to go. The magazine had clout and they'd eat up a controversy like this, gnaw on it and give it so much attention, the sheriff would have to conduct a real investigation. That's why he'd asked Lily Robert down at the café to let him know if someone from the *Connection* showed up asking questions. Not much went on in Beau Pierre that Lily didn't hear about.

He hadn't expected the reporter to be female—or pretty—but it didn't matter to John. He'd said his piece, planted the thought, and that should do it.

Cassie Pierson. The name sounded familiar. Pierson. As in Drake Pierson, Flanders's high-priced, fancy talking attorney. Damn. That's why her name sounded familiar. He'd read an article on the infamous attorney not long ago, and it had mentioned that his ex-wife was a reporter, even called her by name.

All the better. Drake Pierson would surely notice his ex's article and he'd play the suspicion of murder to the hilt.

I'll make Guilliot pay, Dennis. I'll make the sonofabitch pay. And if it's not him that killed you, I'll find the man who did.

He'd see that justice was done. But that wouldn't bring Dennis back. The pain of that hit again, the force of it almost doubling him over.

"MURDER." The word rolled off of Olson's tongue at their Monday morning meeting, and his lips settled into the kind of thoroughly satisfied smile some men might link to sliding their tongue over a dip of Häagen-Dazs ice cream.

Cassie stared at him, amazed once again at the way he transformed from a dull, robotlike creature into a canty, euphoric dynamo the second the possibility of a juicy story made an appearance. Patterson Olson was nearing forty but possessed that nondescript agelessness that let him pass for any age between thirty and fifty.

His muscles were no more defined than Cassie's, though he was lean with thick, brown hair and a classic nose. None of his features set him aside as particularly handsome or unattractive, his most noticeable flaw being a chin that seemed to collapse into his neck.

He picked up a pen, drew a page-size question mark on the top of a yellow legal pad, then pushed the pad across his desk and toward her. "There's your story!"

"A question mark?"

"*The* question. Suicide or murder?"

"There are no facts to back up a murder claim."

"We're not trying the case, Cassie. We're giving our readers information to arouse their curiosity and titillate their minds. They can make their own judgements."

"Based on unfounded rumors."

"Based on facts you're going to gather for us and on information provided by the brother of the victim—a man with his own fascinating story and shaded past."

"Are you sure we're talking about the same John Robicheaux?"

"Don't tell me you don't know who he is?"

"Would I be asking if I did?"

"He was a brilliant trial lawyer. He almost convinced me once a guy was innocent, and I knew for a fact he was guilty."

"Then you know John Robicheaux personally?"

"Professionally. I was working for the *Times Picayune* when he was practicing. I interviewed him a few times."

"What was he like then?"

"Abrupt when it suited him. Persuasive when he needed to be."

"Manipulative?"

"Do you know a trial lawyer worth his fee who isn't?"

"Why did he quit practicing?" she asked, still finding it hard to imagine the guy had practiced criminal law.

"Ever heard of Gregory Benson?"

She tossed the name around in her mind. "Doesn't sound familiar."

"It was eight years ago."

"I was twenty-four and finishing up my master's in journalism at the University of Texas back then."

"Benson kidnapped a ten-year-old girl in south Mississippi and killed her. Only he kept her alive for a few days, raped and tortured her repeatedly before he finally drowned her in the Pearl River."

"Don't tell me John Robicheaux got that guy off."

"Not that time, but he had just six months earlier—won

an innocent verdict on rape and murder charges against Benson in the death of a young teenager in Slidell.''

"Sonofabitch."

"Yeah. That's what a lot of people said. John didn't say anything in his own defense, just gave up his practice and left town."

"I don't blame him for taking down his shingle and moving back to the swamp. I don't see how he can live with himself."

"He was a lawyer, Cassie. He did his job."

"Yeah, sure."

"Don't go all rigid and righteous on me. This is a big story, the kind that can get *Crescent Connection* the type of clout we're looking for. And that will require your being friendly to the guy. Keep him talking to you."

"In other words, you want me to suck up to him."

"That's one way of putting it. And that's just the beginning. I want you to dig into every aspect of the situation. Find out who Dennis was dating, who he might have talked to about Ginny Flanders's death, if he had a drinking or a drug problem. Snoop into every niche and corner of his life, or at least the life he had until the wee hours of Saturday morning."

"That won't be easy. The population of Beau Pierre is primarily Cajun. They'll bond together against an outsider."

"Then don't be an outsider. Become a fixture in Beau Pierre. Get a room down there. Hang out with the locals. Make yourself available. There's always someone who will talk."

"You're not serious about my renting a room down there, are you?"

"Serious as a street flooding in May. Keep me posted on everything. I'd like a couple of stories before Saturday's print deadline. Hell, if this is as big as it sounds, we might even do a special issue on the 'Beau Pierre Mystery.' Sales numbers could swell by a hundred thousand. Dr. Guilliot. The Reverend Flanders's dead wife. John Robicheaux's past. And a possible murder. We've got it all.''

And Olson was going to start salivating any minute—which was reason enough to clear out of his office. She'd go home, pack a few things, then drive down to Beau Pierre and try to find a decent motel with a vacancy somewhere in the area.

But first she had a phone call to make.

Back in her office, Cassie called information and requested the phone number for Minden High School. She'd given up on the idea of joining her mother in Greece, but all the talk of scandals and murderous secrets was upping her apprehension level, probably unnecessarily so.

Her mother was perfectly fine, off with an old high school friend on the adventure of a lifetime. And at fifty-nine, it was about damn time.

Once she had the number, Cassie called the school and made her request.

"Could I ask why you need that information?"

"I have a lost mother," she said, teasing, but was immediately sorry she'd put it that way. The words had an ominous ring to them and they seemed to hang in the air after she'd blurted them out.

She explained about the trip in as few words as possible, focusing on the fact that she couldn't locate an itinerary. Then she gave them both her mother's maiden name and Patsy David. "I'll feel better if I can talk to my mother and be assured that the trip is going well. So if I can get a contact number for Patsy David, I'd really appreciate it."

"I understand. I'd be worried half to death if it was my

mother, but then she's never gone farther than Shreveport
without Dad. Did you check the Minden phone directory
for a phone number for Patsy David?''

"I did. There was no such listing. That's why I thought
I'd see if you had some kind of alumnae records that include a current contact number.''

"We don't that I know of, but I'm new here. Give me
a few minutes and I'll see what I can find out. Would you
like for me to call you back?''

"No, that's okay. I'll hold.''

Cassie scribbled a few notes as she waited, her mind
shifting back to John Robicheaux. She tried to picture him
pleading a case in front of a jury, imagined that hard body
in a suit, the tie a little loose around his neck, his dark
eyes peering into those of the jurors.

"Are you certain you have that name right?''

"Patsy David, class of '64. That's her maiden name, but
I understand she never married.''

"That's right. Patsy David from the class of '64 never
married.''

"Do you have a current name or address for her?''

"Patsy David is dead, Ms. Pierson. She died in a car
accident her senior year of high school.''

CHAPTER FOUR

CASSIE PICKED UP the postcard, this time checking the postmark. It had been mailed from Athens, Greece, on the fourteenth of May, five days after her mother had left Houston. She picked up the second one. Santorini. Mailed May 20.

Her mother had clearly lied about her traveling companion, but not her destination. But if she wasn't with Patsy, who had she gone with and why had she felt the need to lie? Could this possibly be a romantic tryst far from the prying eyes of anyone who knew her?

Cassie tried to picture her mother in the arms of a man other than Butch Havelin. The image was too ludicrous to jell. But then, how much did she really know about her mother these days? She'd been so caught up in her own problems with Drake that she'd seldom gone home for visits and she couldn't remember the last time she and her mother had actually had a conversation about anything more important than plans for holidays or a sale they were having at Nieman Marcus.

But, a lover? It was extremely unlikely.

The phone rang, startling Cassie from her troubled trance. She grabbed the receiver. Surely it was the school secretary calling her back to say everything she'd told her a few minutes ago was a mistake.

"Hello."

"Is this Cassie Pierson?"

A male voice, rich with a Cajun accent. "Yes. How can I help you?"

"I understand from Lily and Robert you were in Beau Pierre yesterday asking questions about the Magnolia Restorative and Therapeutic Center."

"I was. Who is this?"

"Dr. Norman Guilliot. I'm assuming you're interested in the center as a reporter rather than a potential guest."

"I'd like to do a story on Magnolia Plantation for the *Crescent Connection*. We're a cutting-edge magazine that focuses…"

"I'm familiar with the magazine. If you're coming out in the hopes of digging up dirt, then don't waste your time. There is none."

Yet he'd bothered to call her when she hadn't even left a message. First John Robicheaux, now Dr. Norman Guilliot, both going out of their way to look her up. A suspicious happening when dealing with articles involving lawsuits and now possibly a murder.

"No dirt," she said. Unless, of course, she found some. "I'd love to talk to you and do a feature article on your clinic."

"In that case, I'll be happy to meet with you and discuss the center. I don't have surgery scheduled today, so I can see you this afternoon if you like."

"How's one o'clock?" Cassie asked, wanting to act before he changed his mind.

"Fine. Just press the call button and identify yourself when you arrive. I'll alert the staff to expect you."

"Then I'll see you at one," she said.

"I should warn you ahead of time that confidentiality is a basic tenet of Magnolia Plantation, so certain areas of the center will be off-limits. You won't be allowed any contact with the guests."

"I understand."

Off and running, at least as far as the Beau Pierre investigation was concerned, but the planned meeting with Dr. Guilliot did nothing to allay her concerns about her mother. Touring Greece. Having a great time. The postcards said so.

But if everything else about her trip was a lie, then the postcards could be more of the same. Having a great time. Wish you were here.

Cassie wasn't convinced that either statement was true.

THE FIRST FLOOR had a large reception area and just past that a series of small offices. The back of the first floor was guest rooms, or so Cassie was told. She didn't get to tour that part of the house.

The second story had a large, airy sitting room with a TV, a baby grand piano and clusters of comfortable chairs. The dining room was there as well, with a long antique table and several small round tables. And once again there were patient rooms that she was not allowed to tour.

But while the first two floors seemed a Lucullan holdout from the days when ladies had worn full skirts and binding corsets and had danced beneath candled chandeliers, the third floor left no doubt that this was a state-of-the-art surgery center.

"So this is where the miracles take place," Cassie said, as they departed the elevator and started down a spotlessly clean hall, one bereft of the elegant antique furnishings that had characterized the lower floors.

"Interesting that you put it that way," Dr. Guilliot answered. "Modern surgical procedures are nothing short of miraculous. Think how archaic medicine was at the time this old plantation was built."

"But apparently all cosmetic surgeons are not created

equal. Otherwise, you wouldn't have patients coming to a clinic tucked away in a little town like this."

"I like to think I'm worth it, and I'm sure our facilities for follow-up care are second to none in the world."

"Exactly how does that work? Are the patients required to stay here for a certain period of time after surgery?"

"I require a one-week stay for major procedures such as face or forehead lifts. Many patients opt to stay longer, some until the swelling and bruises have completely disappeared. That can take as long as six weeks. Once the bandages and draining tubes are removed they're basically guests in this beautiful, restful setting for the rest of their stay, though I do see them for regular checkups while they're here."

"Do you have male patients as well as female?"

"Certainly. Men like to look their best, too, especially those in the public eye. Entertainers, TV personalities, politicians. We get them all right here in Beau Pierre." The doctor pushed through a set of double doors, then stood aside and waited for her to enter. "We have two operating rooms. This is the first one."

"You surely don't operate on two patients at once."

"No, but occasionally Dr. Walter Gates uses this facility, as well."

"I didn't realize that."

"See, you've learned something already."

"But doesn't he ordinarily work out of Touro Hospital in New Orleans?"

"Normally, but I feel that a surgeon must have a narrow field of specialization if he expects to be one of the very best at what he does. I stick to facial and neck surgery, but if a patient is interested in other types of cosmetic surgery, Dr. Gates will come here and provide pretty much anything else the patient desires."

"So a patient can get the works without leaving Magnolia Plantation."

"Exactly."

"Was Ginny Flanders planning to have additional surgery done?"

He wagged a finger at her. "No discussing the case. Strict orders from my attorney."

When they left the operating room, Dr. Guilliot took her through the recovery area, then led her to a closed door at the end of the hall. "This is my private office," he said, opening the door and revealing a sun-filled room with plush beige carpet and off-white walls.

Obviously a second office, since she'd seen the one on the first floor where he examined and met with new patients. This one was smaller, cozy actually. The large mahogany desk was polished to a brilliant shine and a silver frame held a snapshot of two girls who appeared to be in their early twenties. She guessed them to be the daughters he'd fathered with his first wife.

They talked for a few minutes about the center, including its excellent reputation. When the talk turned to staff, Cassie saw her opportunity. "You must be very upset about the death of your anesthetist."

"What do you know about Dennis Robicheaux?" he asked, his eyes narrowing and taking on an intensity that intrigued her.

"Basically what was in the newspaper, that he shot himself in the head. That he'd been the one to administer the anesthetic to Ginny Flanders."

"Both true, I'm afraid."

"Had he been with you long?"

"Five years, but I knew him before that. He did a clinical with me before while working on his CRNA. He was an excellent anesthetist and a good friend."

"You must have been shocked to hear of his suicide."

"I was quite upset and still am. We're all very close here at the center, Cassie. Is it okay to call you that?"

"Cassie's fine." He didn't, however suggest she call him Norman. She started to anyway, just to see how he reacted, but didn't want to do anything to aggravate him before she got everything out of him that she could. "Did you have any suspicion that Dennis was contemplating suicide?"

"Certainly not. If I had, I would have seen that he got counseling—and that he hadn't gone out drinking with his brother that night. If he'd had more family support instead of…" Dr. Guilliot hesitated as voices and laughter drifted in from the hall. "Better if I don't get started on John Robicheaux. And it sounds as if the rest of the surgical team is in the lounge. I'll introduce you to them."

Cassie would have loved to hear more about Guilliot's theories on John Robicheaux, though in the end she'd make up her own mind about the man, as she would about Norman Guilliot.

They joined the staff in a small lounge area at the very end of the hall. It was basically an oblong kitchen, consisting of a long wooden table with eight chairs, a counter, cabinets, a microwave and a refrigerator.

Cassie made mental notes as Guilliot introduced the staff. Angela Dubuisson was the instrument technician, a registered nurse who'd been with Guilliot for twenty years. Cassie guessed her to be in her mid-forties. Her hair was the color of onyx, and she wore it in a square cut that fell just below her cheekbones, with long bangs she'd pushed to the side and caught in an amber-colored barrette.

Her eyes were slightly darker than her hair, her lashes long and natural, her complexion smooth. She didn't wear any makeup, except maybe a light dusting of powder over her nose and a pale pink lip gloss. She didn't say much except to agree with anything Dr. Guilliot said.

Susan Dalton, the circulating nurse, was pretty much the opposite. She appeared to be in her early thirties and had short blond hair that curled about a heart-shaped face. Her eyes were a deep blue and seemed to be dancing behind mascara-laden lashes. Her nose turned up ever so slightly at the end. Perhaps some of Dr. Guilliot's handiwork. She talked with her hands and eyes, as well as her mouth, and her voice sounded as if she might burst into giggles at any second. Where Angela's femininity was understated and gentle, Susan's was exaggerated, like sparks from Fourth of July fireworks.

Roy Baskins was the temporary anesthetist. At least forty and slim with a face that looked as if it might actually break if forced into a smile, he was clearly not part of the group and seemed to prefer it that way.

Fred Powell was the most difficult member of the staff to get a handle on. He was in his late twenties or early thirties, a fellowship assistant who'd been with the group since January. He was nice-looking, polite, but seemed a tad stuffier than the rest of the group. She knew from media coverage of the trial that he hadn't been at work the day Ginny Lynn Flanders had died. Lucky him.

"Anyone know where I can rent a room for a week or so?" Cassie asked when the conversation lagged. Guilliot's expression went from friendly to guarded in a matter of heartbeats, but he didn't respond to the question.

"I'm not looking for anything fancy," she added. "Just something clean and convenient."

"I don't think you'll find anything in Beau Pierre," Susan said. "There's nothing but those cabins back of Suzette's. I'm sure they smell like dead fish, and you'd have alligators to greet you when you came home at night."

"Why are you looking to stay in Beau Pierre?" Angela asked.

"We're doing a feature article on the town. I'd like to get a feel for the place and get to know the people who live here."

"That should take about an hour," Roy said.

"You can drive back to New Orleans in about two hours," Susan said. "That is where you live, isn't it?"

"I drive over from Houma every day," Fred said. "That's not a bad drive and you can find decent places to stay there."

"I'd rather be closer," Cassie said, though she didn't care for a cabin that smelled of dead fish, or for the company of alligators.

"Will you only be here for a week?" Angela asked.

"Maybe less."

Angela looked to Guilliot then back to Cassie. "My mother and I have a large house. It's old, nothing fancy, but it's only about ten minutes from here. You can stay with us for a week if you like."

The lounge grew quiet at Angela's offer. Evidently the others were as surprised by it as Cassie.

"I'm certain Cassie would prefer a place of her own," Dr. Guilliot said, his tone tinged with authority.

He was right. She'd have much preferred a place of her own, but an invitation into the inner circle of the surgery team was too good to pass up, especially since it was obvious Guilliot didn't like the idea.

"I'd love to stay with you, Angela."

Angela directed her gaze to a half-eaten salad that sat on the table in front of her. "On second thought, it's probably not a good idea. My mother has a tendency to wander the house at all hours of the night. She'd probably keep you awake."

"I can sleep through anything. And I won't be any trouble. I'll take my meals at the café in town and I'll be out most of the day."

Angela looked to Guilliot again. He nodded as if giving approval, providing Cassie with additional insight into the workings of the interpersonal dynamics of the staff. Guilliot was king. The others were loyal—or maybe not-so-loyal—subjects.

At any rate, it was clear Cassie's visit to the plantation had come to a close. Guilliot was still charming on the surface, but Cassie felt a chill now that hadn't been there earlier, and the conversation went from a lull to stone silence.

Suicide or murder?

Suddenly the question seemed to have as many facets as the plantation had rooms. This might prove to be a very interesting week, but as Cassie was escorted out of the plantation, she had an idea that it was the last time she'd be welcomed into the inner sanctum.

The king had granted her one audience, no doubt to make certain she presented him and the center favorably. Now she was on her own.

CASSIE WAS STILL pondering the suicide or murder question as she left the plantation grounds and started back into Beau Pierre. The almost two hours Cassie had spent with Dr. Guilliot had done little to further her investigation into the matter and had given her nothing to spark the article Olson wanted by Saturday.

She needed some real insight into Dennis, needed someone who knew him well to open up and tell her what had really been going on in Dennis's mind before Friday night.

Her best bet would be an ex-girlfriend, someone who

knew all and was no longer emotionally connected with Dennis or involved in the Flanders v. Guilliot case.

And she needed to talk to John Robicheaux. There was clearly no love lost between him and Dr. Norman Guilliot. That in itself had the potential for a fascinating cover story if she could get facts and anecdotes to back it up. The darkly handsome fallen Cajun attorney. The prestigious, charismatic Cajun surgeon who was in the middle of the most publicized lawsuit since the Edwin Edwards trial that sent the former governor to prison. This was as good as it got in the world of reporting.

Yet it didn't fully claim Cassie's mind. Nothing would until she found out why her mother had lied to her and Butch about her trip. She'd put off calling her father, but she couldn't put it off any longer. She drove until she came to the bait/convenience shop she'd spotted on her way out. Her throat was dry, and she needed something cold to drink before she got her father on the line and hit him with the news.

She walked into the shop, took a diet soda from the cooler and exchanged a few words with a gnarly clerk in a stained white T-shirt and baggy jeans before walking to a slightly lopsided picnic table outside the shop. From there she could see the still, murky waters of Tortue Bayou. A row of turtles sat along the bank as if waiting for their ship to come in and a stately blue heron fished in the muddy water, lifting its feet high with each careful step.

Cassie slapped at a mosquito that had settled on her arm, then punched her dad's office number into the keypad of the cell phone, silently praying that for once he'd be in.

"Conner-Marsh Drilling and Exploration. Butch Havelin's office. May I help you?"

"It's Cassie again, Dottie. Tell me Dad is in."

"He's on the other line. If you can hold on, I'll see how long he'll be."

"I can hold, but tell him the call is urgent."

"How urgent? Have you been in a wreck?"

"Not that urgent, but I need to talk to him as soon as possible."

"I'll see what I can do."

A minute later Dottie informed her that Butch would return her call momentarily. She lingered at the picnic table, drinking her cold soda and wondering if her mother had to go through Dottie every time she wanted to talk to her husband. If so, that could explain why she hadn't bothered to call from Greece. It didn't, however, explain why there was no itinerary and no Patsy David.

BUTCH STARED at the phone, dreading making the call to Cassie. He was almost certain this had to do with her mother, a subject which he'd much prefer to avoid. "What's up?" he asked, once he had her on the line.

"It's Mom, Dad."

He groaned inwardly. "Did you talk to her?"

"No. I never located an itinerary. I don't know how to tell you this, Dad, but Mom didn't go to Greece with Patsy David."

"Of course, she did."

"Patsy David is dead, has been since their senior year in high school."

"You must have her confused with someone else, Cassie."

His irritation grew as Cassie detailed her discovery. He'd never thought the Greece trip fit his wife's personality, but he hadn't questioned Rhonda too much about it. He'd been too glad to see her go.

"If you know what this is about, Dad, just level with me."

"I don't have a clue. Not a damn clue."

"Were you and Mom having problems?"

"If we were, I didn't know it."

"Did she seem upset when she left? Distant? Aggravated?"

"No more than usual."

"What do we do?"

Nothing as far as he was concerned, but he knew Cassie wouldn't settle for that. "The postcards all say she's having a wonderful time," he said. "And she'll be back in two weeks. I say we just wait until then to try to find out why she felt she had to lie to us."

"But what if something's wrong?"

"Why would you think something's wrong?"

"She lied to us about who she went with. She didn't leave an itinerary, and she hasn't called."

"That's your mother for you. Sometimes it's hard to figure out why she does things the way she does. But it sounds to me as if she wanted some time alone. I think it's only fair we respect that."

"I'd feel a lot better if I could talk to her."

"She knows where we are if she wants to talk."

"So you think we should do nothing?"

"Right. Just let it ride. If I hear from her, I'll give you a call. If you hear from her, you call me. And in the meantime, don't worry."

"I'm not sure I can do that."

"Try. So, tell me, what big story are you scooping now?"

He only half listened as Cassie told him about Dennis Robicheaux's death. His mind was on Rhonda. He wasn't worried, not in the sense Cassie was, but he did wonder what the hell was going on with his wife.

She could have found out about him and Babs, though he didn't see how that would inspire a trip to Greece. An argument, maybe even a showdown, but not a trip to Europe—unless this was a prelude to divorce.

Talk about gumming up the works. He had no interest in splitting up his 401K at this stage in his life, and if Babs was named in the divorce proceedings, it could cause a lot of talk at Conner-Marsh, a company that wouldn't want even the whisper of a scandal involving its CEO and one of its female supervisors.

An old Beach Boys song knocked around in Butch's head after he'd hung up the phone. *Help me, Rhonda. Help, help me, Rhonda.*

He wasn't sure just what form that help should take, but for starters, she could find happiness and fulfillment in Greece and just not bother to return. He'd miss her sometimes, but he could live with it.

CASSIE TRIED to adopt some of her father's optimism but decided the only way she'd be able to get her mother off her mind was to jump into the job at hand. So as much as she dreaded dealing with the sexy, arrogant Cajun, John Robicheaux was her next logical interviewee.

She had an idea that anyone in town could tell her where he lived, including the fishy-smelling guy inside the store. She finished her drink, tossed the empty can into a rusted trash barrel and walked back inside.

Maybe the fallen attorney would be in a better mood today. And maybe Jupiter would collide with Mars or the bars on Bourbon Street would stop selling liquor on Mardi Gras Day.

CHAPTER FIVE

CASSIE SLOWED as she passed Suzette's. The roadhouse was a low-slung, wooden structure with a tin roof. It looked as if it might have been a bright yellow at one time, but the paint was faded and peeling and the facings around the windows were literally rotting away.

There was a row of rental cabins along the bayou just as Susan had said, half-hidden by cypress trees and palmetto plants. They were rustic at best, but some looked to be bordering on total ruin. She imagined them crawling with spiders and stinging scorpions, with slimy black water moccasins slithering through the swampy grass just outside the doors. Definitely not a place for a city gal like her.

She wondered if John Robicheaux's habitat would be much different. The guy in the bait shop had referred to it as a trapper's shack and warned her to be careful with the same level of caution to his tone she would have expected if she'd said she was going skinny-dipping with a family of alligators.

From being one of the hottest defense attorneys in New Orleans, and probably the state, to living in a shack in the swamp was quite a backward jump. Penance, she suspected, for unleashing a fiendish sex pervert on an innocent little girl.

The sun slid behind a cloud as Cassie turned from the narrow asphalt road onto a dirt one bordered on either side by swampland. There was no shack. In fact there was no sign of human life anywhere, and she had a sudden impulse to turn around and get the hell out before what was left of the road dissolved into the watery morass.

Yet Dennis Robicheaux had chosen to end his life standing in just such a soggy swamp. At least, that was the sheriff's version. But even if you were set on ending it all, why spend the last few seconds of life sinking in the mud instead of sitting behind the wheel of a nice, dry car?

Had he been doing penance, too—for a mistake that had killed Ginny Lynn? Lots of questions. No answers.

The old dirt road grew more difficult to maneuver. Cassie dodged potholes and bounced across deep ruts and places where the road had all but washed out. It crossed her mind that the guy in the bait shop might have seen her as a nosy reporter and sent her on a journey to nowhere.

She shouldn't have had that soda. They always went right through her, and her bladder was already protesting the rough road and screaming for relief.

She was about to turn around when she saw John's black pickup truck stopped in the middle of the road. She threw on her brakes, thinking something was wrong, then realized that her earlier fears were actually true. The road narrowed to a path just beyond the truck and disappeared into the bog.

She spotted the house a few yards off the road. It was built of split cypress logs and stood on short piers that put it just above the swampland that surrounded it. A couple of weathered rockers, some metal pails, a foam cooler and a jug of Kentwood Springs water sat on a porch that swayed to the left like a woman who'd carried babies on her hip for too many years.

Cassie studied the shell walkway that led to the porch as she crawled from behind the wheel of her car. Reaching back into the car, she grabbed her black notebook and started down the path, swatting a vicious mosquito the size of a small helicopter as she did. Like the mosquito, she was unannounced and uninvited. But probably not unexpected.

An attorney, even a nonpracticing one like John, knew that the word murder and the mention of Dr. Norman Guilliot's name would lure a reporter just as surely as his smelly bait lured fish onto his hook.

She rapped on the door of the cabin and it creaked open as if she were being welcomed by some invisible phantom. The eeriness settled in, creeping up her spine like a wet chill on a frosty January morning. She wasn't on the edge of civilization. She'd passed that about five miles back. It didn't get more isolated than this.

Cassie rapped again, then eased the door open a few more inches. "John Robicheaux?" She called his name tentatively. "Anyone home?"

No answer. But the door was open and she really needed to go to the bathroom. Not that there weren't plenty of places to go outside if she dared venture off the shell path. She didn't dare.

She stepped into a rectangular room that apparently served as dining room, den and study. Her gaze settled on a massive claw-footed pine table that stretched along a row of side windows. There was a floor-to-ceiling homemade bookcase on the opposite wall, filled to overflowing with both hardcover and paperback selections. Two worn recliners and a mock leather sofa with a split in the armrest were clustered on the side of the room with the bookcase. A large wooden desk sat against the back wall.

The desk was empty except for a stack of newspaper clippings and a computer. The computer stood out, as if it had been plucked from the modern world and placed in the time warp that had trapped the rest of the surroundings.

The floorboards groaned as Cassie crossed the room to a closed door she really hoped was a bathroom. Luckily, she was right, and indoor plumbing had never looked so good. She took care of business, then washed her hands and dried them on an earth-colored towel—a towel that smelled of soap and spices and musk.

She turned half-expecting to see John behind her, but it was only the smell of him and the fact that she was surrounded by his personal things that made the sense of his presence so strong. His razor, his toothbrush, an open bottle of over-the-counter painkillers.

She left the bathroom and walked to the bookshelf. She scanned the titles and found everything from the classics to Dennis Lehane's newest thriller. Not one law book, though, or anything to suggest John had ever been a practicing defense attorney.

She picked up a homemade cypress frame from the top of the bookshelf and studied the photograph. Two boys, one a teenager, the other a preschooler, stood between an elderly man and woman. The man had on black wading boots, a shirt that was open at the neck and a pair of baggy jeans. Gray-haired, too thin, but smiling big enough to show a row of tobacco-stained teeth. The woman was plump, with salt-and-pepper hair pulled into a chignon on top of her head.

There was no doubt that the oldest boy was John. Hair as black as night, a cocky smile and the same eyes that had seemed to see right through her yesterday. And already sexy, though he couldn't have been more than seventeen or so when the picture was taken. And the younger boy must be Dennis. Adorable, with the same thick dark hair and cocky smile. There were quite a few years between them, yet she got the impression from John that they'd been close.

The Robicheaux brothers. From the swamps to law school and anesthetist training and on their way to the good life. Now Dennis was dead. And John was...

Actually she wasn't sure what John was except angry, grieved and incredibly virile. And in spite of the fact that the door had been unlocked and had opened at her knock, she still felt uneasy at being here when he wasn't around.

Reporters who are scared to take chances end up with predictable, boring copy. That was pretty much the basic rule of journalism, the no guts, no glory edict of reporting. She'd always had more balls than most of the male reporters she'd worked with, but still the sheer isolation of this place was getting to her.

She'd about convinced herself to clear out when she heard footsteps on the porch. She turned as John pushed through the door, then propped a hand on the facing and glared at her. "Why don't you come in, Cassie Pierson? Make yourself at home?"

His stance and voice were intimidating, but she kept her back straight and her own voice just as level. "The door was open."

"Cajun hospitality." Only he didn't sound the least bit hospitable.

She smelled the whiskey on his breath from across the room and knew she didn't want to get into an argument with him. "Your truck was here," she said. "I assumed you were around somewhere."

"I'm around. What do you want?"

"To talk."

"I'm listening."

He wasn't going to make this easy. "Do you remember our conversation yesterday?"

"I'm half-drunk, not addled."

"Do you still think Dennis was murdered?"

"I still *know* that he was. I also told you yesterday that Norman Guilliot would manipulate you and use you the same way he uses everyone else in town. That didn't keep you from going back out there today."

"What did you do? Pay someone to follow me around? Stalk me yourself?"

"Beau Pierre's a small town. News gets around."

"Then I guess there are no secrets in Beau Pierre?"

"Oh, there are plenty of secrets—just not for long. They're like splinters buried under the skin. They fester awhile, but eventually work their way out. Now if you'll excuse me, I need to do some more drinking before this day gets any further along. If that offends you or bothers you in any way, feel free to find your way out of here the same way you found your way in."

"You say Guilliot wants to manipulate me, and that could be true, but what about you, John? Why do you need me?"

"Me? Need you? You've got things way wrong, sweetheart."

"Not the way it looks to me. You followed me out to Magnolia Plantation yesterday and informed me that your brother had been murdered."

"And that means I need you?"

"You knew I wouldn't just walk away from the implication of murder."

"Of course not. No reporter walks away from a chance for a juicy story."

"But you didn't go to just any reporter. You came to me and claimed Dennis was murdered. You got my interest, so now give me facts. Level with me, and I'll give you the press you're obviously looking for."

LEVEL WITH HER. He'd love to, only his mind was so damn twisted today he had trouble putting his thoughts in any kind of sequence that made sense. Caskets and flowers. Tombstones and burial plots. He'd been through this before not so long ago, but then it had been for his grandparents.

The actions were basically the same, but they felt so different. Dennis should have lived years longer, should have had the chance to grow old right here in Beau Pierre.

He poured himself a drink then one for Cassie. Whiskey. Straight up, so it would burn clear down to his belly. He drank his down, then poured two fingers more. Carrying both drinks, he crossed the room and handed one to Cassie.

"To leveling," he said, clinking his glass with hers. "And to justice."

"To justice," she agreed. "And truth."

"Truth—or a story? Which is it you're after, Cassie? You have to make up your mind, you know."

"I'd like both."

He looked up from the whiskey and into Cassie's eyes, the color of spring leaves, ardent, not yet jaded by the heat and merciless beatings of life. He'd been like that once, though he could barely remember it now.

Cassie sipped at the whiskey, making a face as it slid down her throat and probably hit her stomach like hot wax from a dripping candle.

"Why do you claim Dennis was murdered when the evidence points to suicide?" She tossed her head as if issuing a challenge, and wispy tendrils of curly auburn hair danced around her cheeks.

John wondered if she had any idea how sexy she looked when she did that.

"Why murder, John?" Cassie repeated.

He exhaled sharply as he struggled to find the most cohesive thread through his suspicions. "Dennis had plans. Suicide wasn't in them."

"What kind of plans?"

"He was going to leave Beau Pierre."

"Where was he going?"

"The West Coast."

"Did Norman Guilliot know that?"

"Dennis hadn't told him, but that doesn't mean he hadn't heard."

"Was his leaving connected to the Flanders trial?"

"You'll have to ask your friend Norman Guilliot that. Ask him what really happened the day Ginny Flanders died. Get an answer to that, and you'll have the reason why Dennis was murdered."

"Then you think he was murdered because of some mistake he made administering the anesthetic?"

"No. He was killed because he knew what really happened that day. A bullet through the head is the surest way to keep a man quiet."

"But if Dennis wanted to talk, he'd had six months to do it. He could have talked to the sheriff or any of the lawyers handling the case. And you said yourself, he was leaving Beau Pierre anyway."

"None of that changes the fact that my brother was murdered."

"With his own gun?"

"Anyone could have walked in the house and taken that gun, the same way you walked into this house. We don't lock doors in Beau Pierre."

"So you think someone stole his gun, then waited for him on the road that night."

"That's exactly what I think. They forced him into the swamp and then shot him."

The image crept to life inside John's head, the brains

spilling out of Dennis's head, the blood spurting, his life ripped from him in shattered shreds. But the image clouded and merged with one of a little girl, her body bruised and swollen so badly that even the family had difficulty identifying her.

"Are you all right?"

Cassie's voice managed to penetrate the stifling haze that had settled over his mind. "No," he answered. "And I'm not going to be all right until Dennis's killer is in prison. Put that in your article. And when you see your friend Norman Guilliot again, you can tell him for me that if he had anything to do with Dennis's death, he better watch his back every second."

"I'm not your messenger girl, John. I'm sorry about your brother, really sorry, but you can't dictate the content of my articles and you'll have to talk to Dr. Guilliot yourself."

Tough woman. But she didn't look tough. She looked soft, her skin all tanned beneath that white blouse. Her shiny auburn hair pulled back and knotted at the nape of her neck. Full pink lips. And those eyes.

He shook his head, fighting the lust that came from nowhere. He didn't need a woman. What he needed was another drink, a stiff whiskey to dull the pain. He went back to the counter to pour another. "How about you, Cassie? Do you want another drink?"

"No. I need to go now."

"Can't say that I blame you. None of Guilliot's charm around here. No big plantation. No servants. No bullshit."

"I wouldn't go that far." She took a few steps toward the door. "It's none of my business, John, but you look as if you've had enough to drink."

"You're right. It's none of your business."

"It's not going to be easy proving your brother was

murdered. Going at it with liquor-dulled senses and a mind-dulling hangover isn't going to help you."

"You did say you were leaving, didn't you?"

"Yeah. Do what you like. I have a feeling you always do."

He watched her walk out the door and heard her footsteps as she raced down the front steps. His hand tightened on the whiskey glass. He'd drunk his way through the pain for nights on end following Toni Crenshaw's murder. Drank until the images would finally fade and let him fall asleep.

But Cassie was right. If he did that now, he'd be crippling his chances of proving Dennis was murdered. And there would be no way to drink himself past that.

He swallowed hard, then hurled the empty glass against the wall behind the bookcase. Glass rained down on the worn wood floor, shimmering in the late-afternoon sun that poured through the windows.

But John's gaze fastened on the jagged shard that had fallen just in front of the photo of Dennis and him with their grandparents. The glass beneath his boots ground into the floor when he crossed the room and picked up the picture. All the people he'd ever loved, and now he was the only one left. The only one of them who had the least reason to go on breathing had survived them all.

Proof again that there was no justice in life.

But you'll get your justice, Dennis. Someone pulled the trigger that night, and someone will pay with their life. I promise you that, little brother. And this time I won't let you down.

BUTCH HAVELIN pulled into the driveway of his rambling ranch-style house at five minutes before six. It was the earliest he'd made it back to suburbia since being promoted to CEO, except for the times he'd come by to change into formal clothes for a special function. He hadn't planned on coming home tonight at all, but Cassie's phone call had changed that.

Piss-poor timing, but he had to try and figure out what was behind this foolish stunt of Rhonda's. Aggravation ragged him as he opened the door and stepped inside the quiet house. He wasn't the perfect husband, but he wasn't the worst. Rhonda had never wanted for anything. And as for his affair with Babs, Rhonda had lost interest in sex long ago. If she'd found out about the affair, she was probably glad he was getting his rocks off with someone else.

Butch dropped his briefcase on the sofa, then poured a shot of Glenmorangie over a couple of cubes of ice. Fortified, he walked to the master bedroom suite he'd shared with Rhonda since they'd bought the house ten years ago. Decorated to perfection with expensive furnishings and tasteful accessories. Rhonda had done it herself. She'd always been good at that, had never bothered with designers.

She was good at a lot of things. He'd never denied that. That didn't make up for the fact that she didn't know him anymore and didn't want to.

Muscles tight, he finished his drink and lifted Rhonda's daily calendar from the antique secretary in the corner of the bedroom. He scanned the pages for the days preceding her leaving for Greece. A dental appointment. Lunch with friends at the club. Contact lenses to pick up. Manicure and pedicure. So much for the calendar.

He started to pick up the small Rolodex, then decided Rhonda's cell phone would likely give better information. He found it tucked away in the top drawer, then used the menu key to get to outgoing calls. Some numbers he recognized. Some he didn't, but there was no pattern of repeat calls to any unfamiliar numbers.

Next he checked the incoming calls. Still nothing that looked amiss. He turned off the phone and yanked open the top desk drawer.

Rhonda saved everything, which meant every drawer in the house was full. This one held an invitation to a friend's fiftieth birthday party, receipts, menus for local restaurants and a dental appointment card.

He returned the papers to the drawer and opened the one below it. At least he tried to open it. The freaking thing was stuck on something. He squeezed his big hand to the back of the narrow drawer and found the problem. A brown envelope had apparently spilled over from the top drawer and gotten lodged between the two.

Butch pulled it out, then straightened the bent edges of the envelope. It had been sent to Rhonda but there was no return address. The postmark said Sifnos, Greece. He undid the clasp and shook the envelope. A brightly colored postcard fell out. A church painted white and trimmed in a vivid blue with the sea in the background.

He turned it over to see who it was from. There was no message and no address. Strange that someone would mail an unsigned postcard in a brown envelope. Or perhaps Rhonda had just stuck it in the envelope.

Using his thumb, he pressed the crease from the center of the postcard, then stuck it in his shirt pocket. He wasn't sure why, but the postcard bothered him, added a dark shade of mystery to a situation that was already bizarre.

If this sudden trip to Greece wasn't about him and Babs, then Rhonda would have some explaining to do.

And if it was about his affair... Well, he'd face that when and if he had to. With luck, that would be never.

A LIGHT DRIZZLE was falling by the time Cassie reached Angela Dubuisson's place. The house was a rambling

wooden structure, three stories, with steep, wide steps leading to the second floor gallery. It had probably been a
grand structure in its time, but its time was probably close
to a hundred years ago.

The light blue paint was faded and had peeled in spots,
leaving patches of yellowed white paint showing through.
One storm shutter was missing from the long windows
along the second level, and the columns across the front
of the house were seriously mildewed.

Haunted. That was the word that came to mind as Cassie
pulled her car to a stop in the shell drive. Odd, since she
was not one to believe in ghosts, but if she had, this was
the type of place she'd expect to find them. Maybe Dennis's ghost would come calling and give her the insight
she needed. Or the ghost of Ginny Lynn Flanders. Either
ghost would probably have lots to say.

Hopefully Angela would, as well. And if not, staying
here would still beat the ambiance of Suzette's bayou cabins.

A flash of lightning zigzagged across the sky as Cassie
rang the bell, followed by a rumbling roar of thunder.
Summer thunderstorms blew in from the Gulf with almost
predictable regularity in southern Louisiana, frequently in-
tense but usually blowing over as quickly as they moved
in. Hopefully this one would do the same, since Cassie's
luggage was still in the trunk of the car.

Angela opened the front door as lightning struck again,
this time close enough that the following clap of thunder
seemed instantaneous.

"Looks like I made it just in time," Cassie said.

Angela stared at her, unsmiling, looking as if she'd eaten
something that was threatening to pop back up.

"I would have called you," she said, her voice low,
"but I didn't have a phone number."

"Is something wrong?"

She nodded. "It's my mother. I told her we were having a guest, and she got really upset. She's been like this ever since my father died last year. Sometimes she's rational. Other times she's disoriented and frightened of anything unfamiliar."

"So she doesn't want me here?"

"I'm afraid not. And when she's like this, you wouldn't want to be around her."

"Maybe she'd feel better about my staying if she met me."

"No. That's not a good idea. I'm really sorry about this, Cassie, but your staying here just won't work out."

And something about this whole scenario didn't jive. It was clear the others at the clinic hadn't approved of Angela inviting Cassie to share her home. Now it looked as if Angela had succumbed to pressure.

"I called Suzette's," Angela offered. "She has a vacancy in one of the cabins. I asked her to get it cleaned up and to hold it for you in case you wanted to stay there."

"I'd much rather stay here. Fewer crawling creatures, I'm sure."

Angela managed a slight smile, but it didn't reach her eyes. "On the bright side, Suzette's has great food and a nightlife. That is, if you call smoke, beer and fiddle music a nightlife."

"I'm not much of a party girl," Cassie said.

"Me, either. I'm pretty much the town dud. I think you should take Suzette's cabin even if just for the night. The TV meteorologist says there's a line of severe thunderstorms moving in from the Gulf. Driving would be hazardous."

"Who are you talking to, Angela?"

Cassie peeked around the door and saw the owner of

the voice, a nice and very alert-looking woman somewhere around her mid-seventies standing a few feet behind Angela.

"It's a friend, *Maman*," Angela answered.

"What, you got no manners, shay? Tell your friend to get herself out of that storm. The crawfish stew is ready. There's plenty enough for your friend."

Angela stepped out on the porch with Cassie, pulling the door shut behind her. "See what I mean. She's forgotten all about telling me not to let you come here. Her moods are too unreliable for me to risk having a guest in the house. I don't know what I was thinking when I invited you."

"I appreciate the offer anyway. Maybe we can have dinner together one night."

Angela shook her head. "I usually come straight home to be with my mother."

"Then lunch?"

"We'll see. I have to go now. I'm sorry I put you to the trouble of driving out here."

"No trouble. I'm just sorry I can't stay. The house seems charming, and I'd love to get to know you better."

The drizzle had intensified to a downpour by the time Cassie reached the end of the driveway. Looked like Suzette's Bayou Cabins were it—at least for one night.

The prospect was downright chilling.

CHAPTER SIX

THE RAIN didn't let up, making the drive to Suzette's slow and tedious. By the time Cassie arrived, she was more than ready for a soothing glass of red wine and willing to spend the night in her car if it came to that. A stiff back and a crick in her neck beat driving back to the city in this downpour.

There were a dozen cars parked in front of the old clapboard restaurant in spite of the weather. Cassie pulled in between a couple of muddy, dented pickup trucks, both with hunting rifles mounted in the back window, though she doubted June was open season on anything.

Unless maybe it had been open season on anesthetists who knew a dirty secret. The gruesome thought stuck in her mind as she opened the car door, grabbed her purse and made a run for cover.

Raindrops pelted her face and hair and water spilled into her shoes as she sloshed through deep puddles. She ducked under the overhang and stamped off as much water as she could before pushing through the door.

When she stepped inside, all eyes turned her way. Nothing like a clinging wet shirt on a stranger to grab an audience. She avoided eye contact with the gawkers and headed for the long bar in the left corner of the low-ceilinged, rectangular room.

"Hello, reporter lady."

She let her gaze follow the voice and found Fred Powell at the end of the bar, beer in hand.

He tipped his beer her way. "It's a little wet out there."

"You think?"

"Grab a stool and have a drink. It sure beats driving in the rain."

"A drink sounds good." She grabbed a handful of thin paper napkins from the bar, mopped her face and the back of her neck with them, then slid onto the barstool next to Guilliot's fellowship assistant.

The night might not be a total waste after all, she decided. Fred Powell hadn't said much when she was at Magnolia Plantation today but there was nothing like a beer and a smoky bar for getting men's tongues to wag.

"I thought you'd be snug and dry at Angela's house," he said.

"There was a change of plans."

"Oh?"

"Angela thought company might be hard on her mother."

He looked skeptical, but didn't comment.

"I had the feeling Susan and Guilliot didn't think my staying there was a good idea anyway."

"Did you expect them to?"

"I don't know why they should mind. It's Angela's house."

"Entertaining the press is a big no-no these days."

"So you think Guilliot exerted a little pressure?"

"I try not to even think of things that are none of my business. One of the big differences between being a surgeon and a reporter."

"We can't all be surgeons. Somebody's got to keep the public informed."

"Then good luck in Beau Pierre. You'll need it."

The bartender showed up to take Cassie's order. She would have preferred wine, but the offerings were limited and not to her liking, so she settled on a beer.

"Excuse me for a minute," Fred said. "Nature calls."

She watched him as he crossed the grease-stained floor to the men's room. He was tall, lanky and lean with stylishly cut, sandy-colored hair and extremely blue eyes. Not a knockout, but nice-looking, as was everyone at Magnolia Plantation. She wondered if that was one of the qualifications for working there, part of the image Guilliot was going for.

Fred didn't ooze charm the way Guilliot did, but Guilliot wouldn't want an assistant with the same level of charisma he possessed, especially one who also had youth going for him.

Fred wasn't part of the inner circle. She'd picked that up from the brief meeting in the lounge today. But he was at least on the fringes, and he'd known Dennis Robicheaux. Reason enough to linger over her beer and try to keep him talking.

The bartender slid the bottle in front of her. He was a tall guy, muscular, with a crooked nose and acne-scarred face.

"You're new in here."

"My first time."

"You a friend of Fred's, or just another reporter?"

"Couldn't I be both?"

"Not likely. You could be a friend of mine, though. I got no loyalty to Guilliot."

"I thought he was the local legend."

"In his mind. Him, he ain't done nothing for me."

He went back to chat with a couple of guys at the other

end of the bar, and Cassie scanned the room. Most of the tables were empty, but there was a group of guys at a long table near the back, drinking beer and struggling with boiled crawfish. Clearly novices at pinching tails and sucking heads.

There was also a family of six at a nearby table, a young couple holding hands and drinking sodas, and a group of teenage boys playing pool in the back of the room. Brave souls who'd ventured out in the storm, or gotten caught in it the way she had.

"The food's great here," Fred said, returning to his stool. "Love Suzette's gumbo. And if you like oysters or softshell crab, they don't come any better than you get them here."

"Do you eat here often?"

"A couple of nights a week. My girlfriend works late Tuesdays and Thursdays, so I grab a bite before I drive over to Houma. Usually the place is a lot livelier than this. The weather kept most people at home."

"I can't imagine anyone driving anywhere tonight unless they have to."

"Most of the people in here are probably staying in the cabins. Vacationers from the north come down here every summer for a taste of the bayou life."

"Actually I'm thinking of renting one of the cabins," she said.

"Have you seen them?"

"Only from the road."

"I'd think twice about staying in one of them tonight."

"Are they that bad?"

"They're okay for a few nights if you don't mind roughing it. I stayed in one the first week I was with Guilliot, but you'll have to wade through mud and slush to get to them tonight.''

"No walkway, huh?"

"There's a path, but it probably went under water about two inches of rain ago. But if you're serious about renting one of them, there's the woman you should talk to. Suzette herself.''

Cassie watched as a middle-aged woman pushed through the swinging door from the kitchen carrying a tray loaded with hamburgers and fried fish for the family of six. She was pretty in the face and had a saucy gait, but the pants she wore pulled tight across her belly and derriere and she looked as if she'd had a few too many platefuls of her own cooking.

Fred put up a hand and motioned to her when she finished serving the food. She walked over and laid her wrinkled hand on Fred's shoulder. "Too bad about Dennis.''

"Yeah."

"Pisses me off, you know. A good guy like that. Life ain't fair. We shoulda seen it coming. Shoulda stopped it.''

"I don't even know if he saw it coming,'' Fred said.

"He was in here that night, laughing and talking, just like always.''

"I heard.'' Fred nodded toward Cassie. "This is Cassie Pierson, Suzette. She's a reporter with *Crescent Connection*.''

"Another one. Shoulda figured that. Every time we get a stranger by here, they looking for some gossip, them.'' She glared at Cassie. "Why don't you people leave us alone down here? We got enough troubles.''

"I'm not looking to cause trouble,'' Cassie said. "I'd like to rent one of your cabins if you have a vacancy.''

"How many nights?''

"I'm not sure. One. Maybe more."

"You ask me awhile ago, I give you a good one, but the fishermen, they stay another night now. 'Cause of the storm. I got one left, but I'm saving it for someone."

"Is it the cabin Angela Dubuisson asked you to save?"

"*Mais oui.* You the one she called about?"

"Yes."

"That's good. Last one. Way in the back, though." She looked down at Cassie's feet and frowned. "You got yourself some boots?"

Cassie shook her head. "These are the only shoes I have with me."

The woman nodded, as if she expected no better from an outsider like Cassie. "No matter. I find you some boots. You'll stay dry, you."

They discussed price and that worried Cassie even more. What kind of place could she possibly be renting for so few dollars per night? But just as she thought of saying no thanks, a crack of thunder rattled the windows. The storm was far from over.

"I'll take the cabin," she said. "Do I pay cash or credit?"

"Cash is better."

"I'll need a receipt, for expense purposes."

"Sure," Suzette said. "You stay in here awhile. I'll take you to the cabin when the rain lets up."

"Good idea," Cassie said.

She went back to her beer, thinking she'd need it to sleep through a fierce thunderstorm in a cabin stuck in the middle of the swamps. When she finished that beer, she ordered another and a bowl of gumbo that turned out to be every bit as good as Fred had said.

"So what's it like working for Norman Guilliot?" she asked, wiping her mouth on one of the paper napkins.

"The work's interesting."

"And the man?"

"Norman Guilliot's a brilliant surgeon."

"His staff seem to like him. I get the impression they're a very cohesive group."

"It's that kind of working environment."

"How did Dennis fit in the group?"

Fred leaned forward, propped an elbow on the table and looked her in the eye. "What is it you're looking for, Cassie? Dirt on Guilliot? Some reason to place guilt on him for Ginny Lynn Flanders's death? Or is it Dennis Robicheaux you're interested in?"

"I'm looking for the truth."

"Truth comes in a million different shades."

"It only came in blood-red for Dennis."

"Don't go after Dennis. Whatever his reasons were for killing himself, they don't imply guilt in the Flanders's death."

"You sound awfully sure about that for a guy who wasn't around that day."

"He did his job and did it right. And that's all I'm saying about that. Lawyer has an unofficial gag order on us."

"Did anyone at Magnolia Plantation have a reason to want Dennis Robicheaux dead?"

Fred downed a long swig of his beer, then set the empty bottle on the table with a resounding thud. "Where would you ever get an idea like that?"

"He's dead. His brother thinks he was murdered."

"His brother's a drunk."

"Even so, he must have known his brother well."

"John's probably trying to manipulate the insurance company, find a way to a payout."

That was always a possibility, but John had seemed far too troubled to be thinking of insurance when she'd talked to him. Besides, if money had been important to him, he'd have stayed an attorney. "Were you and Dennis friends?"

"Everyone who knew Dennis was his friend. He was that kind of a guy."

"So you don't think Dennis was murdered?"

"Can't imagine who'd have a motive."

She went back to her beer, but felt Fred's gaze boring into her.

"Looks like the rain is letting up," he said. "I think I'll get out of here while there's a break in the storm."

"In that case, I'd better get to the cabin before it starts up again." She scanned the room in search of Suzette.

"Sure you want to stay there alone? You never know what strange creatures may stalk the bayou on a stormy night."

"I'll take my chances."

But the warning stayed on her mind as she went to find Suzette. She would definitely lock her door tonight and wish she were home in her own bed, where visions of swamp creatures would *not* dance in her head.

"How DID IT GO?" Norman asked, keeping his voice low so that Annabeth wouldn't hear him over the television set that was blaring away in the next room.

"I felt terrible about turning her away in the storm."

"It's not as if it were a hurricane. She'll be fine."

"I guess," Angela said. "I hate to think of her staying in those horrid cabins at Suzette's."

"If she finds it bad enough, then maybe she'll go back

to New Orleans and stay there. And from now on, let me handle the reporters.''

''We're not just talking about a reporter, Norman. We're talking about Cassie Havelin Pierson.''

''You're not going to start panicking on me, are you?''

''I can't help it. First Dennis. Now this.''

''I hate what happened to Dennis as much as you do, but it's too late to do anything about it. And Cassie is just down here to do a story. So just stay cool, Angela. Everything is under control.''

''I still don't understand what was so wrong in my asking her to stay here. If she were sleeping under my roof, we'd surely talk. Then at least we'd know what she's up to.''

''Cozy chitchats with Cassie Pierson are not the way to handle this.'' In fact he could think of nothing worse. He'd sooner have Cassie snooping around the center than staying with Angela. She was loyal to the core but this was hard on her. Too much stress could lead her to say something she shouldn't and he could hear the anxiety in her voice over the phone.

''Get some sleep, Angela. And don't worry about Cassie. I'll handle her.''

''If you say so.''

''I do. I'll see you in the morning.''

He hung up and went back into the living room. Annabeth was stretched out on the sofa, immersed in the sitcom she was watching. She didn't look up until the commercial came on. ''I think I'll go with you to Dennis's funeral tomorrow.''

''It's not necessary.''

''I know, but I want to go.''

"Suit yourself, but don't start crying and making a scene. It will just be fodder for the press."

"Surely there won't be reporters at the funeral."

"Don't count on it. Vultures don't show a lot of mercy for roadkill."

"Don't talk like that, Norman. I can't bear to hear Dennis referred to as roadkill."

"It's just an expression. I didn't mean anything by it." He sat down beside her and pulled her into his arms.

"Do you think he was murdered, Norman?"

"Absolutely not. There was no sign that anyone else was around, and he was shot at close range with his own pistol."

"His brother doesn't think it was suicide."

"How do you know what his brother thinks?"

"I ran into him in town today."

"Well, stay away from him. He's nothing but trouble. If you want to go to the funeral, fine, but I don't want to talk about this any more tonight."

Didn't want to talk about it. Didn't want to think about it. He'd be so damned glad when this whole thing was over. The funeral tomorrow would be tough. The whole town would be there, somehow blaming him that Dennis didn't have the balls to take the pressure. Balls. That's what made the difference. The Guilliots had always had balls.

He missed Dennis all the same and Norman dreaded the funeral as much as he'd dreaded anything in a long, long time.

THE CABIN was about what Cassie expected. Two twin beds with lumpy mattresses and clean but worn linens. A functional kitchen that would let her make coffee in the morning. And a bathroom with a toilet and a shower that was little more than a square of tile with a drain in the middle of it surrounded by a faded plastic shower curtain.

The structure looked as if it were about ready to collapse, but it was tight enough to keep out the rain and the larger swamp creatures, such as the ratlike nutrias and the alligators—and hopefully the water moccasins. But it was not pest free. She'd already killed a couple of two-inch black roaches with wings, a southern Louisiana speciality.

And a green-eyed bug she'd never seen before had been waiting for her atop the threadbare spread when she'd entered the cabin. Suzette had knocked it to the floor with her bare hand, then squashed it beneath her white rubber boot. Cassie only hoped there weren't more surprises waiting for her the minute she turned off the overhead light—*if* she turned off the light tonight.

A far cry from the nights on the Adriatic Sea she'd hoped for. But her mother was there, somewhere beneath the stars. Living out a fantasy? Living out a lie.

Cassie's cell phone rang, and she pulled it from her purse, saw the name on the caller ID and realized that as bad as the night was, it had just taken a turn for the worse.

"Hello, Drake."

"What the hell do you think you're doing?"

"Nice to know you haven't lost that old charm."

"Don't start with me, Cassie. I know you were out at Magnolia Plantation today, schmoozing it up with Guilliot."

Oh, geez. Just how many men were spending their time tracking her every move? "How would anything I do possibly be any of your business?"

"Norman Guilliot's been avoiding reporters and refusing to grant any interviews until after the trial. Now all of

a sudden he's giving you a grand tour. You know good
and well that's only because you're still using my name.''

"Actually it's my name, Drake, until whatever time I
see fit to change it. And talking to people in the news is
what I do. It has nothing to do with you.''

"Are you telling me that you're not trying to sway public opinion to Guilliot's side, just to spite me?''

The man's conceit blew her away—and made her furious. "I never gave you a thought, Drake.''

"Don't get entangled in my case, Cassie. Guilliot and
his surgery team committed malpractice and when I get
through nailing him, his reputation will be shot! He won't
make enough money to pay someone to polish the gate on
his little mansion. The fact that his anesthetist killed himself is just further proof of their guilt.''

"If your case is so airtight, why are you worried about
what I'm doing?''

"I'm not worried. I just don't like it. So why don't you
get back to New Orleans and quit flaunting your breasts
in that smoky Cajun bar?''

The guy was unbelievable. No wonder she hadn't been
with a man since the divorce. How could she possibly trust
her instincts where men were concerned after having married him?

"I'll flaunt whatever I want, Drake, in front of whom-
ever I want. You know me. I'm constantly picking up guys
and screwing their brains out. And how could you possibly
know where I am?''

"I make it my job to know about everything connected
to one of my lawsuits.''

He was right. She did know that he was obsessed with
winning in every area of his life except marriage. He'd let
that go down the tube with seemingly little regret. But this

was taking things too far. "So who do you have down here snooping for you, Drake? Suzette? The bartender? Or do you actually have a spy posing as a fisherman in one of these back-to-nature cabins?"

"That's none of your business. Write your little article, but don't try to manipulate the facts or make my client look bad."

"Any other orders?"

"Yeah. Stay away from John Robicheaux. He was a slimeball when he was practicing law, and he's still a slimeball. He'll use you any way he can."

"It's a little late for you to worry about me being used, Drake."

She broke the connection without waiting to hear his retort. Feeling as if she were suffocating in the tiny cabin, she opened the door and stared at the falling rain. Her insides shook from fury and remorse that she'd ever been taken in by Drake Pierson.

What hurt worse was that he was right. His name was the clout that had likely gotten her an interview with Guilliot. But she wasn't doing this to mess up his case. She was merely doing her job, and if that swayed public opinion against him, so be it. She didn't even know what it mattered, except that Drake was making the most of representing the man of God against the evil and filthy rich plastic surgeon.

It was all hype. Reverend Flanders was likely as rich as Guilliot, as Drake hoped to be someday. In the end, none of that would matter. It would all come down to his convincing a judge and jury that Dr. Guilliot and Dennis had made a mistake that caused Ginny Flanders's death.

Something rippled in the bayou outside her cabin. She

stared into the darkness, saw two gleaming eyes and trembled before slamming the door shut and locking it.

She kicked off her shoes, dropped to the bed and closed her eyes. John Robicheaux's face floated through her mind. A drunk who'd thrown his life away, but that didn't mean he wasn't right about Dennis having been murdered. But if he was right about everything, it meant that someone in this peaceful bayou town would kill to keep Norman Guilliot from losing a malpractice suit.

It just didn't add up. No more than her mother's lies about Patsy David and her trip to Greece added up.

Noises filtered through the cracks and crevices of the old cabin. A bullfrog's deep croak. A throaty, bellowing roar that she didn't recognize but that gave her cold chills. The spine-tingling screech of an owl.

Cassie was certain it was going to be a long, long night.

CHAPTER SEVEN

IT WAS PAST MIDNIGHT when Cassie finally fell asleep, and she was sore, tired and irritable when she woke the next morning. She was not only aggravated with Olson for expecting her to stay in a town without a decent motel, but disgusted with herself for ever having the poor judgment to marry a self-serving jerk like Drake Pierson. And as for his name, she would drop it the way she'd dropped him, just as soon as she found the time.

Most of all she was furious with her mother for lying to her and her father. And not a spur-of-the-minute little white lie, either. She'd planned this in advance, gone so far as to give them the name of a nonexistent travel companion. The only thing her mother hadn't given them was an itinerary.

But there had to be some way of tracking her down, even without an itinerary. If she was traveling, she had to be staying in hotels and eating and shopping. All of which meant she'd be flashing her credit cards. And charges to credit cards could be traced.

Cassie stepped into the shower—such as it was—and got ready for another day of life in Beau Pierre. Tuesday. The day of Dennis's funeral. Suicide or murder?

It was a question that might never be answered. Fortunately, the question of her mother's whereabouts would be.

JOHN CLIMBED the steps of the small house Dennis had rented and stopped at the front door, hesitant to push it open and walk inside. It would look like Dennis. Things tossed around. A couple of pairs of shoes kicked off by the door. The guy never had been one for keeping his shoes on.

And it would smell like Dennis. A little heavy on the aftershave. Stale coffee. A few sips of beer left in a can somewhere.

It would be just as always, only Dennis wouldn't step out to greet him.

John took a deep breath and pushed through the door. God, could he use a drink! A taste to wash away the possibilities burning in his mind. But one drink would only lead to another, and another—and when he became sober again, the evidence would be covered by a new layer of haze.

He had to think clearly, had to figure this out. This had Guilliot's name written all over it, but doctors didn't kill over a malpractice suit, not even one as big as this one. There had to be more. Some blatant act of irresponsibility that could cause Guilliot not only to lose the case Flanders had against him, but lose his reputation, maybe even his license to practice medicine.

A dirty secret that had eaten away at Dennis until he could no longer bear to work side by side with Guilliot. One that had him on the verge of leaving the life and the bayou country that he loved. Guilliot must have feared that Dennis would break under questioning during the trial and reveal the truth. So he'd silenced Dennis forever, or else he'd had him silenced.

Fury rolled inside John and if Guilliot had walked through the door right then, he could probably have wrung his neck like a squawking chicken's. But Guilliot wasn't there, and neither was Dennis.

He had to go and put his little brother in the crypt, had to watch him be laid out beside their father and Muh-maw and Puh-paw.

First the funeral. Then revenge.

CASSIE DROVE slowly past St. Mark Church, staring at the parking lot full of cars and the black hearse parked near the back door of the small wooden structure. She was certain there were reporters inside, trying their best to blend in with the legitimate mourners, but she'd never sunk quite that low.

She would like to be a fly on the wall, though. Not out of any need to experience grief vicariously, but to observe the faces of Dr. Guilliot and his staff. John hadn't presented any convincing evidence to sway her to the belief that Dennis had been killed, yet she found herself leaning that way.

A young, fun-loving anesthetist who was liked by everybody just didn't seem the ideal candidate for suicide. Even if the surgery team was found guilty of malpractice, insurance would cover any settlement against Dennis. And unlike Norman Guilliot, he could move on easily enough. Magnolia Plantation wasn't his baby, and he could likely draw the same salary or more at any hospital or clinic anywhere in the country.

She passed the church, made a few more turns and ended up on Bayou Road. It was narrow, bordered on both sides by boggy terrain. Her hands tightened on the wheel, and the muscles in her arms and neck bunched as she approached the spot near the bridge where Dennis had left the road. Someone had nailed a wreath of red plastic roses on a tree, and when she saw it, her eyes grew moist.

She imagined Dennis driving along in the wee hours of the morning under the influence of too many beers. His eyes would have been heavy, his concentration affected by the liquor and the hour. He could have easily drifted onto the shoulder, then gone into a skid and landed in the swamp.

She pressed the accelerator and sped by, turning at the dirt road where Dennis had lived. The house he never made it to. There were no addresses but the house was easy enough to find. The mailbox next to the road was adorned with the same type of plastic wreath that had hung at the crime scene, and someone had left a bouquet of flowers on the steps.

A photograph of the setting would provide a nice human interest touch to the article she'd eventually have to write. The heavy rains last night had left the yard and walkway to the front door a small lake. Cassie would have to buy a pair of boots today. They were a necessity in Beau Pierre, but for now she decided to take photos from inside the car.

Holding the camera outside the open window, she framed the shot so that she included both the flowers and the pirogue propped against the side of the house. Then she took a few more snapshots of the old shrimp boat in need of repair that sat next to the garage.

Cassie returned the camera to its case, jotted a few observations in her notebook, then took out her cell phone. It was as good a time as any to make a stab at reaching Butch. She punched in the number and left a message with Dottie when told her father was in a conference.

Butch called a half hour later.

"Dottie said you needed to talk to me."

"I'd like you to check with the credit card companies for the cards that Mother carries and get a record of her spending. We can likely pin her down to a town with that, possibly even a hotel.''

''Why would I do that?''

''So we'll know she's okay and may even be able to talk to her.''

''It's not as if your mother was kidnapped, Cassie. She planned this trip.''

''But it's so unlike her. She's never gone off like this before and certainly has never gone four weeks without talking to either of us. And she lied about who she was going with.''

''You're really worried about her, aren't you?''

''Yeah, I am.''

''Okay. I've got to get back to the conference room now, but I'll try to find out something after lunch and get back to you.''

''I'd appreciate that.''

''In the meantime, don't let this get to you. Your mother is a grown woman and perfectly capable of taking care of herself. I'm sure everything's fine.''

''But you'll check, right? And call me back?''

''I'll call you as soon as I learn that your mother is traveling around Greece and charging up a storm.''

''Thanks, Dad.''

He was right, of course. She was overreacting, but it was not like her mother to lie, and definitely not like her not to call.

''ARE YOU CERTAIN there are no foreign charges on that account?''

''Not since back in December.''

''What was that?''

''A piece of glassware from Milano, Italy. The charges were four-hundred-and-eighty dollars.''

Glass from Italy. Probably a Christmas gift, or that stupid colored bowl he'd broken while moving it off the dining room table for the New Year's brunch. "Are there any charges for hotels or flights?"

"Not on this month's bill. Actually, there are no charges on this month's statement."

"When was the last charge made?"

"May seventh. Dillard's Department Store. The charge was eighty-two dollars and sixty-one cents."

May 7. Two days before she left the country. Rhonda hadn't gone that long without using her Visa since they'd had it.

"Is there anything else I can do for you, Mr. Havelin?"

"No. Thanks for your help."

He walked to the window and stared out at the view of Memorial Park. No charges on Rhonda's Visa. No charges on their American Express. But she had to be spending, so that left cash or traveler's checks. He walked back to his desk and punched his intercom button.

"Yes, Mr. Havelin?"

"Dottie, get my bank on the phone. I need to check the history on one of my accounts."

"Yes, sir."

The account Rhonda used was actually a joint account, even though for all practical purposes it belonged to her. All Butch did was transfer funds to it once a month, or more often if she ran low. He was exceedingly generous with her, always had been. She could have easily saved enough money to pay for this trip outright.

That was it. A perfect explanation for why there were no charges. This whole thing was some kind of show of independence. Somehow she'd found out about Babs and instead of confronting him with it, she'd taken off, probably hoping to have some kind of wild fling with a Greek playboy to get back at him.

"Line one for the bank, Mr. Havelin."

Butch pushed the button, explained what he wanted to know, then listened while the woman on the other end of the connection rattled off the account history. The last transaction had been on May 6, a cash withdrawal in the amount of fifty-thousand dollars.

He let out a low whistle as he sank into his chair. He'd had no idea she had that much money in the account.

"Everything seems to be in order with that transaction, Mr. Havelin. Is there a problem with it?"

"No." And yes. A real problem. A sane woman did not go to the bank and withdraw fifty-thousand dollars in cash and board a plane for Greece. This was about him and Babs. He was sure of it.

What if she'd left him for good, just walked out of his life never to return again? But she'd never do that for a mere fifty-thousand dollars. Half of all he had was rightfully hers and that would amount to several million.

Rhonda would have some kind of explaining to do when she got home. Patsy David. No itinerary. Traveling with that kind of cash. No matter how pissed she was that he'd had an affair, it was no call to pull a stunt like this.

Only, what if he was wrong? Suppose she was in some kind of trouble? Suppose she'd gotten mixed up in something and was afraid to tell him about it? What if she didn't come home at all? What if she was…

Dead?

He wrapped his hands around his skull, squeezing as if they were a vice. God, he didn't need this kind of worry now. He dreaded calling Cassie back with this information. She'd be more upset than ever and there wasn't a lot he could say to make her feel better about this. He was about to make the call when Babs stepped into his office.

"You look like hell. What's wrong?"

"This mess with Rhonda."

"What now?"

"She took fifty thousand in cash out of her account and she hasn't used her charge card since she left."

"Why would she carry that much cash on her? That's dangerous."

"I don't know why she's done any of this."

"I know you're upset, but you better get your act together. We've got a meeting with the directors of Cabot in less than an hour, and you better be on your game if you expect this thing to fly. You're the only one they listen to. Your future is riding on this merger."

"Thanks for sharing that."

"You know it's true."

"I know."

His whole world had slipped right off its axis and was spinning out of control. But Babs was right. He had to get his act together and walk into that meeting in less than an hour as if he held all the aces. Never let them see you sweat.

Rhonda had been gone for four weeks. Even if something was wrong, another few hours wouldn't make a lot of difference. He'd deal with that and with Cassie later.

CASSIE SPENT the rest of the afternoon playing the role of any good reporter. She had lunch at the Corner Café in town, making small talk with the waitress and another customer and catching scraps of every conversation she could while pretending to be immersed in a paperback book she'd read before.

All the talk was of the upcoming trial and Dennis's suicide. As far as she could tell, no one else had reached the conclusion that Dennis had been murdered. The consensus of opinion seemed to be that the stress of the trial and accompanying publicity had driven Dennis over the edge.

Cassie kept a couple of interview appointments after lunch, one with an ex-girlfriend of Dennis's who lived just outside of Larose, the other with a distant cousin who still lived in Beau Pierre but was old and ailing and hadn't made the funeral. Both ladies had only glowing reports of Dennis. He was fun, smart and didn't have a mean bone in his body.

But neither were all that surprised he'd caved under pressure. It was the Robicheaux curse. When she'd pressed for more information on that, they'd backed off, but she suspected they were referring to John's giving up his law practice and moving back to the bayou country where he'd grown up.

Evening was coming now. The sun had started its descent and the temperature had dropped a few degrees but the humidity was over ninety, making the air feel like steam every time she stepped outside the car.

She turned off five miles out of town, taking the parish road that led down to St. Mark Church and the cemetery a half mile past it. The ground was drier here, and she parked under a sweet gum tree and stepped out of her car. There were a few in-ground graves, but most people were buried in stone mausoleums, probably to make sure the bodies didn't wash away in a flood and go floating down the bayous.

Stepping carefully, she made her way through the cemetery to the only tomb covered in fresh flowers. The Robicheaux mausoleum was relatively small and not as elaborate as some of the others. It was a simple stone structure with a four-foot-high brass cross above the door and the names of the dead etched on marbleized plaques. Leon and Mary had died a year apart. One, two years ago, one, three. They had both been in their seventies, the grandparents whose names had been listed in Dennis's obituary. Tommy Jo Robicheaux was their father. He'd died thirty years ago.

Cassie did some quick figuring in her head. Tommy Jo would have been forty-one at the time, and Dennis would have been only two. There were no other names, though she was certain the obituary had said both parents were deceased. But for whatever reason, Dennis's mother did not share the family burial tomb.

There were several large bouquets of lilies and chrysanthemums and one smaller bouquet of daisies and mixed blossoms. But it was the one, long-stemmed white rose lying in the grass by the door that caught Cassie's attention. It was fresh with drops of moisture still clinging to the stem, as if someone had come along minutes ago and dropped off the blossom.

Cassie felt weepy thinking about who might have left it, and wondering if they'd actually come back to the grave after everyone else had left to say a private goodbye. She took out her camera and snapped a half dozen pictures of it from several different angles.

She felt almost guilty, but she *was* a reporter on assignment. And if the rose touched her, chances were it would touch her readers.

Her cell phone rang as she started to walk back to the car. Her dad. Finally.

"Were you able to track Mother down?" she asked before he'd finished his hello.

"No, sweetheart. No luck at that."

"But you did call the credit card companies?"

"I called them. The cards haven't been used since two days before your mother left on her trip."

"That can't be. What is she using for money?"

"Cash."

Cassie listened to the account of the fifty-thousand-dollar withdrawal as a new wave of apprehension swelled inside her. "Something's wrong, Dad. Mom wouldn't take that much money in cash. And she wouldn't have lied to us, not unless something is really wrong."

"She did it, Cassie. That's all I can tell you."

"What if she was coerced into this, or threatened?"

"There's no indication of that. Your mother wanted to take a trip on her own and she did it."

"What about the money?"

"It was hers to do with as she wanted."

No. She wasn't buying this. She couldn't. "There must be more to this. Was she upset when you made the travel plans?"

"If she was, I didn't know about it, and don't lay this on me, Cassie. I'm not the one who left town. I'm here and trying to do my job."

His job. How could he even think of that when they were discussing whether or not her mother could be in serious trouble, maybe even in danger?

"Does Conner-Marsh come before my mother?"

"You know better than that. Look, Cassie. We're both upset but striking out at each other isn't going to help. Your mother will be home next week and she can explain this herself."

"What if she doesn't come home, Dad? What then?"

"She'll be here. Now, how's the job going? Are you still in Beau Pierre?"

"Yeah." She tried to talk about the situation with Dennis's death and her interactions with John and Dr. Guilliot and some of the others in Beau Pierre, but she just couldn't get past the newest news—or no news—on her mother.

"I need to go, Dad."

"Okay. I have to fly to London first thing in the morning and I won't be back until Saturday, but if you need me while I'm gone Dottie will track me down."

"Do you have to go this week with all that's going on with Mom?"

"It's my job, sweetheart, just like being in Beau Pierre this week is your job. You take care. And don't worry about your mother. I'm sure she'll be able to explain everything when she gets home."

But Cassie was worried and plagued with vague suspicions that refused to fully materialize but that clouded her mind. She brushed away the gnats that were flying around her face then looked up at the sound of the old black pickup truck bouncing down the dirt road.

John Robicheaux. The last person she needed to face at a point when she felt more vulnerable than she had at any time since her separation from Drake.

Even overcome with grief, John would still be pushy and demanding. She'd like nothing better than to disappear. Unfortunately that wasn't an option, so she took a deep breath, stuck out her chest and struck a self-confident pose as he strode across the cemetery at a fast and furious pace.

CHAPTER EIGHT

CASSIE WAS PREPARED for some arrogant comment about her presence at the cemetery and for John to hurl accusations that she was using the circumstances surrounding Dennis's death to build circulation numbers for *Crescent Connection.*

But he didn't say a word as he approached. He just stared at her with those dark, piercing eyes until he stooped and picked up the solitary rose.

"Did you bring this?"

"No," she answered. "It was here when I got here."

Blood pooled on his index finger from the prick of a thorn but he didn't seem to notice. "It all comes down to this," he said. "In the end all of life comes down to a lonely graveyard. Did you write that in your article for next month's edition, Cassie Pierson?"

"I haven't finished the copy."

"When you do, have the guts to stand to tell the truth even if you're the only reporter who does. Say that Dennis's blood is on someone's hands."

"I know how hard this must be, but—"

"How would you know?" John stepped closer. The muscles in his face were pulled taut and his hands were clutched into fists as if he was about to slug someone. "How could you possibly know? Have you lost everyone in your life who meant anything to you? Have you just buried a brother who had no cause to die except some damn surgeon with an ego the size of the Superdome decided he was dispensable?''

"No."

"Then you don't know what this is like for me, so don't stand there and pretend that you do."

Any other time she would have lashed back, but she didn't have the heart to do it when she knew he had to be hurting so bad he could barely stand it.

"What will you do now?"

"What will I do?" He tossed the rose to the ground and wiped the blood he'd finally noticed on his jeans. "Go fishing, I guess. That's a Robicheaux for you. Cram us between a rock and a hard place, slam us into the ground and kick our face in the mud, and we go fishing—or get drunk."

"I meant, what will you do about proving this wasn't suicide?"

He turned away from her and studied the new nameplate on the marble plaque as if it had the answers he was looking for. "Keep searching for evidence...and for someone who'll talk. Dennis wasn't the only person besides Guilliot in the operating room the day Ginny Flanders died. Hopefully at least one of them has a conscience not fully controlled by the great Norman Guilliot."

"Then you're still convinced this has to do with Ginny Lynn Flanders?"

"What else is there?"

"The usual reasons for murder. Money. Maybe jealousy. Everyone says Dennis had a way with the women. Could he have been fooling around with the wrong one?"

"I thought about that. But when a man kills out of jealousy, he usually finds you with his woman or finds out you've been with her and goes ape. He'll bust open your head with his fist or shoot you in the parking lot. He doesn't work things out to the tiniest detail. A man crazed with jealousy doesn't steal your gun ahead of time and wait for you in the swamp in the middle of the night."

"Some men might."

"Not this time. The timing is too critical. The trial starts in less than two weeks. This is premeditated murder, planned and carried out without the slightest hitch. But I don't expect you to believe that."

"I'm trying to keep an open mind."

"*Mais,* yeah. Reporters do that all the time."

She ignored the comment, but this time it took more effort. "I don't see the motivation for Guilliot to commit murder. Doctors face malpractice suits all the time. The insurance pays off the claim and they go on with their work. They don't kill people."

"This is no ordinary suit. It's the story of the decade. You people made it more that way with your hype. If Guilliot gets a guilty verdict, the whole world will know, and they're not going to flock to his bayou resort and pay exorbitant prices to risk dying on the table."

"*You* people?" There was a limit to how much she could take without calling him on it. "So you just lump all reporters into one barrel and label them poison?"

"I don't print the labels."

He met her gaze again, and the hurt in his eyes sucked the ire right out of her. "I don't want to argue with you, John."

"Might be a good time. The way I'm feeling right now, you might actually win." He stuck his hands in his pockets. "I'm getting out of here."

"Are you really going fishing?"

"Why not? See you around, Cassie Pierson."

She nodded and watched him walk away. He shouldn't be alone tonight. He should have family around to share old memories of Dennis, should have friends to touch his shoulder when they passed and be there if he wanted to talk.

But he had no family. And he'd evidently shut the old friends out of his life, probably when he'd come home to drown in remorse.

So he was alone. Like she'd be tonight, wondering where her mother was and fighting the fear that something was dreadfully wrong.

"John. Wait up."

He stopped and she ran to catch up with him. "Take me fishing with you."

His eyebrows arched. "Business or pleasure?"

"Neither."

"Then why do you want to go?"

Because she was hurting, too. Because she hated the thought of going back to the cabin on the bayou and spending the evening alone. "I like fishing."

"Sure you do. Dressed for it, too." He stared at her feet, then shrugged. "Come along if you like," he said. "If you start acting like a reporter, I can always throw you overboard."

There wasn't the slightest indication that he was joking.

JOHN POLED the narrow pirogue almost silently through the still, murky waters of the bayou, but the night was far from quiet. The background sounds were ever-changing—the high-pitched hum of tree frogs, the deep-throated croak of bullfrogs, the screeching call of owls out looking for their prey.

The splash as an alligator slithered from the swampy banks into the water. Cassie kept a wary eye on it. "Aren't you frightened of the alligators at all?" she asked.

"No." He looked as if even asking him were an insult.

"Would that one attack you if you jumped in the water right now?"

"Most likely he'd swim away. But he might attack, if he felt threatened."

"Or if he was hungry?"

"There's easier meals for them to find than a grown man."

"Then they're not usually aggressive?"

"No. Unlike humans, they don't just go after everything that gets in their way."

"The way you think Dr. Guilliot does?"

"A man doesn't get to the top of his game unless he goes after it relentlessly and without mercy."

"Were you like that once, John?"

He nodded. "A million years ago."

"Yet it still eats at you and controls your life?"

"You sound like a reporter looking to find out the answer to your own question about swimming with a gator."

"So what subjects am I allowed to talk about?"

"Fishing is a silent sport."

They didn't talk again for a good thirty minutes. Neither did they fish. John just poled through the water, turning as one bayou fed into another. At times the poling seemed to go easy, but at other times the waterways were so clogged with water hyacinths, irises and other plants that he seemed to be pushing across dry land. And all the time they were going deeper into the dark swamp.

"I can't imagine how you ever learned to navigate these waters."

"I grew up here. It's my hood, you know."

"Have you ever gotten lost?"

"A couple of times, when I first started taking the boat out on my own."

"What did you do?"

"Kept poling until I found something that looked familiar."

He was talking again, and this time she'd be careful to avoid any mention of his having ever been an attorney. "How old were you then?"

"Seven or so."

"You're kidding, right?"

"Mais, non, chère."

"Now I know you're putting me on."

"Not so much. My roots run deep. My grandfather was a trapper back in the days you could make a decent living at it. After that he got him a shrimp boat and took to the bays. Brought in enough money to keep us fed and clothed and somehow saved enough to put both Dennis and I through college."

"What did your dad do?"

"He did some fishing during the week. Spent his weekends gambling away what he'd made at the card tables or playing craps."

"That must have upset your mother."

"I didn't have a mother."

The tone of the response let her know the question-and-answer routine was over. She wondered if it would be different if she weren't a reporter, or if the barriers were always in place so that there was no chance anyone ever got too close.

"Not you, huh, Cassie."

"Not me, what?"

"No drunken, gambling dad. No runaway mother."

Missing. The word cut into her, sharp as a knife. It was far too close to the truth.

John stared at her, no doubt reading her distress. "Now I'm overstepping my bounds. Forget it. Your past is your business."

But she couldn't let go of the thoughts that tumbled through her mind now. They came to life and took hold, more confusing than ever. It might actually help her get a handle on the situation if she spoke her suspicions out loud.

"My mother is missing," she said. "Or maybe she's not. But there's no way I can get in touch with her." She shook her head, already sorry she'd brought it up. Said out loud, the situation sounded even more bizarre than it did tumbling around in her brain.

"Then I take it she's not living at home."

"She was until four weeks ago. She flew to Greece for a six-week vacation, and no one's heard a word from her, except for postcards."

"She's probably having too much fun to call."

"I'd like to think that."

"But you don't."

"There's more." She outlined the scenario with the few facts she actually knew, including the lie about the old high school friend. "It's probably nothing. I'm just a little paranoid about the whole thing."

"I wouldn't call that paranoia. I'd say you have reason to be concerned. What does you father think about the situation?"

"He doesn't seem too concerned about it."

"Does your mother travel a lot?"

"She used to go with my father on business trips, but she doesn't do that much anymore. When her parents were alive, she'd fly to Florida to visit them occasionally, but she's never been out of the country without Dad, and never been anywhere for more than a week or two without him."

"Odd that all of a sudden she'd take off for six weeks and lie about her traveling companion."

"Even more odd, since I've never known my mother to lie about anything."

"Then she must have a good reason for doing it now—or else she thinks she does."

"I wish she'd shared that reason with me."

"Obviously she didn't think she could."

"Obviously. The only explanation I can think of is that she's going through a middle-age crisis or having a tough time with menopause."

"You wouldn't be so worried if that's all you're thinking."

John Robicheaux surprised her. Not only had he listened to her concerns, he saw straight through to the apprehension beyond her words.

"I can't help but think she could be in some kind of trouble," Cassie admitted.

"Any chance she's having an affair?"

"She's almost sixty."

"Women in their sixties still have sex, Cassie."

"Not Mom."

"I wouldn't bet on that."

"I didn't mean that the way it sounded. I'm sure she and Dad have sex, but she's not the kind to screw around."

"Sometimes the quiet ones surprise you."

"Well, she's not buying thong panties at Victoria's Secret. I can assure you of that, though she does like to shop. That's another thing that really puzzles me. Why isn't she using her charge cards?"

"She has fifty-thousand dollars in cash. I take it your father's not worried about the money?"

"He says it was hers to do with as she wanted. He's too involved in his career to worry much about anything else."

"What's his career?"

"He's the new CEO of Conner-Marsh."

"A man at the top of his game," John said.

There wasn't a hint of accusation in his tone but John's earlier comment still hung in the air.

A man doesn't get to the top of his game unless he goes after it relentlessly and without mercy.

John stopped poling and sat down on the narrow wooden seat across from her. "Have you checked with all the airlines to see if your mother actually left the country?"

"She's sent postcards with Greek postmarks."

"That only proves that someone mailed them from Greece. It doesn't prove your mother did."

"The messages are in her handwriting. I'm almost certain of that. And her neighbor took her to the airport."

"If it were me, I'd still check with the airlines."

John reached across the space that separated them and lay his hand on top of hers. The touch was unexpected and the warm rush of heated awareness caught her off guard. Still she turned her hand over and clasped his, letting their fingers tangle so that she could hold on tightly. A quick squeeze and then she let go.

John was too much a man for her not to feel some sexual awareness but she couldn't let it go beyond that. They were both needy tonight, their emotions raw and their vulnerabilities exposed.

But when this situation was past they'd have nothing in common. She was determined to hit life full-stride, recover the self-esteem she'd lost in the marriage and put Drake Pierson totally behind her.

John's life was a wrecked train that would probably never get back on track. He had too many old demons to fight and he drank too much to put up much of a battle.

Only, he wasn't drinking tonight. He was focused, dealing with his grief straight-on and even that hadn't kept him from noticing how upset she was or listening attentively to her problems.

John Robicheaux was a complex man.

"I'm a little hungry," he said, apparently not dealing with any of the issues his brief touch had broached for her. "What about you?"

She looked around. "If I were hungry, what would we eat?"

"Suzette's is just around the bend."

That surprised her. She'd thought they'd been traveling deeper into the swamp and never dreamed they were near civilization. "Are we on the bayou that runs behind the cabin I'm staying in?"

"We are now. It's not nearly as far by boat as it is by car."

She was hungry, but doubtful that spending more time with John tonight would be a good idea.

"I had a big lunch," she lied, "and I need to get home."

"I can drop you off by pirogue."

"What about my car?"

"I'll bring it over in the morning."

Dinner with John Robicheaux. A glass or two of wine, and then he'd walk her back to her cabin. He might even kiss her, though surely men in the throes of guilt didn't think of having sex.

Who was she kidding? Men thought of sex no matter what they were facing. And if his almost casual touch had affected her, there was no telling what a kiss would do to her in her current emotional state. It was far better not to find out.

"I'd rather go back to your place and get my car tonight."

"Suit yourself." He turned the pirogue around and headed away from Suzette's. He didn't say anything else, but the mood had changed. He withdrew into the brooding silence she'd come to associate with him.

Moonlight painted silvery streaks across the murky water and the tree frogs still filled the night with their serenade. But the bayou seemed far more mysterious and frightening now. The water was alive with alligators and the screeching of an owl sounded almost ominous as John took a narrow offshoot that brought them into an area where the cypress trees grew so thick that the needled branches all but blocked the rays of the moon.

Something cold and heavy settled inside her. It was almost tangible, yet still shadowy and foreboding, like a surreal premonition that the news from the airlines would not be good.

ANNABETH STEPPED into the bathroom and tugged her black bikini panties down to see if she'd spotted yet. She was two weeks late getting her period, and that hadn't happened since she was a teenager.

Good news. There was no sign of blood.

Pregnant. She was almost afraid to even think the word for fear it might jinx her. She'd given up hoping for it, but people always said that when you gave up working on it, that's when it happened.

And she definitely wasn't too old. Women in their late-thirties had babies all the time, and she was only thirty-six. If she needed help she could hire a nanny, but she was going to do the fun things herself. She'd rock it and feed it and play with it.

If it was a girl, she could buy all sorts of adorable outfits. And she'd seen the most terrific nursery furniture on the E channel. She couldn't remember whose baby it was for, but it was one of the stars they'd interviewed.

And here she was getting all excited when being late might not mean anything. All the stress could have messed up her system, but being pregnant and having a baby would help her get over it.

It would take Norman some time to adjust to the idea of being a father again after all these years, but once he did, he'd be excited, too. It would give him something to look forward to when the trial was over and their lives got back to normal.

As it was, he was a walking time bomb. The only time he ever seemed his pre-Ginny Lynn self was when they were having sex and not always then.

But a baby would change everything. She'd wait a few more days, then she'd go to the drugstore and buy one of those pregnancy tests. Or maybe she wouldn't wait. She could get one tomorrow.

She rubbed her flat stomach and thought of it swelling to the size of a beach ball. Gross. But a baby would be worth it. And she wouldn't be one of those women who just let themselves go after giving birth. She'd exercise and get her figure back. Life would be good again, just the way she'd planned all along.

She pulled up her panties and went back to the living room where Norman was waiting for the start of the ten o'clock news. Watching it was a ritual now that he was mentioned almost every night. She'd love to crawl in his lap right now and tell him that she just might be pregnant.

But better to wait until she was sure.

"I'D LIKE TO RECONFIRM a flight returning to Houston from Athens, Greece on June eighteenth."

"Can I have your name?"

"Rhonda Havelin."

"Is that connection through London or Amsterdam?"

"London." She had a fifty percent chance of being right.

"Do you have the confirmation or flight number?"

"I don't have that with me. I was hoping you could find the information from my name." Actually she knew they could. She wasn't even sure she needed to lie about her identity to check a reservation, but she wanted to avoid any unnecessary hassles.

"I'll need to put you on hold for a minute while I check for that reservation."

"That's fine." Cassie squirmed in her chair and doodled on the pad at her fingertips while she waited, too nervous to sit still. This was the fourth airline she'd called. The first two had no reservations for Rhonda Havelin. The third explained that their computers were down and she'd have to call back in an hour.

"I'm afraid there's nothing in your name, Mrs. Havelin."

"Oh, dear. Maybe it is Amsterdam where I catch that connecting flight."

"No, I checked that, as well. Are you certain that June eighteenth is the correct return date?"

"Fairly certain." It was definitely the date her mother had given her. She knew because it was the day before Butch's birthday, and she'd said she wanted to be home to celebrate it with him. But then her mother had lied about other things, so she may have lied about her flight, as well.

"I do have a return flight for a Rhonda Havelin on June eighteenth, but it's a direct flight from New Orleans."

"Could that be the last leg of the trip?"

"No. This is part of a round trip. The outgoing flight was Houston to New Orleans on May ninth."

"Are you certain of that?"

"That's what's coming up on the computer."

"Mrs. Rhonda Havelin, 2864 Jonquil Drive, Houston, Texas?"

"That's the address that's listed. It would help to straighten this out if I had your reservation number."

"I'll locate it and call you back."

Cassie slumped to the side of the bed, nauseous and confused, and wondering if she knew her parents at all. The anguish became a hard knot in her chest as she headed for a hot shower. If the airline was right, even the trip to Greece was likely a lie.

FRIDAY, JUNE 11, three days since Dennis's funeral and the first day they'd scheduled surgery since his death. That had been yet another mistake, Norman decided, as he tried to eat his lunch in the midst of the bickering that had started in the operating room and increased at a steady pace.

"Why can't we have normal chickory coffee like we used to instead of this flavored crap?" Fred complained.

Susan poured herself a cup of the brew and added a pinch of sweetener. "You can have any kind of coffee you want if you weren't too lazy to make it."

"And take away the only job you're good at?"

Guilliot tried to ignore the bickering and eat his sandwich, but it was getting damn hard to do. The entire surgery staff was falling apart on him, crumbling like that tasteless cake Annabeth had served him last night. The only good thing was that the new anesthetist didn't hang around much once his day was through, so he didn't know half of what was really going on on the third floor.

"Doesn't anyone around here put things back where

they found them?'' Angela said, sticking her head around the doorway and peering into the lounge.

"Cut the anyone trash, Angela. We all know who you're talking about so if you want to diss me, diss me.''

"Okay, Susan, why isn't Janelle Carson's file where it belongs?''

"Because I'm not through looking at it.''

"Fine. I was just asking. You don't have to snap at me.''

"Why not?'' Fred asked. "That's all you two do anyway. This place sounds more like a kindergarten than a clinic.''

Susan yanked the door of the refrigerator open and pulled out an anemic-looking salad. "You're not exactly a barrel of fun yourself, monkey boy.''

"I could just take the afternoon off,'' Angela said. Her voice was shaky, and Guilliot hoped to hell she wasn't about to burst into tears. If she did, he was taking the afternoon off, too. He'd drive the Porsche into New Orleans and get sloppy drunk in some two-bit strip joint.

A nice thought, but he couldn't do that. Sure as he did, a reporter would show up and snap his picture for the *Times Picayune*. He couldn't even get drunk at Suzette's. Drunks had a tendency to talk too much, and he couldn't risk letting anything slip out. How many times had he warned Dennis of that?

"Take the afternoon off,'' he suggested, working to keep his voice calm. "You, too, Susan. Go shopping or just relax. Both of you do whatever it takes to make sure you have it together when the trial starts.''

"I'm together,'' Susan said. "It's Angela and Fred who can't speak in a civil voice.''

"The trial has nothing to do with me,'' Fred said. "I'm not named in the suit and I haven't been subpoenaed as a witness." He slammed his coffee cup down and glared at Susan as if daring her to say something else.

Guilliot steamed. He'd had it with the lot of them. No longer hungry, he dumped the last half of his roast beef po'boy in the trash can and marched out. He went into his office and closed the door behind him, wondering if things would ever be the same again.

His intercom buzzed. "Your wife is on line one," the receptionist said.

"Tell her I'm with a... No, never mind. I'll take the call."

"Are you busy, sweetheart?"

He exhaled slowly and let the sultry timbre of her southern drawl coat his ragged nerves. "I just finished lunch."

"How did surgery go?"

"It went well. The patient's in recovery."

"Good."

"So what are you doing today?"

"I ran a couple of errands this morning. And this afternoon I'm getting a manicure and making crawfish pasta."

His favorite, and one of the few dishes Annabeth could actually do a halfway decent job on.

"And for dessert, I'm thinking something hot and juicy and naked."

"Nice to know someone's in a good mood today." Especially since she'd been in a rotten one ever since Dennis's death.

"I have a surprise for you."

"The dessert sounds like surprise enough."

"No, it's much better than that. But that's all I'm saying until you get home. Will you be late?"

"Not now," he said. "How could I be?"

"I'll be waiting."

He hung up the phone and leaned back in his chair. The only surprise he wanted was for all of this to be over.

There was a soft knock at the door, hopefully not more whining. "Come in if you're smiling."

"I could be," Susan said.

"What would it take to make that happen?"

She stepped inside, stopping to close and lock the door behind her. "A little afternoon delight would help." She sashayed across the room, her hips swaying and her blond curls bouncing around her baby blue eyes.

His body hardened. She could be so damn sexy when she wanted to be, and she apparently wanted to be right now.

"I thought you'd given up afternoon delight," he said.

"A temporary condition that I'm ready to remedy." She pulled up her skirt and perched on the edge of his desk, giving him a peek of the good stuff. If she'd had panties on earlier, she'd shed them before coming in.

He slid his hand under her skirt, played with her for a second, then dipped two fingers inside her. She was already wet, as if just thinking about him had gotten her juices flowing. That was a big turn-on for him. Always had been.

Susan and Annabeth both knew how to push his buttons. And he knew how to push theirs.

She put a finger beside his, feeling herself right along with him before she stopped to unbutton her blouse, slowly, letting the fabric fall away and exposing her bare breasts.

He nibbled one and then the other, but he didn't want to waste time on the preliminaries today. It was the first time in over a week that he'd been with Susan, and he wanted her mouth on him. He just wanted to get it off with her and feel the release.

He unzipped his trousers and leaned back in his chair. "Take care of me, baby," he whispered. "Take care of me."

And like a good nurse, Susan did.

ANGELA BLEW HER NOSE, then wiped her face with the wet paper towel. She hated that she'd gotten upset. It just made this harder for Norman and this was difficult enough for him as it was. He'd done what he had to do. She understood that. He had such talent and skill. He couldn't be expected to follow the same rules normal people did.

She'd stop and apologize before she left. She stepped to the door, started to knock, then realized that someone was in the room with him.

"Take care of me, baby. Take care of me."

She heard his words and the soft moans. But it wasn't until she heard Susan's voice paired with Norman's moan that she realized what was going on.

Her hands shook and fell to her side. She was shaking and fighting tears as she took the elevator to the first floor and rushed past the office staff without a word.

Susan and Norman.

How could he do this to Annabeth?

How could he do it to her?

CHAPTER NINE

IT WAS LATE Friday afternoon and Cassie was driving south on Highway 308, back toward Beau Pierre and her rented cabin in the swamp. She still hadn't heard a word from her mother or talked to her father about the round-trip flight the airline claimed Rhonda had booked to New Orleans. She'd tried to reach him a couple of times in London, but hadn't succeeded. Not that it mattered all that much. She was certain his response would be the same as it had been with every other complication. Wait and see.

Besides, the more she thought about it, John could have touched on the truth the other night. She doubted seriously her mother was having an affair, but even though her father hadn't admitted it, she and Butch could be having marital problems. If so, this could be her mother's way of finding the time to think things through.

New Orleans would make sense for that. It wasn't that far from Houston if she'd changed her mind before the six weeks were up, plus it was where Cassie lived so it would be a logical choice for a permanent move if she decided on a divorce.

If not New Orleans, which her mother had always found a little daunting, the bedroom communities of the North-shore had charmed her. It was easy to imagine her mother taking up residence in Covington or Madisonville—less than an hour outside New Orleans but miles away in terms of culture, entertainment and crime statistics.

And if her mother had rented an apartment there to see if she could live and make it on her own, that would adequately explain her failure to get in touch with Cassie.

A neat package. The problem was it was all conjecture. Nonetheless, it would all come to a head next Thursday when her mother was due to arrive back in Houston.

Six days away and only four days before jury selection for the Flanders v. Guilliot case was set to begin. At that point, Cassie's research in Beau Pierre would no doubt come to a close. The action would have moved to the courts. And Cassie would be back in her own town house where the water ran hot until she was out of the shower instead of jumping from scalding to icy and back without warning.

Her sojourn in the bayou cabin hadn't been as traumatic as she'd expected that first night. A couple of cans of bug spray had gotten rid of most of the six- and eight-legged creatures, and she'd almost gotten used to having a parade of alligators, snakes, nutria and ducks swimming past her door instead of the tugboats, barges, ferries and cruise ships that traveled the Mississippi River.

The pressing problem of the moment was that she still hadn't written the copy for the upcoming issue of *Crescent Connection,* even though her article was due on Olson's desk by five o'clock, exactly—she glanced at her watch— ten minutes from now. Suicide or murder? Yet, how could she ethically plant the idea of murder in her readers' minds when she hadn't found one iota of evidence to back the claim?

She hadn't talked to John since Tuesday night. She'd left messages for him to return her call. He never had. He was brooding, mysterious and hard-edged, sociable only when he chose to be. He'd chosen to be that night, had given her a glimpse of the man behind the gritty facade.

What she'd seen and heard convinced her he was not nearly as far from the astute, discerning attorney he'd once been as she and many others thought.

But he still had provided no real motive for murder.

Cassie slowed as she neared the cutoff for the road to the cemetery where Dennis was no doubt already decaying in the family crypt. She was exhausted, but still she was drawn to the place, as she'd been for the past three days. Each day there had been one lone white rose lying in the grass in front of the mausoleum. She felt compelled to see if one was waiting today.

She made the turn then punched her boss's office. As much as she hated to, she had to let him know that the copy was not going to be there on time.

"FedEx delivery just came," Olson said, not bothering with a customary hello. "I'm shuffling through your pictures as we speak. Love this lone white rose lying in the grass by the mausoleum."

"Thanks."

"Any idea who left it there?"

"No, but there's been a new one there every day."

"Could be the murderer. That would make great copy."

"And make for a stupid murderer."

"Hey, we're talking copy, not police work. But you never know. He could have been killed by a jealous lover, caught in a twisted love triangle. Readers love that secret lover bent."

"So far no one's admitted to being a lover. At least, not a current lover."

"You can still plant the idea in the readers' mind without actually saying it. And speaking of the article, I hope this call is to say you're about to fax it to me. I'd like to get the layout done tonight."

"That's the bad news."

"I don't like bad news, Cassie. Bad news gets me extremely agitated."

Then he'd just have to be agitated. "The article's not written."

"So, go ahead. Tell me how you broke both arms and you're having to type the article with your right foot."

"Actually, the right foot's sprained. I'm typing with my left foot."

"You used that excuse last month. Did you interview that woman in Baton Rouge?"

"Today, and one in Lafayette, as well. They both raved about Dr. Guilliot's skill with a scalpel and I have to admit, they looked great. No sign of scars and both of them could have passed for being ten years younger than they are."

"No complaints, huh?"

"Not a one. They both remarked on how professionally they'd been treated and raved about the excellent care they'd received during recuperation at Magnolia Plantation R & T."

"How's that going to fit in with your murder/suicide question?"

"It isn't. And neither does anything else I've uncovered. There's no evidence at all to suggest murder. I think we should trash that whole idea."

"Work with me here, Cassie. There has to be something. The guy's dead from a bullet to the head."

"Which is the extent of the evidence."

"Does his brother still think he was murdered?"

"He did the last time we talked."

"Then if nothing else, give his side of the story."

"Even if no one else in Beau Pierre shares his view?"

"Why not? Build him up. An ex-attorney with a jaded past trying to see justice done. The readers will love it."

"You're not going to dig up his past for the issue, are you?"

"Of course. What's the guy like now? As ratty and unkempt as I've heard?"

Ratty, unkempt and so virile he fairly oozed testosterone. "He's not so bad. I don't think you should bring up John's past. None of this is really about him."

"Sure it is. It's about whatever you say it's about. Say, you're not falling for the guy, are you?"

"Me?"

"I've heard those hot-blooded Cajun guys are hard to resist."

"So you still want the focus to be on the murder/suicide question in spite of the lack of credibility?" she asked, changing the subject back to one that didn't get her hot and bothered.

"Do you think it's possible Dennis Robicheaux was murdered?"

She pondered the question and all its implications, trying to be honest. Was it possible that there was more to Beau Pierre than a friendly little Cajun town? Possible that Magnolia Plantation Restorative and Therapeutic Center held a cache of deadly secrets that someone would kill for rather than have them come to light? Possible that John Robicheaux of the dark, piercing eyes and whisker-studded face knew more about Dr. Guilliot's potential for evil than anyone else imagined?

"Either you do or you don't," Olson said insistently. "Which is it?"

"I think it's possible."

"Then let's go with it."

"Dr. Guilliot will be furious. He'll cry libel."

"The louder he yells, the more readers we'll pick up. Now get to work, Cassie. I need that article."

"You'll have it before noon tomorrow."

"No later. I've got a magazine to get out."

Yes, Ogre, she mouthed as her phone started beeping. "Gotta go. I have another call coming in." She switched to the next caller, as always hoping it was her mother but no longer expecting it to be.

"Is this Cassie Pierson?"

The voice was male, but so muffled she could barely understand him. "Who is this?"

"Doesn't matter."

"What do you want?"

"I need to talk to you."

Her pulse quickened. "Does this have to do with Dennis Robicheaux?"

"It's related. I can't talk about this over the phone. I need you to meet me somewhere."

The guy had definitely piqued her interest. "Where do you want to meet?"

"There's a marina in Cocodrie. Meet me there tomorrow morning at twelve. We'll take a boat out."

"I'm not keen on meeting people who don't identify themselves. If you expect me to show up, you'll have to be more specific. What is this about?"

"It's about...Rhonda Havelin."

His voice had lowered to no more than a whisper, but it turned her blood to ice water.

"What do you know about my mother?"

"I'll call you tomorrow just before twelve and tell you where I am. Be in Cocodrie when I call. Alone. And don't tell anyone about this call."

"What do you know about my mother?"

The connection went dead.

The cemetery was just a few yards in front of her, but instead of stopping, Cassie whirled the car around in the driveway and started back to Beau Pierre. All the conjecture about her mother's being safe was just so much hogwash.

Something was wrong. But what? And why?

Cassie had heard of Cocodrie before, but she wasn't sure exactly where it was. All she knew was that it was on the edge of the swampy land that dissolved into the Gulf of Mexico. It was not a place her mother would have ever willingly chosen to go.

Tomorrow noon seemed an eternity away. She had to talk to her dad, had to let him know. Cassie's heart was racing when she reached Suzette's and her stomach churned so that she was afraid she'd throw up in the parking lot. Leaning forward, she propped her head against the steering wheel as the stranger's voice echoed in her brain.

Someone knocked on the window of her car. "Are you all right?"

She looked out the window. Fred Powell. She nodded and opened her door. "I'm fine," she said.

"You don't look it."

"Guess it's the heat." She threw her feet to the shell parking lot and stood by the side of the car.

"You coming in?"

"No. I'm just going to my cabin."

"I'll walk with you, make sure you get there okay. You don't look too steady on your feet."

"That's okay. Actually, I'm not going to the cabin now. I forgot something I needed from the grocery store. I want to get it before they close."

"I'll drive you if you want."

But she didn't want. She didn't want to hear his voice or attempt inane conversation. But as much as she didn't want to deal with Fred, she still wasn't ready to be alone.

"Thanks for the offer, but I'm fine." She crawled back

behind the wheel, closed her door and backed from the parking lot. She turned south, heading for John Robicheaux's shack in the swamps without even knowing when she'd made the decision.

ANNABETH SHOOK the martini, poured the drink into a crystal glass and carried it back to the den where Norman was sitting on the leather sofa and watching the evening news. As excited as she was, she was also nervous, mainly because the timing was so bad.

The trial had gotten to Norman and now he was faced with Dennis's death and trying to get used to working with a new anesthetist. Not the best time for hitting him with a life-changing surprise, especially when he'd never really wanted more children.

He claimed he'd done the parenting bit in his first marriage. But she wanted a baby more than she'd ever wanted anything. And the drugstore kit had tested positive.

A baby. She'd be satisfied now. Everything she'd done to make her life with Norman work would be worth the cost.

She pressed the glass in his hands and sat down beside him, glad she was wearing the shoulder-baring sundress he'd bought her the last time they'd gone shopping in New Orleans. It showed off her tan to perfection and did nice things for her breasts.

"I love you," she whispered, putting her mouth to his ear. "Are you ready for your surprise?"

NORMAN HATED surprises, and he had an idea this one was going to be worse than usual. Annabeth was fidgety and trying too hard to please him. That was never a good sign.

"Why don't we wait and you can tell me the surprise after dinner?"

"I'm too excited to wait." She snuggled close beside him, let her breasts brush his arm while she ran her hand up and down his thigh. Even having been with Susan just a few hours ago, her actions would have ordinarily made him horny and ready to deal with the surprise, but with the stress he was under now, once a day was pretty much it for him.

Annabeth slid the TV controls from his hand and pushed the power button. He watched as the screen went black, then pulled her onto his lap. He might as well make the most of the moment. It didn't look as if it were going away.

"So what is this big surprise?"

"I'm pregnant."

He heard the words, but they didn't sink in, at least not at first. When they did, he just stared at her, wondering how in hell she'd come to a conclusion like that. "You've got to be mistaken, sweetheart."

"No. I'm two weeks late for my period."

"Lots of things can cause that. Stress, for one, and we're dealing with more than our share of that." Poor Annabeth. He actually felt sorry for her. He knew how much she wanted a baby, but it wasn't going to happen. He was fifty-eight-years-old and he had no intention of spending his sixties raising kids.

"You can't be pregnant, baby."

"I thought that at first, too, but I am. I bought one of those pregnancy kits at the drugstore. It tested positive."

The pressure started to build at the base of his skull and in his temples. He stuck a thumb under Annabeth's chin and forced her to meet his gaze. "Are you certain?"

"I haven't seen a doctor yet, but I'm two weeks late and I tested positive."

He jumped up, letting her fall from his lap to the floor. "Who's the father, Annabeth?"

"You are, Norman. You know that. It couldn't be anyone but you."

His world had been falling apart for weeks. Lie by lie. Death by death. But nothing had made him feel as cold and empty as the gall knotting in his gut right now.

"Who are you sleeping with, Annabeth? I want to know and I want to know now!"

"You. Just you."

"You're a lying bitch."

She winced as if he'd hit her. He did want to hit her, wanted to knock her across the room and hear her head slam against the wall.

"Why are you doing this to me, Norman? Why are you saying these things?"

She was crying, whimpering like a kicked dog. "Easy. I can say these things real easy, Annabeth. I had a vasectomy five years ago."

"A vasectomy? How could you? You knew how badly I wanted children. You knew it when you married me." She turned on him then, started beating her fists into his chest.

He grabbed her hands and held them. "How dare you berate me when you've been spreading your legs for some other man."

"What about you, Norman? Do you think I don't know that you and Susan leave the office sometimes for two or three hours at a time? Do you think I don't know what you do when you go up to New Orleans on your so-called business trips? What about you?"

She was wailing, her voice grating on his nerves so bad, he had to struggle not to rip her tongue from her mouth.

"There will be no baby in this house, Annabeth. Not in nine months. Not ever."

He pushed her back onto the sofa, knocking his martini from the coffee table in the process. The liquid flew into the air, spraying the front of his shirt. He watched the two olives roll off the edge of the table and plop to the floor. He squashed them into the carpet with the toe of his shoe, then kicked the damn table over on top of them before stalking out of the house.

She wasn't the woman he'd thought she was, and he didn't know if he'd ever be able to crawl into bed with her again. But he would find out who she'd slept with. And the guy would rue the day he'd screwed around with the wife of Norman Guilliot.

Sure he had his little indiscretions, but that was different. Men needed more sex, but he wasn't in love with the others. He never cared about anyone but Annabeth.

"YOU WORK LONG HOURS for a reporter," John said, opening his door and staring at Cassie without inviting her in.

He was barefoot, shirtless, the snap on his worn jeans open. She stared, the hot blast of awareness colliding with the cold apprehension that had brought her here.

"Can I come in?"

"Yeah." He held the door open while she stepped inside. "You don't look so good."

She wished she could say the same.

John grabbed a pile of magazines from the sofa and stacked them on the coffee table, then motioned for her to sit. He slouched against the bookshelf. "What's up?"

"I was hoping we could talk, but if you have plans, I can come back another time."

"It depends."

"Depends on what?"

"Depends on what you want to talk about."

"About Dennis," she said, choosing an obvious topic.

"Then I have plans."

"What answer were you looking for?"

"The truth."

"What makes you think that isn't the truth?"

"You got trouble written all over you, Cassie. Not mine or Dennis's, but yours. Is this about your mother?"

She almost blurted out the details of the telephone call, but caught herself just in time. If she told John the total truth, he'd likely try to talk her out of going to Cocodrie alone or else follow her there and ruin everything.

"I called the airlines as you suggested," she said, deciding to try a partial truth. "Apparently Mom didn't leave the country. The only flight she'd booked was a round trip to New Orleans."

"And that's what has you pasty white and looking like you just made a pact with the devil himself?"

"No. I mean yes. In a way."

"Don't know how you're going to make it in the reporting business if you don't learn to lie better than that."

She shook her head. "You don't miss a thing, do you?"

"I've been known to miss it all. But you're easy to read."

"I guess I'm simple and uncomplicated."

"I'd never say that, *chère.*"

"What would you say about me, John?"

"On a scale of one to ten?"

"On the scale of your choosing."

"I'd say you're a…" He shook his head. "I'd say a smart guy wouldn't go there. How about a drink? I don't have any hard liquor, but there's wine. Not the finest stock, but it's drinkable."

No hard liquor. That surprised her. "Wine sounds good."

"Chardonnay, Merlot, a Cab?"

"Whatever's open."

"A corkscrew's not that difficult to operate."

"Then I'd like the Cabernet."

"I'll grab a bottle and some glasses and we'll take it out to the dock. There should be a breeze along the bayou. There usually is by evening. It will be a good place to *not* talk about whatever's bothering you."

She paced the room when he left, ending up at the old, scarred desk. She stared at the newspaper clipping on top of the stack.

Toni Crenshaw's Body Found By Fisherman In Pearl River.

She picked it up and read the account of how Gregory Benson, a man found not guilty on a molestation charge just months before had kidnapped the ten-year-old girl and held her captive in his house, raping her repeatedly and beating and starving her before strangling her and dumping her frail, lifeless body in the river.

She jumped at the sound of John's footsteps returning with the wine. The clipping slipped from her fingers as she turned toward him.

"Reading the gory details?"

"It was out. I couldn't help seeing it."

"I guess not."

"It was a long time ago, John."

"I bet the Crenshaws wouldn't agree with you. I bet they see the tortured body of their little girl every time they close their eyes."

"Gregory Benson was a vicious, crazed man."

"Only on the inside where no one could see. On the

outside, he was just a man like any other. Evil doesn't have a face, Cassie. All it has is a black, rotted soul.''

His eyes were glazed, as if his own soul had been taken over by some creature from a darker world. She could only imagine the torment he must put himself through every day of his life, blaming himself for what had happened to that little girl.

He was a beaten, anguished hull of the man he must have been before he'd represented Benson and gotten the man off only to have him kill a child. And still she was more attracted to him than she'd been to any man since…since Drake.

The wise thing to do would be to leave right now before she wound up in his arms—or in his bed. She was too vulnerable tonight to leave herself open to temptation.

But she couldn't bear the thought of being alone, so she took the glass from his hands and followed him out the back door to watch the sun slide beneath the horizon on a dock at the edge of the swamp.

CHAPTER TEN

CASSIE SAT next to John, her legs dangling over the end of the short dock, her feet swinging about a half foot above the surface and not three feet from where a large turtle had just poked its head out of the murky water. Thankfully, there was a slight but very welcome breeze.

"The heat takes some getting used to," she said.

"It's no hotter here than it is in New Orleans."

"True, but we spend most waking summer hours in air-conditioned buildings. In Beau Pierre, the outdoor life seems to go on as usual."

"It's the air conditioning that spoils you."

"Could be."

They were talking of the weather, the subject people always reverted to when more relevant topics came with too many complications. Her mother. His past. Dennis's death.

"How much longer will you be in Beau Pierre?" John asked, apparently ready to move beyond the topic of the temperature.

"I'm not sure. I could be going back to New Orleans as early as Monday, but it's more likely I'll be here until Wednesday."

"When is your mother supposed to return?"

"Thursday."

"Will you go to Houston for the homecoming?"

"I'll at least go to the airport for the flight Continental

Airlines has her booked on." But tomorrow's meeting in Cocodrie might change everything. She pulled her feet back to the dock and hugged her knees to her chest, fighting the urge to spill her guts.

"And how did the article go?" John asked.

"I haven't written it yet," she admitted. "But I plan for it to say that you believe your brother was murdered and that you think the murder is related to the Flanders v. Guilliot trial."

"All true. And what do you plan to say about the famed surgeon?"

"I don't plan to mention him by name, but I'll say you think Dennis was killed because someone was afraid he knew too much and that he'd talk. Our readers are smart enough to figure the rest out for themselves. They'll make their own decisions about whether or not they buy into your theory."

"You're obviously not convinced."

"I think it's possible, but I've talked to a lot of people in Beau Pierre this week, John. No one sees the doctor the way you do."

"The people who know him best aren't going to talk. Certainly not his surgery team. They're named in the suit."

"Then how can you be so sure one of them didn't kill Dennis?"

"Guilliot's got the most to lose if the trial goes against him. The others may lose their jobs, but they'll find new ones. No one will remember their names or that they're connected with the trial. Guilliot will lose his whole lifestyle if his reputation is ruined. He'd be just another surgeon in a hospital somewhere, not ruler of his kingdom."

She nodded. "Dr. Guilliot did seem a little bigger than life in the Magnolia setting, and most of the locals see him as a celebrity of sorts, the town's claim to fame."

"And how do they see Dennis?"

She'd have to tread lightly there. The people of Beau Pierre liked Dennis but few saw him as together as John did, and he was nowhere near as high on their list as Guilliot. "They said Dennis liked to pass a good time."

"I'm sure that's not all they said."

"Some said he drank too much. Several mentioned the fact that he liked women—the married ones as well as the single ones."

"He wasn't always smart about whose legs he crawled between." John finished off his glass of wine and poured another. "Dennis wasn't perfect, but he didn't kill himself. He didn't deserve to be killed, and I'm not giving up on this until I find out what really went on in that operating room the day the preacher's wife died."

"But nothing you want to share with me." She took another sip of her wine. This was getting them nowhere and she was tired of trying to concentrate on Dennis Robicheaux when her mother was foremost on her mind.

"Let's not talk of problems for a while, John. Not mine or yours."

"Fine by me, but I predict you'll have difficulty with that."

He gulped down his wine as if it were medicine, then lay back on the dock and closed his eyes.

She studied his sun-bronzed face and the deep wrinkles that had settled around his eyes even though he wasn't much over forty. The bayou surroundings suited him, fit him the way his skin fit his lean, hard body.

She scooted farther back on the dock so that she could stretch out beside him and hopefully let the peaceful atmosphere ease the tension that had settled in her shoulders and the back of her neck.

Her full skirt bunched under her as she lay down, and

she tugged it loose, tucking it under her legs so that it didn't catch the wind and inch up her thighs.

John opened his eyes at the movement, but closed them again without saying a word or giving any indication that he liked or didn't like having her so close.

She wondered if he'd ever let any woman get really close in any way that mattered.

"Why didn't you ever marry, John?"

He opened his eyes and rolled over on his side, facing her. "Is this for the enquiring minds of the *Crescent Connection* readership?"

"It depends," she said, playfully mocking him.

"On what?"

"How juicy your answer is."

"Then I'm safe."

"So what's the story?"

"I never had time for working on a relationship when I was at Tulane. I had less time after I started working as an attorney."

"And since you've been back in Beau Pierre?"

"No way I'd marry any woman with standards low enough to settle for me."

"But you have dated?"

"Dated? No. I gave that up when I graduated from college. I never cared much for it anyway. All those expectations. It's a woman thing."

"You surely don't expect me to believe you haven't slept with a woman since you graduated from college or even since you moved back to Beau Pierre?"

"You didn't ask if I'd *slept* with a woman. You asked if I dated."

"Touché."

"So what about you, Cassie? What was it like being

married to the dashing and brilliant attorney Drake Pierson?''

"Mostly it sucked, but it had its moments."

"Yeah. Enlighten me. Tell me what kind of moments stick out in a woman's mind."

John sat up and refilled both their wineglasses, sliding hers next to her fingertips while she stared at a lizard who'd joined them on the deck. She wasn't intentionally avoiding John's question, but at this point, trying to remember something momentous about her life with Drake was difficult.

"We went on some interesting trips. A honeymoon in Hawaii. Cruising in the Caribbean. Snow skiing at Lake Tahoe."

He reached across the space that separated them and let the tips of his fingers slide through a lock of hair that had slipped from the knot at the nape of her neck. "Those are places, not moments."

The back of his hand brushed across her cheek and the awareness level spiraled out of control. These were the moments John was talking about, times when her breath caught in her throat and her heart seemed to skip around in her chest.

"Did Drake thrill you when he kissed you, Cassie? Did you ever want to make love to him so badly that you lost all control and did it right out in the open, not caring who saw or who knew?"

"No, of course not. Drake wasn't like that. Drake was…"

John's hand cradled her head, and he pulled her closer, leaning over her so that his lips were inches away from hers and she could feel his breath on her skin. This wasn't about Drake. It was about her and John and an impossible situation that had pushed them together when…

His lips brushed hers, and for a second she lost all power

to think or to reason. She would have kissed him and forgotten all the questions of right and wrong, but John pulled away.

Neither of them said a word, but he stood and stepped to the end of the dock, staring out at the almost-still waters of the bayou. His hands were gripped into tight fists and the muscles in his shoulders and arms were flexed and taut.

"Do you want me to go?" she asked, in a voice that sounded as if it had slid over sandpaper.

"That's up to you. But if you stay, I don't think we're going to make it through the night on conversation."

"Then I better go."

"Your decision."

She started back toward her car, knowing it was for the best, but aching to finish the kiss that had never really gotten started. But they wouldn't stop with a kiss any more than they'd stop with conversation.

They'd make love, and her life that was already so complicated she could barely sleep or concentrate would become even more convoluted. She couldn't deal with that now. Not with the dread surrounding her trip to Cocodrie tomorrow. Not when she didn't really know or understand John Robicheaux or sometimes herself. She'd changed since the divorce, couldn't get her hands around what she expected or wanted from a man anymore.

She crawled behind the wheel and turned the key in the ignition, gunning the engine. She did a U-turn and sped away, escaping one of those moments that John had been talking about, the kind that would have lived in her memory forever.

It just might anyway.

JOHN POLED his pirogue down the bayou as he had so many times over the past seven years, seeking the solace of familiarity and the coolness of the evening breeze. It didn't help tonight.

It had all caught up with him. His dad's death. His mother's walking out and never coming home again. Toni Crenshaw. Dennis. Land mines he couldn't avoid or run from. And now there was Cassie Pierson to add to the mix.

He'd tried all week to get her out of his mind, but she'd refused to leave. He liked her style, her verve and her intelligence. But none of that was what he'd been thinking about on the dock this evening when he'd run his fingers through her hair or even before that when he'd been lying beside her with his eyes closed and trying hard to keep from having an erection.

If she'd stayed tonight, they would have made love. He could have seen what her breasts looked like outside that crisp white shirt. He could have freed her hair from those combs and run his fingers through it, could have watched it fall about her bare shoulders.

No fighting off the erection now. It was pushing hard against his jeans. In spite of all he was dealing with, in spite of the fact that there was no way on earth a woman like Cassie could fit into the mess he'd made of his life, he wanted her.

He wanted her in a way he hadn't wanted any woman in a long, long time—if ever.

Thankfully, she'd had the sense to walk away.

He stayed on the bayou another thirty minutes, thought of going down to Suzette's for dinner, but didn't want to risk reliving the memory of being in there that last night with Dennis.

He pulled his pirogue in beside his dock, started to get out, then froze as a woman stepped from the shadows.

"What are you doing out here this time of night, Annabeth?"

"I had to see you, John."

Not a good sign, unless she'd learned something about Dennis's murder and had come to tell him. He tied the pirogue to the pier that held up the dock, then stepped onto the bank. "Does Norman know you're here?"

"No. No one does. I need a place to stay, John. Not forever, but for a while."

"Why?" John grabbed her arm, but when he pulled her close, he could see that she'd been crying. "What's happened, Annabeth? What did you find out? Did your husband kill Dennis?"

"I'm pregnant, John."

"Pregnant?"

"Pregnant. And it's not Norman's baby."

THE ARTICLE was finished, faxed and on its way when Cassie began the two-hour drive to Cocodrie. It had taken her most of the night to write and, as far as she was concerned, the article was still a piece of journalistic garbage. It lacked substance and mood. It captured nothing of the mystery she'd hoped for.

There simply weren't facts to back up John's allegations of murder, and while his theory of a dark, deadly secret as the motive sounded halfway credible in conversation, it looked ludicrous in print. Worse, she knew she hadn't been objective. Nothing about her feelings for John Robicheaux was rational or objective, so how could she possibly present him that way?

But the biggest hindrance to the writing was the dread concerning the meeting she was on her way to now. She'd been apprehensive before yesterday's phone call from the mysterious stranger, but then she could at least come up with scenarios that made a semblance of sense, scenarios that didn't put her mother in danger.

Now she was afraid to conjecture.

She took highway 308 north, though Cocodrie was west of Beau Pierre and as far south as you could go without a boat. Roads were limited in this part of the state since there was more marshland than people and laws designed to protect the limited wetlands discouraged new construction.

A few miles outside of town she passed the massive gate to Magnolia Plantation and then crossed the bridge over the offshoot of Bayou Lafourche, which ran behind the clinic. Roads that she'd never traveled before last week were becoming familiar now. She slowed at the sight of flashing blue lights up ahead.

When she got closer, she could see that the lights were from two state police cars parked on the shoulder of the road. The uniformed troopers were at the edge of the bayou, bent over something in the water. Two teenage boys were with them and a couple of dirt bikes were lying on the ground beside them.

The pickup truck in front of Cassie pulled off the road and a young guy in jeans and a muscle shirt jumped out and ran to join the officers.

She threw on her brakes and pulled in behind the pickup truck, a typical reporter reaction. She had three hours to make the drive to Cocodrie, plenty of time to check this out. Grabbing her notebook, she headed toward the action.

One of the state troopers was waving his arms by the time she reached the group. "Will you folks just get back? This isn't the kind of thing you really want to stand around and admire."

"What is it?" the guy asked.

"It's a wrist with part of a hand attached," one of the teenagers said. "Me and my friend here found it. We were just kicking around at a king snake and…"

"I stepped on it. Man, it was gross."

Cassie peered around the trooper. He was digging around in the mud at the foot of a cypress tree, but the body part was lying in the grass in full view. There wasn't a lot of it left, and what was there was black and swollen. If it hadn't been for the thumb and two fingers that were still attached, she'd have never taken the remains for human.

She sucked in her breath and tried to ward off the nausea. "Who called the troopers?"

"I waved some guy down who was driving by, and he called them," one of the boys said. "He didn't hang around, though. He said it gave him the willies."

The young man in the muscle shirt stood at the trooper's elbow. "What do you think happened?"

"Looks like the victim got attacked by gators," he said.

"That don't happen too often down here." The young man leaned over for a closer look, as seemingly unperturbed as if they were discussing a dead fish. "More likely someone fed him to the gator after they'd whacked 'em. Surprises me there's that much left."

"It was buried in the mud right at the bank. Only reason I found it was 'cause I booted up a clod of mud when I was kicking at the snake."

"Are you from around here?" the trooper asked, directing his question to the guy from the pickup truck.

"Down the road. Near cut off."

"Do you know of anyone who's gone missing lately? Male or female? There's no way to tell from this."

"A couple of slutty girls from down the bayou came up missing last fall, but they were always running away. Druggies. Now they probably up in New Orleans turning tricks in the French Quarter, them."

The trooper nodded. "This one's fresher than last fall. Could be as fresh as last month."

Cassie turned and strode back to her car. She'd have to catch Olson, let him know to throw out that copy and wait for an update.

John's theory of a dirty secret that someone would kill to keep hidden had just gained a lot more credibility, and the new article was already taking form in her mind.

Cassie raced back to the car for her camera. She needed pictures and quotes from the troopers and the boys who'd found the body part. She had to move quickly.

There was still a man in Cocodrie to meet.

CHAPTER ELEVEN

CASSIE ARRIVED in Cocodrie thirty minutes before the appointed time. She had no idea where to go until she received further instructions, so she pulled into a service station for a diet cola. She picked up a package of cheese crackers, as well, since she'd eaten only about two bites of cold toast for breakfast and had completely missed dinner last night.

She'd give the crackers a try and hope they stayed down what with the anxiety about the meeting and the image of the body part wreaking havoc on her equilibrium.

Back in the car with her snack, she nibbled on a cracker and pulled out the spiral notebook. Olson had been thrilled over the prospect of a decent article to replace what he called "amateurish dribble," but he wanted it pronto.

This time when she started writing the words flowed. The cell phone rang. The pen fell from Cassie's shaking fingers as she grabbed for it. "Hello."

"Hi, Cassie. It's Dad."

She glanced at her watch. Still fifteen minutes to spare. "I thought you weren't getting home until late this afternoon."

"We finished our meeting and I caught an earlier flight out than I'd planned."

"How did it go?"

"Great. The merger is back on track. If all goes well, we could be signing the final paperwork by August."

"That must make you feel good."

"I'm too tired to feel good, but I'm relieved to have the worst of this behind me. Have you heard from your mother?"

She hesitated, feeling guilty that she wasn't leveling with him, but she couldn't get into all of this now. The phone had to be free for the stranger's call. "I haven't talked to her. Have you?"

"No, but I might have a new postcard. I'm going through the mail as we speak. Yep, here's one...and another. That's it. They were both mailed from Crete. One from Iraklion. The other from Ayia Galini. She wrote she's having a great time, she's fascinated with the Minoan ruins and that she'll be home soon. Sounds like everything's fine with her."

"Sounds that way," she agreed.

"I don't understand what the confusion is with the Patsy David thing, but Rhonda will explain it when she gets home and we'll have a good laugh over it."

"I hope so." She'd never hoped for anything more in her life. "Can I call you back in half an hour, Dad? I'm in the middle of something really important now."

"Sure, baby. I'm going to jump in the shower and then catch a quick nap. I'm getting too old for continent hopping with no time to recuperate from jet lag between hops."

"Keep your phone with you, Dad. Please. I really need to talk to you, just not right this minute."

"I'll be here."

She felt as if she'd been cut off from a lifeline instead of a phone connection. She'd been angry at him more than once during this ordeal for his seeming lack of concern, but he sounded relieved when he'd talked of the newest postcards.

He might not be the perfect husband, but he was basically honest and good and he'd always been there for Cassie. He still was. She held on to that thought as she waited for the next call. The minutes ticked past. She tried to write again, but she'd lost all focus. There was nothing to do but wait.

And wait. And wait.

By twenty minutes past the scheduled time, there was no call.

HE PEERED through the lens of his high-powered binoculars, watching Cassie as she banged her fists against the steering wheel. She was frustrated, but so was he. She'd come just like he'd instructed, but she hadn't followed the rest of his orders.

She'd run straight to John Robicheaux last night, and he was likely the one she'd been talking to on the phone a few minutes ago. The guy was no doubt around here somewhere, watching to see who approached Cassie's car and ready to follow if she drove away.

Cassie Pierson, smug and secure in her little reporter world. That would all change when she learned the truth of what had gone down in Beau Pierre—if she ever learned the full truth. Chances were she never would.

Chances were she'd never live that long.

You should have listened to me, Cassie Pierson, and come alone so we could have a nice, long talk somewhere beyond the eyes and ears of Beau Pierre.

He was almost sure someone was watching her all the time in Beau Pierre, every minute of the day. The stakes were too high for anyone not to know what she was up to. If she'd just followed his instructions, he could have explained everything to her, and all he'd wanted in return was the guarantee that she'd never divulge her source.

An Important Message from the Editors

Dear Reader,

Because you've chosen to read one of our fine romance novels, we'd like to say "thank you!" And, as a **special** way to thank you, we've selected <u>two more</u> of the books you love so well **plus** an exciting Mystery Gift to send you — absolutely <u>FREE</u>!

Please enjoy them with our compliments...

Pam Powers

Lift here

How to validate your Editor's
"Thank You"
FREE GIFT

1. Peel off gift seal from front cover. Place it in space provided at right. This automatically entitles you to receive 2 FREE BOOKS and a fabulous mystery gift.

2. Send back this card and you'll get 2 brand-new *Romance* novels. These books have a cover price of $5.99 or more each in the U.S. and $6.99 or more each in Canada, but they are yours to keep absolutely free.

3. There's no catch. You're under no obligation to buy anything. We charge nothing—ZERO—for your first shipment. And you don't have to make any minimum number of purchases—not even one!

4. The fact is, thousands of readers enjoy receiving their books by mail from The Reader Service. They enjoy the convenience of home delivery...they like getting the best new novels at discount prices BEFORE they're available in stores... and they love their Heart to Heart subscriber newsletter featuring author news, horoscopes, recipes, book reviews and much more!

5. We hope that after receiving your free books you'll want to remain a subscriber. But the choice is yours— to continue or cancel, any time at all! So why not take us up on our invitation, with no risk of any kind. You'll be glad you did!

GET A *Free* MYSTERY GIFT...

SURPRISE MYSTERY GIFT COULD BE YOURS **FREE** AS A SPECIAL "THANK YOU" FROM THE EDITORS

DETACH AND MAIL CARD TODAY!

Yes! I have placed my
Editor's "Thank You" seal in the
space provided above. Please
send me 2 free books and a
fabulous mystery gift. I
understand I am under no
obligation to purchase any
books, as explained on the
back and on the opposite page.

PLACE
FREE GIFT
SEAL
HERE

393 MDL DVFG   193 MDL DVFF

FIRST NAME	LAST NAME

ADDRESS

APT.#	CITY

STATE/PROV.	ZIP/POSTAL CODE

(PR-R-04)

Thank You!

The Reader Service — Here's How It Works:

The secret would be out, and no one would blame him. But she hadn't followed his instructions. He could call and tell her that, but why bother! She could sit here and stew, then figure it out for herself.

"So you're on your own, Cassie Havelin Pierson. Heaven help you."

CANDLES AND LAMPS turned low provided the illumination. Sultry mood music provided the background. Babs provided the exhilaration.

Her tanned shoulders were bare and the slinky white sundress she wore not only accentuated her tiny waist and perky breasts but the high slit in the long skirt revealed inches and inches of seductive, luscious thigh. Butch's guess was that there was nothing beneath the dress other than a light spray of perfume.

No wonder he loved spending evenings here. It was every man's dream to step into a love nest and know that he'd never be disappointed—and never disappoint.

"You're early," Babs said. "I thought you were going to take a nap."

"I had to pass on that. A problem came up."

"That quickly? The merger team was all smiles when we left them in London."

"This had nothing to do with the merger." He walked to the bar and splashed a couple of fingers of his favorite scotch over ice. "What can I get you?"

"Nothing yet." She adjusted the volume on the CD player and turned the lamps even lower. "You must have talked to Cassie."

"I did." He took the drink to the overstuffed sofa and sat on the far end, knowing Babs would curl up beside him. God, he'd miss this.

"So what's the latest on Rhonda?"

"It looks as if she may not have gone to Greece after all."

"You're kidding, right? You have postcards."

"Postcards, but no flight, at least not one that Cassie could confirm."

Babs dropped to the other end of the couch and curled up with a throw pillow instead of him. "If she didn't go to Greece, where is she?"

"According to the airlines, she booked a round-trip flight to New Orleans."

"This is even more ludicrous than the story about the dead high school friend."

"I know. I'm totally confused now. So is Cassie, and she's worried sick over her mother."

"She should be. The woman sounds as if she's going nuts. Maybe it's menopause. Some women go off the deep end with that."

"I thought she went through it ten years ago when she lost interest in having sex."

"Or maybe she only lost interest in having it with you. She may be having a wild, passionate affair with someone in New Orleans. When's the mystery flight home?"

"Thursday."

"Meet her at the airport and demand answers. Then whatever the problem is, you just have to deal with it."

She made it sound much easier than it was in his mind. He didn't even know what solution he was looking for.

He loved Rhonda in a special way that nothing would ever change. They'd been together for thirty years. She'd given birth to his daughter, had stayed up all night with him when he'd fallen from the horse on vacation and wound up in an emergency room of a hick-town hospital. She'd stood beside him at his mother's casket.

He'd never wish anything bad on Rhonda. He just didn't

like her company much anymore and didn't get the feeling she cared too much for his. She didn't laugh at his jokes or show interest in anything he enjoyed. It had been years since she'd gone with him to an Astros game, years since they'd gone mountain biking or deep-sea diving or taken walks in the moonlight. And making love with her held about the same thrill as watching the cracks in the hard Texas dirt dry up after a rain.

"There's more, isn't there?" she asked, reading his mood the way she always did.

"There's more."

She listened without saying a word until he'd reached the point where Cassie had waited for an hour for the man's phone call before she'd given up and driven back to Beau Pierre from Cocodrie.

"So what are you going to do?"

"I contacted a detective in New Orleans. I'm flying there on Monday to meet with him."

"Wouldn't it make more sense to wait until Thursday and see if she's on that flight?"

"Cassie doesn't think so, and I'm inclined to agree with her. If something is wrong then the sooner we act on this the better. It's already been almost six weeks."

Babs scooted closer and laid her hand on his arm. "Do you think this has to do with us, Butch? Could she have found out that we're seeing each other and planned this scheme to pay you back?"

"That's crossed my mind."

"You don't think she's in real danger, do you? She hasn't been kidnapped or…"

"I can't imagine that she has, but I don't know. If all she wanted was a separation, I don't understand why she didn't just say to. But then Rhonda's always had her own way of looking at things and they seldom make sense to me. One time they found a lump in her breast, and she wasn't even going to tell me about the biopsy—she wouldn't have if she hadn't had an allergic reaction to the anesthetics and almost died.''

Even Babs looked worried now. ''Suppose it's something like that again? What if she has cancer and doesn't want you and Cassie to know she's going through chemotherapy?''

''I'd hate to think she'd go through something like that alone, but I wouldn't put it past her. That's why I hired the detective. I just don't know what to believe right now.''

''What do we do about us, Butch?''

He cradled her in his arms and buried his face in her hair. This was hard, so much more difficult than he thought it would be when he first became involved with her.

''I think it's best if we don't see each other outside the office until this thing is settled, Babs. I hate for it to be this way, but I think it's best for both of us.''

She nodded but held on to him so tightly he could feel her fingers digging into the muscles in his arm. He'd expected an argument from her, maybe even hysterics or tears. But hysterics weren't Babs's style.

''I know you're right,'' she whispered, ''but stay tonight, Butch. Give me one more night in your arms and then don't wake me when you leave. I don't want you to see me cry.''

''One more night,'' he agreed.

He didn't mean the parting to be forever, but he couldn't get past the feeling that it would be, or that he'd never again feel as needed or as loved as he did in Babs's arms right now.

CASSIE STOOD on the narrow front porch of the rented cabin, coffee in hand, observing the Sunday morning activity along the bayou. A blue heron stood on the bank, one leg up, as if waiting for the next beat of a dance tune. Four baby ducks swam in a row behind their mother and one more straggled behind. One log was lined with turtles sunning themselves in the morning sun. Another log floated in the tall grass in the boggy area a few yards from where she was standing.

She stepped toward the bank, and the second log came to life, swishing through the weeds and diving below the surface.

An alligator. Shivers slithered up her spine and she stood frozen to the spot, not moving until the gator surfaced again. He was farther down the bayou now, but close enough that she could still see the bony armor along its back and the shovel shape of its gray-green snout.

John had indicated they weren't all that dangerous, that they'd choose easier meals than an adult, but the badly chewed and decaying hand that the boys had found was adult-size. The image stuck in her mind, and she lost all taste for the coffee and the day.

Not that she'd had much taste for the day to begin with. There was no getting her mother off her mind anymore. Cassie was relieved that Butch was hiring a detective, but the fact that he was that concerned only increased Cassie's fears. They could both be overreacting. If her mother was on Continental flight 622 to Houston next Thursday, all would be well.

If she wasn't…

If she wasn't, the real fear would set in.

Cassie poured the coffee onto the ground and went back inside. She stepped out of her shorts and wiggled the T-shirt over her head. A quick shower and then she'd find a more constructive way to spend her day than watching alligators take their breakfast swim and worrying about things she could do nothing about.

Cassie pushed back the plastic shower curtain, stepped onto the cracked tile floor and twisted the knobs. She adjusted the temperature toward hot, then jumped back as a blast of near-scalding water pounded her on the back. Too hot or too cold were the only temperatures available in the cabin. Add that to the ever-growing list of things she wouldn't miss when she left Beau Pierre.

As to the things she would miss, that was easy, though ludicrous. She was going to miss John Robicheaux. Actually she missed him already. She'd half expected him to call when he'd heard the news of the body part that had been found in the bayou.

He hadn't.

But then she'd been the one who had walked away Friday night, so maybe he was waiting for her call. Sunday morning with John Robicheaux. It had interesting possibilities. Tingling sensations not associated with the water temperature danced along her nerve endings, and she knew that if she went out to his house again, they'd make love.

The sex would be great, but after that, things would get awkward. They had nothing in common but the situation in Beau Pierre and a super strong case of lust. It couldn't be more. Their lives were at opposite ends of the spectrum. There was nowhere for the relationship to go.

She stepped out of the shower and grabbed one of the thin white towels, rubbing her body vigorously. The mirror over the sink was cheap glass that gave her face and the wall behind her a wavy appearance. She leaned closer to get a look at her eyes. Not nearly as wrinkled as John's but he probably had ten years on her. Ten hard years.

Still, here she was at thirty-two, afraid to kiss a man because it might go further. Afraid to make love with John even though her desire for him on Friday night had all but consumed her.

Marriage had done this to her. Living with Drake had robbed her of self-confidence and made her afraid to trust her judgement or take chances.

It was time to move past that, and she wanted to. She really did, but it seemed a lot easier said than done. Like falling off a horse, Janie had said. You fall off, you get back on. You lose your confidence with one guy, you find it with another.

Cassie didn't expect a guy to give her back her self-confidence, but the divorce was final. She was a free woman—a free and horny woman who hadn't been touched in any kind of intimate way since she'd walked out on Drake fourteen months ago. And she'd never needed a man more than she did right now.

Hurrying before she backed out, she called John's number and waited. The phone rang six times. Her finger was on the button to end the call when someone answered.

"Hello."

The voice was soft and breathy. And female.

Cassie broke the connection and hurled the phone to the bed. Sonofabitch! All that emotional haggling with herself about whether or not she should risk seeing him again, and he was home going at it with someone else.

As far as she was concerned, fate had stepped in and kept her from making a big mistake.

Cassie sat at a back table in Suzette's, nursing her iced tea and occasionally spooning bites of warm, rum-covered breaded pudding between her lips. Mainly she was people watching. Suzette's was always a good place for that and Sunday noon was no exception.

There were several family groups, a few singles and some couples. Most people who came in seemed to know each other and thought nothing of yelling out greetings or even making conversation with someone at the next table or across the room. A few even waved and spoke to her, but no one approached her table. In spite of what Olson had said, spending her days and nights in Beau Pierre had not kept her from being an outsider.

"You want more tea?"

"No, thanks."

"You're that reporter lady staying down in the cabins, huh?"

"I am. My name's Cassie Pierson. What's yours?"

"Celeste."

The waitress was young, sixteen at the most, with long black hair and incredibly thick lashes. Cassie had noticed her in here before, usually working nights and always in a pair of low-riding black shorts and some kind of stretchy top that showed a lot of cleavage for a girl that young.

She wore a short denim skirt and a cotton shirt today, not nearly as revealing as her usual attire, but she still got stares from half the men in the place.

"Do you live in Beau Pierre?" Cassie asked when the girl continued to stand at her table.

"In Galliano. It's not far. My husband brings me to work and picks me up. He don't trust these guys down here."

"You're married? You seem so young."

"I'm seventeen in two weeks."

Which was very young, not that Cassie had made a great choice in husbands by waiting until her twenties.

"Have you worked here long?"

"Just a week. I started the night that guy killed himself."

"Dennis Robicheaux?"

She nodded. "I waited on him and his brother that night."

The girl glanced behind her then turned back to Cassie, tangling her hands in her hair. "I heard 'em talking."

Keep it nice and friendly. The girl's nervous enough. Don't frighten her into silence. "You must have heard something interesting."

"I don't guess it means nothing now, with him killing himself and all, but the man that killed himself made a phone call while his brother was in the men's room."

"What was the call about?"

"He told someone not to worry about Cassie Pierson, 'cause you'd never figure things out. I saw your name on the list of people staying in the cabins later. That's when I remembered what he'd said."

Cassie tensed and squeezed her hands around the glass of tea.

"Are you sure he said Cassie Pierson?"

"I'm sure he said Cassie. That's my sister's name, and that's when I started paying close attention, but I'm pretty sure he said Cassie Pierson. I remembered 'cause I don't know no Piersons and I was wondering who he was talking about."

This was too bizarre. She'd never been in Beau Pierre back then, didn't know Dennis, hadn't been assigned to this case. And yet Dennis Robicheaux had mentioned her name the night he was murdered—said not to worry about her because she'd never figure things out.

The dirty secrets of Beau Pierre. They'd become personal now, reached out and pulled her inside. Only how could they? She struggled to hide the apprehension and fear that swelled inside her and made it difficult to breathe.

"Did Dennis's brother mention me?"

"No, just Dennis, and he stopped talking and put the phone away when his brother came out of the bathroom."

"Was anyone else at the table with Dennis when he made that phone call?"

"No." She glanced behind her again. "I got to get back to working. Suzette don't like it if I talk too long to the customers when we're busy. Told that to me two times today already."

"Thanks for the information," Cassie said, striving to keep her voice calm. "And if you think of anything else Dennis said in that phone conversation, call me. It's important that you call me."

"That's all I heard."

Reeling from Celeste's words, Cassie finished her tea and was about to leave when Norman Guilliot stepped through the door. The room grew quiet and all eyes went to him. He waved and shouted greetings to everybody and the noise level shot up again.

He worked the room like a politician, stopping to talk to everyone and ruffling the hair on kids' heads. Cassie watched the show and wondered just how much of it had to do with the trial. The people in here couldn't influence the jury, but what they said about him to reporters did influence public opinion, and he was out to do more than win. He needed to come out the wounded hero in all of this. That was tough work when he was facing a well-loved TV evangelist like Flanders and a high-profile attorney like Drake.

"Nice to see you again, Cassie."

"Thanks, but you could have seen me anytime. All you had to do was return my calls."

"I've been busy. And so have you. Word is you've talked to pretty much everyone in town."

"I like to be thorough."

"Some folks think you're stirring up trouble by buying into the trash John Robicheaux's been talking. I guess you'll give his side of all this in the next edition of *Crescent Connection.*"

"John has a right to his opinion. I have a right to report it. *Crescent Connection* has the right to print it."

"Dennis wasn't murdered."

"How can you be so sure, Dr. Guilliot? You weren't there. No one was, unless there was a killer."

"I knew Dennis well. He had lots of problems."

"Like what?"

"I know he dropped out of school for a year after he did a clinical with me. I think he went to get help with a drug problem. Were you aware of that?"

"No, I didn't know that." And John certainly hadn't mentioned it. "No one else in town mentioned a drug problem."

"And they never will, not to an outsider."

"They admitted to me that he was a womanizer."

"I'm sure they didn't use that word. Drinking too much, liking the women. It's not that big a deal down here. We tend to pass a good time here."

"So what's your point, Dr. Guilliot? What does a drug problem in the past have to do with Dennis killing himself? Was he on something here? Did he screw up with Ginny Lynn's anesthetics? Is that what killed her? Because if that's what you're saying, you'd best settle your case with Reverend Flanders out of court."

"Make no mistake, Cassie. Dennis's work was always impeccable, as is everyone else's on my staff. I'd never have let him into my operating room if I had suspected differently."

"Then why tell me about the drug problem?"

"Because Dennis tried to kill himself then, too. And he

would have, if a good friend hadn't stepped in and stopped him.''

''Who was the friend?''

''It damn sure wasn't John. He was off wallowing in self-pity and drinking himself into oblivion. I was the one who saw that Dennis got proper care and stayed with him until he came to his senses. He checked into a drug rehabilitation center in New Orleans the following week.''

''And you think it follows that if he tried to kill himself before, he'd try it again.''

''He would if he was having the same problem.''

''What makes you think he was?''

''The autopsy that John insisted on showed prescription painkillers in his blood. Ask John about that when you see him again, Cassie. Ask him for the whole truth. I just thought you should know all the facts before you write your article and send it out to the public.''

''It's a little late for that, Dr. Guilliot. Why didn't you mention any of this when I met with you last Monday?''

''I didn't see the autopsy report until I met with my lawyer yesterday.''

That made sense. All of this made sense, but none of it explained enough.

''I feel I have to warn you to be careful around John Robicheaux, Cassie. He manipulates and lies and he can't be trusted. Dennis would have been the first to tell you that.''

''More tea?'' Celeste asked, stopping by the table again.

''No, I've had enough.'' Had enough of everything about Guilliot, and John and body parts in the bayou. Had enough of Beau Pierre.

''I hope I didn't ruin your dessert,'' Guilliot said, glancing at her half-eaten bowl of bread pudding.

''I was through with it,'' she said.

"Then I'm glad I caught you before you left."

"How did you know I'd be here?"

"I was driving by and saw your car."

He stood, ready to leave now that he'd said what he wanted to say.

"One question, Doctor."

"I'll be glad to answer if I can."

"Why is it that I'm getting all this attention? There are countless reporters in this town every day trying to dig up a story. Why didn't you go to them with this instead of taking the trouble to look me up?"

"I like you, Cassie. You have spunk. And I think you're letting John Robicheaux influence you."

But this was about more than manipulation. For some reason she'd been singled out both by John and Dr. Guilliot. At first she'd thought it was because she'd been married to one of the attorneys involved in the trial, but that wouldn't explain Dennis's comment about her the night he'd died.

What had he been talking about? Who had he been talking to? The questions were disturbing and filled her with a cold fear she couldn't shake, not even when she'd left Suzette's and stood in the bright noonday sun.

Whatever the mystery was, Dennis had claimed that Cassie Pierson would never figure it out.

She was determined to prove him wrong.

IT WAS NEAR DUSK when Cassie drove to the cemetery. Shadows were deepening to the point that it was difficult to see where she was stepping as she got out of the car and followed the path to the mausoleum where Dennis was buried. Cemeteries didn't bother her at all during the day, but they became eerie just before dark, and she kept looking to make sure no one else was around.

This could have waited until morning, but she was in the area and she was really curious to find out if someone was still leaving a white rose in front of the Robicheaux mausoleum.

She was almost close enough to tell when she heard the rumble of a vehicle on the road and then the squeal of brakes. A streak of fear shot through her and she almost ducked behind one of the stone structures before she realized how ridiculous she was being.

This wasn't a New Orleans cemetery where tourists were warned not to venture alone even in daylight, let alone at dusk. Beau Pierre was a safe, friendly town.

Except for the body parts floating in its bayou.

The thought did nothing to calm her nerves as she waited to see who was joining her. An owl hooted what she could have almost sworn was a warning, followed by the loud crack of gunfire.

The bullet whizzed past her head

CHAPTER TWELVE

CASSIE FROZE for a fraction of a second, then ran, darting through the cemetery in a zigzag pattern, around and between the mausoleums. She imagined the shooter right behind her, but she didn't dare stop to see if he was actually there.

There was no fence to mark the boundary of the cemetery. It just fell away into the swamp. Her right sandal disappeared into the bog and she felt the mud squeeze between her toes and something sharp and painful dig into her heel.

The second shoe was sucked away as she hit standing water that splashed up her legs and wet the hem of her long, full skirt. She dodged low-hanging branches of cypress trees as best she could, but there was no escaping the prickly briars.

She wiped at her face, trying to dislodge the spider webs that caught in her eyelashes and clung to the sweat that poured from her like rain. Her foot tangled in a briar that didn't let go, and this time she fell against the trunk of a towering cypress.

Gasping for breath, she listened for footsteps. The swamp was alive with noises. Sucking, rustling sounds that could be anything. Even alligators.

They'll attack to protect their nest or their young.

Both could be nearby, feet from where she stood, yet

invisible in the growing darkness of the swamp. She didn't dare stay here—and didn't dare move.

Something cold and slimy started crawling up her leg. A snake, a very long snake. She began to shake uncontrollably, then grabbed for it. Her hand closed around it, and she tried to pull it loose and sling it away from her. It dropped its hold on her leg, but curled around her arm, still inching upward. She gasped and tried desperately to keep the scream locked in her throat, but it escaped and echoed through the swamp.

She heard the footsteps then, running toward her. She tried to run, but she'd sunk too deep in the mire. And the snake's tongue was flicking like a satanic lover.

"Cassie!"

John's voice, or else she was hallucinating—or already dead. She started to call to him, then stopped. For all she knew, he could be the one who'd tried to kill her. But why? Unless the hidden secrets of Beau Pierre were his.

She turned away at the bright, blinding beam of a flashlight.

"Cassie! What happened? What are you doing out here?"

She didn't answer, just stared at him pleadingly, both hands locked around the snake that was curled around her arm.

"Let go of the snake and it'll fall loose, Cassie. It's not poisonous. Just let go of it."

John's voice was calm, so low she could barely hear it above the hammering of her heart. She released her hold then gritted her teeth and waited for the snake's next move. It fell to the ground and slithered away.

She slumped against the tree, then slid slowly to the swamp. Every part of her body ached, and her throat felt as if she'd swallowed a hot stone and it was stuck halfway down her esophagus.

John yanked off his shirt and used it as a cloth to wipe her face and eyes. "Are you hurt?" he asked.

His voice was strained as if his vocal cords were stretched too taut. He took her hands and tugged her to a standing position. She ached to fall into his arms, mud and all, but suspicion held her back.

"What are you doing here, John?"

"What am *I* doing here?"

"How did you know where to find me?"

"I stopped by the cemetery and saw your car. When I didn't see you anywhere, I followed your tracks into the swamp. Now why the hell are you here?"

"Someone took a shot at me in the cemetery. It missed, and I took off running."

"Did you see who fired the gun?"

"No."

Something rustled the grass behind John. "Let's get out of here. This is no place to be at night." He handed her the flashlight. "You hold this."

John scooped her up in his arms.

"I can walk," she said.

"Not the best place to hike barefoot."

He kept her in his arms and took off tramping through the swamp. Nothing made sense. Absolutely nothing. So she just held the flashlight tight in her hands and aimed the light in front of them. One beam in a world of black.

"Nice to be saved by a man with strong arms who knows his way out of a swamp."

"Would have been. Too bad you got stuck with one who relies on the stars for direction."

She glanced upward. There wasn't a star in view. If he wasn't kidding, they were in big, big trouble.

"I THOUGHT I'd run much farther than that," Cassie said when they reached the cemetery minutes later. "It seemed like miles."

"Miles, and you'd have had to walk back on your own." John set her on her feet, thankful she was as light as she was. Chivalry was hard on the back. "Now that your breathing is somewhere near normal, tell me exactly what happened."

"I was driving nearby and decided to stop."

"Any particular reason why you'd come back here?"

"I wanted to see if someone had left another white rose."

"And had they?"

"I didn't see one, but someone has been leaving them here, not every day, but almost every day."

"Can we skip the rose part?"

"You asked. Anyway, I heard a vehicle coming down the road and the squeal of the brakes when it stopped. I kept waiting to see who was there, but I never saw anyone. And then I heard the shot and felt something whiz right by my head."

"But you didn't see the vehicle or the person?"

"No. The tall mausoleum toward the front of the cemetery blocked my view of the road."

In which case they might not have been firing at her. It could have been teenagers out getting in a little target practice. There had been that kind of vandalism out here before.

"Show me exactly where you were standing," he said, once they reached the family burial vault.

"In front of the mausoleum. I don't know exactly where."

John directed a beam of light over the door, then

scanned it across the stone wall. There was no sign of a bullet hole.

"What are you looking for?" Cassie asked. "Because I'm not interested in staying around to see if the sniper makes a return visit."

"I'm looking for the bullet or the bullet hole. That might tell what kind of weapon the guy was using." He scanned the bronze cross with the light, and there it was. A solid dent that hadn't been there before. Head high.

It hit him full force then. Cassie was alive by inches, maybe less. Not only had the bullet struck dangerously close, it had ricocheted, giving it another chance to strike her.

She would have been dead, her brains spilled the way Dennis's had been. Someone was desperate. And desperation produced the most dangerous situations of all.

He knelt in the grass and searched for the bullet. Cassie joined him, but even with the flashlight it was tough to see well enough to find a bullet that could have fallen most anywhere.

Finally, they gave up the search. He'd look again in the daylight, but even if he found it, he doubted Babineaux would make any attempt to match it to a weapon. The sheriff was tucked away in Guilliot's pocket.

Cassie didn't say a word as they walked to the car, and he had no idea what she was thinking. He did know that somehow she'd entered into the circle of danger. Either she'd found out something in her interviews without realizing it, or someone feared that she would. But the bullet had been more than a warning. It had hit too close for that.

They were nearly to the road when Cassie broke the awkward silence that had settled between them. "Why me, John? Why am I being singled out for all this special attention? Both you and Guilliot looked me up. Now someone tries to kill me. I can't believe every reporter who drives into Beau Pierre gets this kind of reception.''

"Whoever shot at you tonight thinks you know something, and I'm not ruling out that Guilliot took that shot.''

"What about you, John? Why did you seek me out that first day when you followed me out to Magnolia Plantation?''

"Maybe I liked your looks.''

"You were too upset that day to be thinking about my looks.''

"I figured Guilliot would target you for his campaign to label Dennis as a sick, troubled guy who couldn't take the stress of the trial. I don't want my brother's name and reputation slandered by the man who either killed him or had him killed. And I wanted you to plant the suspicion in everyone's mind that Dennis was murdered,'' he said, seeing no real reason to lie.

She opened her car door, but didn't get in. "I tried to see your side of the story, and you thanked me by feeding me half truths.''

"What are you talking about?''

"Why didn't you tell me Dennis had attempted suicide before?''

"So that's what this is about. You talked to Guilliot, didn't you? You talked to that arrogant, lying bastard and you believe him over me. I thought you were smarter than that.''

"Then don't tell me half truths and try to manipulate me.''

"Dennis never tried to kill himself. He took a combination of painkillers and alcohol and passed out in his truck outside Suzette's. Guilliot found him, took him into his clinic and took care of him.''

"Was Dennis addicted to painkillers at the time?''

"Yeah. He had a drug problem. That was six years ago. He went through rehab and he'd been clean ever since. And the trace of drugs found in his system at the autopsy was from a prescription Guilliot had written for him for headache pain. Any other of Guilliot's garbage I can clear up for you?"

"No. Look, I'm sorry, John. Really sorry. I didn't say any of that right, but my nerves are on edge and I had a really rough evening."

"*Mais* sho'. Now we both have."

He tried to tamp down the anger, but he couldn't. The whole world was going crazy instead of just him for a change. He didn't expect any more of Guilliot, but he hadn't expected Cassie to turn on him like that. He'd thought...

It didn't matter what he'd thought. She was a reporter, and he was part of her research. End of story.

"Thanks, John. You saved my life and I do appreciate it even if it didn't sound that way."

"My mistake. A smart guy would never save a reporter." He turned and stalked to his car, hating that she'd gotten to him. Hating that she was still getting to him. Hating even worse that the anger swelling in his chest like a heart attack about to happen wasn't going to get her off his mind.

Nothing would until he knew for sure who was behind the bullet that had missed her by inches. When he did, he was dead certain he'd have Dennis's killer, as well. And somewhere in the mix, he'd find Guilliot.

And for once in his life John wouldn't fail. He'd see Guilliot in prison—or he'd see him dead.

But how the hell would he keep Cassie safe in the meantime?

EVERYTHING HIT Cassie at once and her hands shook so badly that for a minute, she thought she'd have to pull the car onto the shoulder of the highway and wait until she regained control. She took deep breaths then lowered the window so that the air hit her in the face and cleared out some of the fetid odors that clung to her clothes.

A hot shower would take care of the mud. She wasn't certain any amount of water or soap could remove the stench. And she was fairly certain nothing would ever remove the memory of how the snake had felt slithering up her body and winding around her arm.

She'd be in the swamp yet if John hadn't gone searching for her. He'd not only saved her life, he'd ignored the mud and the stench of her and literally carried her back to dry land and safety.

For repayment, she'd attacked him like some Shakespearean shrew. Two nights ago she'd been fighting to keep from throwing herself into his arms. Tonight, she'd been in his arms and had struck back at him with accusations about his brother's drug problems when Dennis had barely had time to turn cold in the grave.

Her feelings for John were entangled in a web of conflicting emotions that seemed to fly at her from all directions and not settle anywhere. Only, how could her physical attraction be so strong for a man she didn't fully trust? How could she even fantasize about making love with a man who'd had a different woman between his sheets last night?

Thirty minutes later, she parked the car in the parking lot at Suzette's and took her flashlight from the glove compartment and her new mud boots from the trunk before starting back to the cabin. Hot or cold, she couldn't wait to step under the shower.

Olson wanted her on the inside. Well, she was there, no

longer just a reporter gathering facts, but sucked into the danger. She had to figure out why and how and she had to do it quickly before she was dead herself and the only person she'd be interviewing would be Dennis and maybe the person who'd become food for the alligators.

Lost in her thoughts, she pushed open the door.

And stepped into her next nightmare.

The cabin had been trashed. Her clothes had been pulled from their hangers and thrown to the floor. The drawers in the one small chest had been yanked out and dumped upside down.

Her first impulse was to scream. The second was to fall across the bed and bawl her eyes out. But her body kept moving, and neither the scream nor the tears came. From the looks of things, the goon who'd done this had come through the window. It was still open and the screen had been removed. Probably took the guy under a minute.

She was tired, caked in mud and smelled like rotten fish. Now she had this mess to contend with.

She wished she were home, wished she'd never heard of Beau Pierre or Norman Guilliot or Ginny Lynn Flanders. If she'd known all this was coming, she'd never have even become a reporter. She'd have chosen a safer, calmer career, like fighting roaring forest fires or test-driving fighter planes.

She walked to the bathroom. First a shower, then she'd deal with the mess. The clothes were replaceable. The only things of real value here were her...

Her laptop. She spun and took a quick look about the room. Anger exploded inside her. They'd trashed her room and they'd stolen her computer and her stacks of notes. Wrecking the cabin was no doubt secondary to the real intent. They'd come for information.

Now they had it all. The notes from her interviews.

Computer files of the copy she'd submitted and all the ideas and thoughts she'd typed in whenever she'd had a spare minute.

She opened the door and stepped into the night, wondering if the thieving varmint was out there, crouched behind the fronds of a palmetto plant and hoping to see her go running off in fear. Raising her fist in the air, she scanned the surrounding area then stared straight out at the bayou.

"Come out and face me, you scum coward. Tell me to my face what you want from me."

The night was incredibly quiet, or it seemed that way after her taunting screams, but amazingly no one came out of the other cabins to see why she was yelling. She went back inside, slammed the door behind her and locked the deadbolt, though that was obviously a waste of time.

Well, screw the thief and Beau Pierre. But the fire went out of her anger as she stepped under the spray that ran cold tonight. She stood there, shivering, trying to make sense of things, but all she felt was a clutching sensation in her stomach and a tightening in her chest.

As the water finally grew warm, her mind went back to the time in the swamp and the snake that had wrapped itself around her arm. She'd never been so scared in all her life. And then John had stepped in and taken control. John Robicheaux, the attorney who'd freed a monster and run from life. Angry, grieving, John Robicheaux—the most unlikely of saviors.

A burst of scorching water shot from the rattling pipes and she jumped back to avoid the burn. A sign from above. Mess with John and she'd really get burned.

When the water cooled again, she tilted her head backward and let it cascade over her face and run down her body. The water ran almost black as it circled and disappeared down the drain.

She'd been that dirty, and still John had picked her up and carried her from the swamp.

The pipes began to squeal. She turned the knobs and the noise quieted enough that Cassie heard the rapping at her door. Her heart jumped to her throat. She'd screamed at the man to show himself. He might be about to oblige.

She stepped from the water and grabbed her robe, looking around for something to use as a weapon. There weren't a lot of choices. She decided on the lamp, yanking it from the wall and holding it over her head as she moved to the door with adrenaline rushing so strong it felt like it might take her head off.

"Who's there?"

"John. Open the door, Cassie. I need to see you."

She dropped the lamp, opened the door and fell into his arms.

CHAPTER THIRTEEN

JOHN WAS STUNNED by the reception, but he realized pretty quickly it was due to more than just his irresistible charm when she pulled away and he got his first glimpse of the damage.

"Are you okay?" he asked for the second time that day, again dreading that her answer might be no.

"I'm a little shaken, as you probably noticed when I hurled myself into your arms. But I'm not hurt."

"What happened?"

"I found the cabin like this when I returned tonight. Well, except for the lamp. I was going to use that to smash the skull of whoever was at the door if it turned out to be my nemesis returning for more fun."

"Glad I identified myself quickly." He glanced around the room. It had the look of teenage hoodlums looking for cash or something that would easily convert to cash. They didn't get a lot of that down here, and even if they had, he'd have doubted this was random. "What's missing?"

"My laptop. All my notes. All my disks. Whoever broke in knew exactly what he was after," she said. "I guess trashing the rest of my things just provided a little extra thrill."

"Or maybe someone wants to frighten you into leaving town."

"Then the shot may have been a warning, as well."

"Not with a bullet that missed by a fraction of an inch."

"That doesn't make sense," Cassie argued. "Danger would normally escalate, wouldn't it? The warning would come first. Then, if I didn't heed it, the action would become deadly."

"Always happens that way in the movies," he agreed. "How long had you been away from the cabin?"

"Most of the day."

"Then the burglar could have found something in your notes that made him think you know enough to be dangerous. That could have inspired the attempt on your life at the cemetery."

He walked about the room, examining the damage, trying to make sense of what this was about or who had been here, his attention caught by a pile of silky panties that had been dumped to the floor under a window.

"He dumped all the drawers out," Cassie said when she saw him staring at her intimate apparel.

"Dumped them out, but it doesn't look as if he even picked up one pair of panties for a closer look."

"So the thief isn't a pervert," she said. "Is that supposed to make me feel better?"

"Or it could mean that the intruder wasn't a man."

He moved to the clothes that had been pulled from the hangers and thrown to the floor. Some were streaked with mud, as if someone had kicked them. He stooped and picked up a white dress.

"Fairly clear footprint on this, and small."

"I may have stepped on it," she said.

He stared at her bare feet. "What kind of shoes did you have on?"

"None. I slipped out of the mud boots before I even opened the door. And I'd lost my sandals in the swamp." She walked over for a better look at the shoe.

"Most definitely a woman's shoe print," she agreed.

"But if the woman is the same person who took a shot at me, she'd have to be a very good shot."

"You could find a lot of women like that in Beau Pierre. But don't jump to conclusions. The M.O. is very different."

"You sound like a cop," she said, dropping to the bed.

"No. A defense attorney. You think alike, just at cross purposes."

Her accusation hit him where it hurt. That was what he was doing, had been ever since he'd heard about Dennis's death. He was falling into the old mind-set, getting pulled back into fragments of a life he wanted no part of.

"I don't see how any of this can be connected to my questioning people about Dennis. And yet it has to be," she said.

John stood there, hating that he was being sucked into all of this, but he'd vowed to find Dennis's killer and he couldn't just up and run away. And deep down he knew it was more. He'd never wanted to be needed by anyone again. Never wanted to care.

But there sat this auburn-haired reporter in a scruffy white robe and there was no way he could walk away and leave her to face this by herself. Damn Cassie. How had she gotten to him without even trying?

He took a deep breath, then joined her on the edge of the bed. "You must know something, Cassie, some scrap of information that has someone running scared enough to try to kill you."

"But I don't know anything, John. If I did, I'd go to the cops. Of course, I will now anyway. I'll have to report the shooting and break in."

"Maybe it's part of something else and you don't know you know it. The problem now is staying alive long enough to figure it all out."

"And I suppose you have answers for that, as well."

"I have a couple of ideas."

"I'd love to hear them, but not tonight. I've had just about all the fun and excitement I can take in one twenty-four-hour period. I want a glass of wine and a very soft mattress with sheets that crinkle when I crawl between them. I want my own things around me and no alligators and snakes outside my door. I'll come back and report everything to the sheriff tomorrow, but tonight I just want to go home."

She was ready to go back to New Orleans. He should let her. It would make this a hell of a lot easier on him in the long run. But the danger for her wouldn't stop at the parish line. The stakes were too high now.

"Come home with me, Cassie. The sheets aren't that great. The mattress has a few lumps. But come home with me, at least for tonight."

"And do you wash these sheets between guests, John, or do the women just run together like the stains left from making love?"

He pulled away, as much from the change in her tone as her words. Both were edged in bitterness. "Did I deserve that?"

She stood and walked to the window, staring out into the darkness instead of looking at him. "No. You can live your life as you like, have all the women you can get. It's none of my affair."

"I didn't invite you over because I was looking for a good lay, Cassie. But for the record, I haven't been with a woman in almost a year. Now, is that loser enough for you?"

She turned and finally met his gaze. "What about the woman who was at your house early this morning?"

"So that was you who called and hung up."

"I didn't want to disturb you if you were in the middle of something."

"There was nothing happening to disturb. The woman you talked to was Annabeth Guilliot."

"Dr. Guilliot's wife was at your house?" She turned her gaze back to the darkness outside her window. "You know what, John? I don't really want to know the answer to that question. This is all far too complicated for me. So why don't you go now?"

"Annabeth spent the night, but it was because she was frightened and near hysterics."

"And she came to you?"

"She's pregnant and Guilliot isn't the father."

"You're not making this any better, John."

"Annabeth is pregnant with Dennis's child."

"Oh, no. What will she do?"

"I'm not sure." He crossed the room and lay his hands on Cassie's shoulders, as always reeling at the feelings that came from being so close. "Get some clothes on, Cassie— or not. We have lots to talk about. I'm too hungry to do it without food and there's a pot of gumbo waiting at my place, and a mattress with nice, *clean* sheets."

NORMAN SURFED the channels, settling briefly on a late-night movie where a couple were going at it hot and heavy. Most nights he would have watched for a few minutes if only to ogle the half-naked female, but tonight even that didn't interest him. He kept surfing, finally sticking with a tennis match being played somewhere where it was already tomorrow. Lucky them.

Annabeth had come home midmorning. No pleading. No apologies. She'd merely strode into the house as if she'd gone to get her nails done instead of having spent two nights at that rundown shack in the swamp with John Robicheaux.

She'd tried to make conversation with him a couple of times. He'd walked away, a far saner move than other options that appealed to him. She had him over a barrel, hitting him with news like this right before the start of the trial. Kick her out and Drake Pierson would have her testifying for the Flanders team and making him look really bad, especially in light of John Robicheaux's accusation that Norman had killed Dennis.

So he couldn't kick her out, not yet anyway. He switched channels again, then tossed the control to the coffee table when Annabeth joined him in the den, wearing a red, lacy teddie, as if she thought that would make a difference.

She walked over and stood between him at the TV. "Can you turn that off for a minute, Norman? I'd like to talk to you about something."

"You have nothing to say I'm interested in hearing."

"Don't do this, Norman. Please. Don't just shut me out."

"What happened?" he asked, tired of her standing there looking pitiful. "Did John Robicheaux throw you out?"

"How did you know I'd been at John's?"

"Word gets around. I have to hand it to you, though. You did a great job of keeping your affair quiet before. I had no idea you were playing around in the slums."

"I never slept around. I was with one man."

"One man, a dozen. The number doesn't change anything."

"You've been with other women since we've been married, Norman. I knew and I didn't say a word. If I forgave you, why can't you forgive me one mistake? Give me a chance to make this right."

"I never asked you to forgive me, Annabeth. This is my house, and my money keeps it going. You were free to walk out any time things didn't suit you here." He stood and walked to the kitchen for a tall glass of water.

She followed him to the kitchen and grabbed his arm. "I love you, Norman. Please give me a chance."

"I love you, Norman." He mimicked her words, then shoved her away from him. "I was just down in the swamp sleeping with the father of my baby, but I love you."

"John Robicheaux's not the father."

"I'm sure he'll be pleased to hear that."

"Dennis is."

The water glass slipped from his hand, crashing into the sink and shattering into fireworks of broken glass. "You're lying, Annabeth. Dennis and I were friends. He wouldn't have gotten involved with you."

"We didn't mean for it to happen. It just did."

He stared at her, wanting to slap her across the wall for lying, but one look in her eyes, and he knew she was telling the truth or else she was a very good liar. His wife and his friend.

"Where did you do him? Here? At his place? Where?"

She exhaled slowly as if pushing bad air from her lungs. "The first was here, the week you were at the conference in Las Vegas. He came by to drop off some paperwork Drake Pierson had asked him to fill out about the medications he'd used on Mrs. Flanders. We didn't mean for anything to happen, I swear. It just did."

"In my own house. In my own bed, I guess."

"No."

"In one of the guest rooms?"

"Don't do this, Norman. I love you. I'll..."

"You'll what?"

"I'll have an abor—" She started to cry.

"Just don't do this, not after all I've done for you."

He pushed past her and walked out the door. He hated Annabeth for what she'd done. Hated her and...and loved her. God help him, he did. But he would never forgive her.

"Don't go, Norman. Please don't go."

But he was already gone in his mind and that was where all divorces started. *Damn you, Dennis. I trusted you. We were a team.*

Norman started the engine of his Porsche, yanked it into reverse and spun out of the garage. Once on the highway, he gave Susan a call. "You got a spot in bed for me tonight, sweetheart?"

"Norman?"

"Yeah. It's been a hell of a weekend."

"Bad timing."

Which meant she wasn't alone. Sonofabitch. But that didn't mean he was out in the cold. There was always the one woman who'd never turn him away. Twenty years of loyalty. Twenty years of waiting. She might get lucky tonight.

But he changed his mind and drove to the edge of town, took the turn down the bayou road to the spot where Dennis had killed himself. Norman parked there, on the shoulder near the spot where Dennis had run his car off into the swampy bog.

He wanted to scream. He wanted to cry. He wanted to bang his head against the steering wheel. Instead he just sat in the dark and thought back to the day it had all gone wrong.

He had to get Cassie Pierson out of town and off this assignment for good, before she started putting all the facts together. She was the one person who could destroy them all. All but Dennis. He was gone, except for the part of him that lived inside Norman's wife.

The irony of that was the cruelest blow of all.

CASSIE WOKE to the smells of fresh-brewed coffee and frying sausage. She stretched between the sheets, and her muscles protested. The run through the swamp had left its mark in more ways than the scratches on her legs, arms and face. And with the memory of the swamp, it all came back. The shooter. The trashed cabin.

The fact that she'd spent the night at John's place.

She stretched again, slower this time, and tried to remember exactly how she'd ended up sleeping in the one bed alone. They'd eaten gumbo. She'd sipped wine while John had talked of schemes and conspiracies and ugly secrets. He'd talked on and on, and...

She must have fallen asleep on his sofa. Her hands flew beneath the covers to check out her attire. She was still wearing the T-shirt she'd thrown on last night back at the cabin, and a pair of panties. No bra. No shorts.

She flushed with embarrassment and an unexpected blast of desire as she imagined his hands reaching beneath her shirt and removing the bra. He'd also removed her shorts. Had he copped a feel? Or at least had a quick look? And did she care if he had?

She slipped from the bed, found her clothes draped over a chair by the window and pulled them on. She decided not to bother with a bra. If he'd removed it last night, he could surely handle her coming to breakfast without one.

"Something smells good," she said, stepping into the cozy kitchen.

"Boudin and eggs."

"And coffee."

"Lots of coffee. Hope you like it strong."

"Not particularly, but I can weaken it with milk—if you have milk."

"I've got some. Gave up beer for breakfast."

"What a man."

John poured her a cup of coffee, then pulled a half-empty gallon jug of milk from the refrigerator. "Smell it before you pour it in your coffee. I've been known to keep food in there until it starts growing."

She checked the date and smelled it. "Seems fine to me," she said, adding it to coffee that was so thick she half-expected it to support the spoon on its own.

"How do you like your eggs?" he asked. "Over easy? Scrambled? Blackened?"

"Blackened eggs?"

"Just teasing, *chère.*"

"Over medium. Do you want me to fry them?"

"No. I've got it covered."

"Then I'm going to go splash some water on my face."

"The bathroom's all yours. There are clean towels on the counter and toothpaste by the toothbrush holder. I put your hanging toiletry bag in there so you could get to it easily."

"You are on top of things."

"There's method to my madness. Or maybe it's madness to my method. We'll know better after we see if it works."

She should have known there was a catch to the excellent treatment she was receiving.

SITTING ACROSS the breakfast table from Cassie was a lot more difficult than John had anticipated. Could be the hair, he decided. Long and thick and falling about her shoulders. Or the T-shirt with the outline of her nipples showing through.

More likely it was the fact that it had taken all his control last night to undress her and carry her to his bed and

not crawl in beside her. The urges hit stronger when he
thought about sliding those shorts over her hips and leaving those lacy little panties in place. Nice that he was sitting down with a table to block the view. Otherwise, it
would be impossible not to let her see exactly how she
affected him.

And if she knew, it would spoil his whole plan.

"You're a good cook," she said, sopping up the last bit
of egg yolk with her toast.

"Learned it from Muh-maw. She could take anything
Puh-paw brought in from the marsh and turn it into a
feast."

"Did you always live here?"

"It's all I remember. My mother walked out on us when
I was eight. My dad quit his job working for a shipbuilder
up in Bridge City and brought me back here to live."

"But Dennis is more than eight years younger than you.
Is he only a half brother?"

"Technically. It never seemed that way. Mostly we
were both raised by our grandparents."

"Why did you come back to the cabin last night,
John?"

He leaned back in his chair. Too many reasons to count
but they all boiled down to two. "I wanted to see you and
I didn't think you should be by yourself."

"I can never figure you out, John. At times I think you
actually like me, and then you do or say something that
makes me think I'm being manipulated by you, that whatever I'm mistaking for attraction is part of some game plan
that you have for avenging Dennis's death."

"I never figure myself out." How was that for avoid-
ance? A better answer might be to just jump her bones
right here and now. Let all the sexual energy she generated

loose and make love to her on the kitchen table. Or the floor. Or the sofa. Or the bed. Or all of the above.

And if she kept looking at him with those big green eyes, he might not be able to stop himself from doing it. But she did stop. She pushed back from the table and started collecting the dirty dishes and carrying them to the sink.

"You can't stay at Suzette's any longer, Cassie. It's not safe. And you can't just wander around the way you've been doing, strolling through isolated cemeteries and driving down deserted back roads."

"It just doesn't make sense. I'm not worth the trouble of being shot at or having my notes stolen. I'm just like the dozen or so other reporters who are in and out of this town every day."

"Someone is convinced you know something."

"You think I do, too, don't you John? You wouldn't keep bringing this up if you didn't think that. You think I know something that can help you find Dennis's murderer."

John took the clean wet plate from her hand and dried it. "I think you could know something, and I do want something from you."

"I knew it."

"I want you to go back to the Magnolia Plantation, but this time I want you to go with me—unannounced and uninvited."

"You mean break in?"

"That's what I mean."

She pulled her hands from the water and dried them on the towel he was holding. "I'm a reporter for a respectable magazine. I am not about to risk my job and end up in jail breaking into a medical clinic."

"It was just an idea."

"A crazy one. Breakfast was great, John, but I'm out of here." She turned and headed back to the bedroom.

He followed her. "Okay, forget breaking in. I'll do that on my own. But don't move out."

She stared at him as if he'd lost his mind. "I have never moved in. I spent one night here because I was too exhausted and exasperated—and probably too stupid to turn down your invitation."

"Don't move in. Definitely don't move in. I didn't mean to suggest that you do that. I'm just suggesting you stay here until you're through with the Beau Pierre assignment. You'll be safer. You'll have *clean* sheets. And, hey, I'll toss you for who cooks breakfast."

"There's no way I'm breaking into that clinic, John. So if that's your motive for getting me to stay here, forget it."

"It's forgotten. I'd still like you to stay."

"What do you hope to gain by breaking in there?"

"I want to find out for myself if there's information somewhere about what really happened the day the preacher's wife died on the table."

"I'm certain if there was something incriminating, it's either in the hands of Guilliot's attorney or it's been destroyed."

"If it's an official notation in with the official records, but that doesn't mean I wouldn't locate something unofficial that would help me figure out what went wrong."

"Why would you need me for that?"

"Because if something we came across had a connection to whatever it is you know, you might pick up the clue that would make all of this fit together."

"*I don't know anything.*"

"Maybe not, but someone with a gun thinks you do."

"I'll stay here until Wednesday, if your offer is serious

and no strings attached, but I won't even consider breaking into Magnolia Plantation.''

"Fair enough.''

Two more nights with Cassie in his bed. That would work out great for protecting her from a killer. He just wasn't sure who was going to protect her from him. Or more important, who was going to protect him from himself.

CHAPTER FOURTEEN

CLAYTON JACOBBI'S office was in one of the older buildings on Camp Street, a part of downtown New Orleans that was once inhabited primarily by derelicts who slept on the streets and lined up for free food from soup kitchens. The area had been cleaned up over the past few years, and what had formerly been known as the warehouse district was now officially called the Arts District.

Norman liked coming to the city. He liked visiting the gentlemen's clubs on Bourbon Street, liked eating in the restaurants and going to an occasional Saints or Hornets game. He hated coming to Jacobbi's office.

The law offices were stuffy with a kind of pseudo-sophistication that Norman found more stifling than the outside humidity. The walls were too dark, the carpets too plush, and everyone wore dark-colored business suits. It wasn't natural to wear suits when the temperature outside was in the high nineties.

Mostly he hated coming here because the place intimidated him. Clayton Jacobbi worked for him, but the way the guy gave orders, you'd think Norman was his flunky. At Magnolia Plantation, the world revolved around Norman. In the law offices of Jacobbi, Frische and Caldwell, Norman was just another client who needed someone to save his ass.

"Sorry to keep you waiting, Dr. Guilliot," Jacobbi said,

finally appearing in the small conference room where the receptionist had planted Norman.

"No problem, as long as I get back to the clinic by one o'clock. I have appointments this afternoon."

Jacobbi glanced at his watch. "I'll have you out of here by eleven. What we need to do this morning is go over how we're going to handle the suicide of your anesthetist again. This is the biggest complication to the trial to date. Drake Pierson is going to play it as a blatant admission of guilt on Dennis Robicheaux's part. We have to give the jury a believable alternative."

"I told you he had a history of problems with alcohol and addiction to prescription drugs. He had both in his bloodstream the night he killed himself."

"That's still going to play into their hands. Either you had an addict working with you, or Dennis was so disturbed over some error of judgement made in the operating room on the fatal day that he went back to an old addiction."

"He was upset because of the constant press."

"Not good enough."

"Ginny Flanders died on the operating table because she had an undiagnosed heart condition. She wasn't aware of the condition herself, so there was no way I could possibly have known it."

"That's your contention. Drake Pierson is going to try to prove that you should have had a cardiogram run on a woman her age before you operated on her. Not only that, but he's going to say that if you had stopped the procedure at the first sign of patient breakdown, she wouldn't have died."

"So what do you suggest?"

"I think we should sacrifice Dennis for the good of the rest of you. If there was any mistake made that day, let it be his, but not because of drugs, since that falls back on irresponsibility on your part."

"You want to blame all of this on Dennis?"

"I think it's the smart move. He's dead. The rest of you are alive and you're fighting for your careers and your futures. If you go down in this, the bad publicity is going to destroy you. You or Dennis. That's how I see it."

"What do you need on him?"

"A breakup with his girlfriend. A big gambling loss. A family problem."

Sleeping with the surgeon's wife. Getting her pregnant.

Guilliot felt his stomach tighten and he stared at the pattern in the drape until he could get his feelings under control again. He wasn't going into court and admit that some guy half his age who Guilliot had thought a friend had knocked up his wife. But Annabeth might. If she got on that witness stand, she might get scared or angry and say anything.

"I know we talked about my wife taking the stand on my behalf," Guilliot said, "but I've changed my mind about that."

"You may need her. A trusting wife can go a long way with a jury—if we get the right jury."

"She's been upset since Dennis killed himself. I'm not sure she'll hold up well."

Jacobbi scribbled down some notes. "That could be a problem. What about Angela Dubuisson?"

"Use her to full advantage. She's loyal to the core. We've been together twenty years and knew each other growing up. We're both from Beau Pierre."

"And Susan Dalton?"

"She's still a go."

"I'll need to meet with both of them before the end of

the week. Once the jury selection starts next week, things will move fast."

"It's been six months. I'm ready for fast, as long as you still think we have a good chance of winning this."

"A good chance—as long as we play our cards right and nothing new pops up. And believe me, six months may be the shortest time on record for a case like this to make it to trial."

"Back to Dennis," Norman said. "If I can find a woman who claims she had broken up with Dennis and that he was distraught and begging her to get back together, would that help?"

"It would be perfect."

Good. Money could easily buy that.

"Let's go over the questions you'll likely get from Drake Pierson again," the attorney said. "I'll ask. You answer just as if you were on the stand. And don't forget to be careful of any body language that would make you look nervous."

"Does the jury ever listen to the evidence?" Guilliot asked, feeling the frustration building like a giant firecracker about to blow in his head.

"They listen, but they gather as much subconsciously as they do consciously. It's a show. You and Reverend Flanders will be the stars. Pierson and I will be the supporting cast."

Norman's cell phone rang. He checked the incoming number. "I'll need to get that. It's from my clinic."

"Go ahead. Patients first."

He answered the call. "Hello."

"I think you should come back to the clinic as soon as you can, Norman."

"Is there a problem with one of the patients?"

"No, everyone's fine. The facelift patient from yesterday is sitting up watching television, and last week's patients are all healing well."

"I'm with my attorney, Angela. It's an important meeting."

"Then come in as soon as you can. This isn't about a patient, but it is an emergency. A very *serious* emergency."

His hands began to sweat. "I'll be there by one."

The rest of the meeting with Jacobbi was a wash. Serious could mean anything. Or it could mean everything. In which case, Dennis's death wouldn't be an issue at all.

IT WAS 12:35 p.m. when Norman drove through the gates of Magnolia Plantation Restorative and Therapeutic Center. He slowed the car in spite of the anxiety that rode every nerve. He'd sunk every penny he had into buying and restoring this place—his entire inheritance, and all the money he'd made by wise investments during his early years of surgery.

And then he'd made the money back tenfold because he gave patients what they couldn't get anywhere else. There were a few other surgeons as talented as he was, a few who had his charisma, but no one else had a fully operating southern plantation for patients to live in while they recovered. Guilliot provided the services of a five-star hotel with the ambiance of *Gone With The Wind*. All they needed was cash and lots of it.

He'd reached the pinnacle of plastic surgery and he wasn't going to take a plunge because of one lousy mistake, the kind any doctor could have made. He didn't know what the emergency was that had Angela so upset, but if he was a betting man, he'd say it had something to do with Cassie Havelin Pierson or John Robicheaux.

Norman parked in his space near the back door and took

the elevator to the third floor where he was sure Angela would be waiting. He went straight to his office. She was looking through a patient file at his desk, but she jumped up when he walked in.

"You have to do something, Norman. You have to stop her."

"Stop who?"

"Susan."

"Is that what you called me about? You had me down-right panicky thinking something big was up, and it's another spat between you and Susan?"

"She's going to talk, Norman."

"She can't and you know it. She's in this as deep as we are."

"Then she plans to lie about her part in this."

He shook his head. His surgery staff used to be a team. Now it was opposing armies trapped in the same foxhole. He dropped to his chair. "What makes you think she's going to turn squealer?"

"I heard her talking on the phone when I passed her office. She was setting up an appointment to meet someone in New Orleans Saturday morning. It sounded suspicious so I checked the caller ID, then called the number back. It was the office of the *National Enquirer*."

BY WEDNESDAY afternoon, Cassie's primary fear had switched from worrying about being shot at to wondering what she'd do if her mother wasn't at the airport the next afternoon. There had been no more incidents in Beau Pierre. In fact, the town seemed the quiet, safe community tucked away in the Louisiana Bayou country that tour books touted it to be.

Well, except that the hand that had been found in the mud along the banks of Bayou Lafourche had yet to be identified and the rest of the body had not been located. And while the town seemed safer, John was still convinced that she needed his protection.

She didn't know how much longer she'd last taking moonlit rides in his pirogue, sharing morning coffee with him, watching him walk around the small house after a shower with his hair wet and him wearing only a pair of snug-fitting jeans. And sleeping in his bed.

The attraction she'd felt the day they'd met had grown steadily stronger until now it was as if the shock and awe of arousal started the second she walked in the door and didn't cool until she finally fell asleep. Then it started all over again when she opened her eyes in the morning.

All it would take to push them over the limit of control was for her to let him know she was ready. And she was so far past ready that she'd come close to having an orgasm last night just watching him fry fish.

There was no reason for them not to make love. They were consenting adults with no ties. But every time she came close to stepping inside his arms or initiating a kiss, she panicked and walked away. What was holding her back? Fear? Doubt? Or just the inability to move on?

She parked in front of the combined food market, service station and barber shop and went inside to pick up something for dinner. It was her turn to cook. No problem. She was a whiz at opening cans. The store was practically empty. It shouldn't take her but a minute to pick up what she needed and get out.

After that she had only to make a quick stop at Suzette's and her work day would be over. If Celeste wasn't working tonight, she wouldn't stay, but if Celeste was working, she had a few quick questions to ask of the waitress.

"What you got there, Angela?"

"It's a new kind of frozen peas, *Maman*."

Cassie looked up to see Angela Dubuisson and her mother, in a bright pink warmup suit, standing a few feet away. "Hello, Angela. It's nice to see you again."

"Hello, Cassie."

"How are things at Magnolia?"

"Busy."

"I'll bet, especially with the trial starting next week."

"Been long enough getting here," the older woman said. "Me, I don' want nuttin' ta do wit dem lawyers."

"This is my mother," Angela said. "*Maman*, this is Cassie Pierson."

The woman looked her over. "You dat reporter lady what causing all the trouble?"

"I'm a reporter," Cassie said. "I'm not causing any trouble that I know of."

"I heard about you. You went to everybody's house, you. You don' come see old Cotildo. You think I don' know. Me, I know."

"She's very busy, *Maman*. You can talk to Ms. Pierson some other time. I'm sure she needs to get started back to New Orleans. Why don't you go and choose a box of cereal?"

"Hmmpf! Cereal. Just say you don' want me around. That's fine." She walked off but stopped at a display of cake mixes, in listening range.

"I'm sorry," Angela said, keeping her voice low. "You see what I mean about my mother. She's a dear, but she gets more crotchety every day."

"I understand. I'm sorry we didn't get to know each other better, though. Why don't we have lunch one day?"

Angela hesitated. "I really don't think I can."

"Dr. Guilliot's orders?" Cassie asked.

"Attorney's orders. Will you be in Beau Pierre much longer?"

"This could be my last day, but I'd come back to meet you for lunch, or you could drive to New Orleans and we could do lunch up there."

"Maybe when this is all over, if you still want to have lunch then."

"Sure."

"I'm sorry about having to go back on my offer of a place to stay."

"Me, too. Your house looked much nicer than those cabins behind Suzette's."

Cassie had the feeling that talking to her was making Angela very nervous. She kept looking around as if someone was going to jump from behind a stack of cans and punish her for talking to Cassie. But if Angela had nothing to hide, why would any of that bother her?

"How's the new anesthetist working out?" Cassie asked, hoping somehow this would lead to a discussion of Dennis.

"We haven't found a permanent one yet. I have to go, Cassie. See you around."

"You take care, Angela."

Angela hurried away and Cassie saw her leading her protesting mother out of the store with no bags of groceries in hand. If Dennis knew something that had gotten him killed, then Angela must know it, too. Maybe that's why she was so nervous. She could be afraid of going against Guilliot in any way.

But Dennis hadn't gone against him, as far as Cassie could tell, and he was dead while Angela was still alive. That was what was wrong with John's theory that the good surgeon was behind all of it. The theory left too many variables unaccounted for, and it definitely didn't explain why Dennis had mentioned her name the last night of his life.

Like Cassie's mother's disappearance, the questions about the situation in Beau Pierre only produced more questions. And the answers, if they came at all, were always wrong.

"I HOPE YOU'RE CALLING with good news," Butch said, taking the call from his newly hired private detective. "Have you located my wife?"

"Not yet. New Orleans is a big city, especially when you add the Northshore to the area where she might be."

"Did you try all the hotels?"

"Every last one of them. She's not registered in a hotel and hasn't been at any time over the past six weeks. I've checked most of the apartment complexes, as well. Nothing. We're working on new wireless contracts for the area now, in case she got a new cell phone."

"What about the hospitals?"

"I checked those first, so I guess you can count that as your good news."

"I hope this is all a waste of time," Butch said. "I guess we'll know tomorrow."

"I'll be at the airport for her scheduled flight. If she's there, I'll call and give you a heads-up."

"My daughter Cassie will be at the airport, as well. She booked a flight on the same plane. If her mother's on the plane, she's flying over with her."

"And if not, I'll be out combing the streets again. In the meantime, I'm showing her picture around the Quarter."

"I doubt that will provide results. I've taken her to New Orleans with me a few times for conferences and she always insists we stay outside the French Quarter. She never feels safe there."

"But you just never know. A couple of other quick questions. Does you wife have a gambling problem?"

"No. We've been to Vegas a couple of times, but not in several years. When she was there, she fed a couple hundred bucks into the slots, but that's it."

"What about religion?"

"We're Methodist."

"Then she hasn't joined any of those weird cults that believe the world's going to end next week or gotten involved in some kind of voodoo."

"No. She shops. And reads. And goes to museums. That's pretty much it."

"I'm guessing she didn't run away for six weeks to go to a museum."

"I haven't a clue why she left home, but I'm counting on her being on that flight on Thursday. If she's not, I expect you to find her so I can get some answers."

"I understand, Mr. Havelin. Like I told you, nine times out of ten, there's a man involved, and if the picture you gave me is accurate, she's still a nice-looking woman."

They finished the call and Butch hung up his office phone. It was after six. Most of the staff had left for the night, including his secretary. He imagined that Babs had left, too.

In the past she wouldn't have gone home without telling him she was leaving and checking out his plans, but since their talk the other night, their encounters had been all business.

Breaking up with her was supposed to have been so easy. When the time came, he'd planned to say goodbye and walk away. Now the time had come and he'd walked away—at least for the time being—but it was about as easy as having open heart surgery without getting anything for pain.

Still, he was worried about Rhonda. It wasn't like her to lie. It wasn't like her to leave the country for six weeks. It wasn't like her to just disappear.

After thirty years you'd think a man would know his own wife.

THE HUMIDITY and temperature were still in the nineties when Cassie pulled into the parking lot at Suzette's. She dreaded killing the engine and stepping into the heat, but she wanted to talk to Celeste again before the dinner crowd claimed all her attention.

She hadn't mentioned to John or the sheriff the fact that Celeste had overheard Dennis use her name the night he was killed, yet it had been on her mind constantly. She'd been too aggravated with Babineaux after the way he'd handled the shooting at the cemetery and the break-in at the cabin to trust him with the disturbing information. He'd investigated the incidents, but suggested that she was blowing things out of proportion. He said it was likely some teenagers who'd been out to antagonize a reporter and that they'd never meant to hurt her.

She wasn't sure why she hadn't mentioned Celeste's comment to John. She trusted him, at least she thought she did. Her feelings about him were so confused at this point that it was difficult to know how she really felt. The sexual attraction was all but overwhelming, but how could she trust her feelings when her emotions were in such turmoil.

Her life had been solid and secure when she'd met Drake, and still she'd made a huge mistake. Looking back she didn't know why he'd married her when he had no intention of being faithful. She'd asked him that after the divorce was in process but had never gotten a straight answer.

A couple more cars pulled into the parking lot. She

killed the engine, climbed out of the car and headed toward the front door of Suzette's.

Cassie scanned the restaurant and quickly spotted Celeste waiting on a table of four men who looked and smelled as if they'd just stepped off a shrimp boat.

Cassie took the nearest empty table in spite of the smell, hoping that meant Celeste would be her waitress.

"I heard what happened the other night," Celeste said when she stopped at Cassie's table. "Messed your cabin up good, huh?"

"Real good, and the person who did it stole my laptop and notes."

"Had Suzette hopping mad. She screamed at the sheriff when he came in Saturday night. Said he better watch her cabins."

"Good for Suzette."

"Staying at the dead man's brother's house now, huh?"

News did get around in Beau Pierre, and Celeste didn't even live here.

"I'll be staying in my condo in New Orleans after tonight."

"So you came in for your last meal at Suzette's?"

"Actually, I came in to see you, but you can bring me a diet soda over ice."

Celeste nodded. "I'll get it and stop by your table in a few minutes."

"I'd appreciate that. I only have a couple of questions."

Celeste dropped the soda off on the run, but Cassie knew she'd stop and talk when she got a minute. She was in no rush. It was her last night at Suzette's, so she might as well soak up the atmosphere and the spicy odors coming from the kitchen.

Someone fed the jukebox and a Cajun ballad blared over the noise of friends laughing and chattering and sucking the juices from crawfish heads. A week and a half in Beau Pierre had been an experience she'd remember.

"I got only a minute. Suzette don't like me to keep the customers waiting."

"I understand. I know you hear a lot of stuff working in here."

"Everybody talks all the time. Lots of talk about you."

"What kind of talk?"

"Mostly stuff about how you look, you know how men talk. Women and fishing. That's all most men in here know about. And some of them, they think you're messin' with John Robicheaux's mind."

"They underestimate John Robicheaux if they think I can do a lot of messin' with that hard head of his."

Celeste laughed but glanced around the room. "I gotta get back to work."

"I know. Mainly I came in to see if you'd remembered anything else Dennis had said about me the night he was killed."

"No. I mean he could have said a lot more, but I didn't hear nothing else. I was working and it was real noisy in here that night."

"Okay. One more quick question. Does anyone have an idea who may have trashed my cabin? Not evidence, just talk, like they do in here."

"No one. Not even the sheriff. They say it's a mystery."

"I'll be here a few more minutes. If you think of anything else people have said about me, especially about my figuring out something or the break-in, let me know."

"Yes ma'am."

Celeste looked to the door as it opened again, then shot the newest arrival an overly friendly smile. Cassie's jaw dropped. Speak of the devil. Drake Pierson in the flesh.

She rummaged in her purse for change to pay for the

soda. If she hurried, she could scoot out the back door before he noticed her. It had been a tough week, and she wasn't sure she could handle dealing with Drake right now.

She wasn't fast enough. He spotted her and headed straight for her table.

"Hello, Cassie."

"Hello, Drake."

He pulled out a chair and joined her without waiting to be invited. "You're looking great."

So that's how it would be tonight. Last time it had been all accusations. This time, sweetness and light, which meant he wanted something.

"Thanks," she said. She sipped her soda, noticing how out of place his designer shirt and expensive trousers looked in Suzette's. "What are you doing in Beau Pierre, spying on your spy?"

Drake took a paper napkin from the dispenser and rubbed at a greasy spot that had been left on his side of the table. "I'd like to check the climate of my opponent's before a trial. How have you been?"

"I'm doing fine."

"And your parents?"

The question of the day. Leave it to Drake to ask it, though he couldn't possibly suspect the angst surrounding the correct answer—not that she'd dare go into her mother's disappearance with him.

"They're okay."

"Good. That's good."

"How's the Flanders trial going?" she asked

"Extremely well. I understand you've become close to the dead anesthetist's brother."

She grew uneasy, felt almost guilty, which was really absurd considering Drake had never stopped having intimate friends even when they were married. "John's a friend." She pulled some money out of her wallet to pay for her drink. "Nice running into you," she lied, "but I need to go."

"Sure. You've got plans. I understand." He reached across the table and put his hand on top of hers as she lay the money on the table. Odd how his touch meant nothing now.

"I need to ask a favor, Cassie. I wouldn't, but it's important, could even be a case breaker."

"What would this favor entail?"

"I need John Robicheaux's testimony. Or at least some kind of statement from him as to why he thinks his brother was murdered."

"I don't speak for John."

"But you can talk to him and persuade him to at least hear me out. Otherwise, I doubt he'll take my call."

"So, all you want me to do is impose on my friendship with John to help your case. That is what you asked, isn't it, because I want to be sure I have this straight."

"You're twisting things, Cassie."

"So like me to do that, isn't it? I just twist things all around and completely misjudge your unselfish requests. How did you know I'd be here, Drake?"

"Actually, I stopped in to talk to a friend, but I was going to give you a call later."

"Another friend you need a favor from?"

"You used to be a lot nicer, Cassie. Just talk to John for me. For old times."

"For old times," she repeated as he stood and walked away. He stopped when he passed Celeste, leaned over and said something that produced a satisfied smile on her face before going to the bar. The bartender greeted him like an old friend—or one of his paid spies.

Same old Drake. But not the same old Cassie. She wasn't tied to him in any way that mattered anymore, didn't respond to his touch and saw right through his flimsy manipulations. It was a very freeing discovery to make.

And all of a sudden she couldn't wait to get back to John's. She had a request to make of him, a very personal request, and it had nothing whatsoever to do with Drake Pierson.

And if he turned her down, she'd just have to take things into her own hands. She knew just where to start.

CHAPTER FIFTEEN

CASSIE WAS LEAVING Beau Pierre tomorrow. There would be no undies hanging over John's shower curtain to drip in his hair when he crawled in the shower. No toothpaste cap left askew on top of the tube. No sleeping on the sofa. And no chattering and asking questions when he was trying to watch the evening news.

God, he was going to miss her! The old home place had come alive with her in it. Now it would go back to being just the shack he crashed in at night.

The attraction between them was so real it sucked up the air and made it hard to breathe when they stepped too close to each other or let their arms or fingers brush in passing. But Cassie had been right in keeping her distance. If they kept it under wraps, the desire wouldn't consume them and there would be no aftermath to face.

And with women there was always an aftermath. They thought passion possessed magical powers that made everything right. Men were smarter than that. They saw passion as a consumable quality. You used it up, and then it was gone.

And in the end nothing ever changed. He'd still be a failure. Cassie would still live in her world. He'd still live in his. Just him and the swamp and his old buddy, Jack Daniel's.

And this was way too much thinking for one night. Besides, it was getting late. Cassie should be back by now.

He walked to the front porch, took a look around and breathed easier. She was tearing down the old dirt road, spitting gravel and spraying mud.

One more night. A long one he suspected, since he was already feeling the pangs of arousal. He watched her park and jump out of the car, her skirt dancing around her shapely legs as she ran up the walk, her perky breasts jiggling seductively.

She climbed the steps and threw her arms around him and pressed her lips into his. He stumbled backward, but held on, lifting her off the porch while his mind went reeling.

"Make love to me, John. Right here. Right now."

"Cassie, do you know…"

She covered his mouth with hers. "Don't talk about it, John. Just do it."

And all the bunk he'd preached to himself all day flew out of his mind so fast he didn't even feel it blow past his ears.

THEY NEVER MADE IT to the bedroom. Cassie couldn't have cared less. They were a whirl of arms and legs and kisses, tangling and clinging and exploring. She was so hungry for every part of John that she couldn't have slowed things down if there had been a reason to.

She ended up pushed against the living room wall, her shirt still on, its buttons scattered around the floor. John's hands were everywhere at once. On her breasts, her back, sliding between her thighs as he nudged her panties away so that he could slip inside her. She was crazy with wanting him and with the need to stop holding everything inside.

Once he was inside her, she pushed when he did, thrusting and moaning, the ache so sweet she could barely stand it. The orgasm started then, building like an explosion on a short, frayed fuse. She didn't know if they came together or if she started and it set him off, but she could feel his heart beating against her chest and hear his breath, as sharp and quick as if he'd been running.

"Wow!"

A one word response, but it was better than she could do right now. She put her head on his shoulders and kissed his neck just under his ear, while the heated wetness of him grew sticky between her legs.

To say she'd never made love this savagely would have been the understatement of the year. She hadn't really believed anyone did it like that except in X-rated movies.

"And here I thought reporters only did it in print," John said, pulling away and tugging his jeans and shorts back over his hips.

"That was just the teaser," she whispered, "the little statement in front of the article that gets you excited about what's yet to come."

"Yeah. Well guess what? It's working."

JOHN WOKE in the middle of the night stretched out in his own bed with Cassie cuddled next to him. She'd left off the T-shirt tonight. There was nothing between their bodies but some sweet smelling lotion she'd rubbed on her legs and then let him smooth on to her back—and her front.

He let his thumbs brush her nipples. He couldn't see them under the sheet but he knew exactly what they looked like, felt like and tasted like now. He didn't know what had changed things for Cassie, what had made her decide that tonight was the night, but he knew they'd been moving toward this moment ever since they'd met.

Cassie squirmed beside him. He kissed the back of her neck and cradled her breasts in his hands. She was still leaving in the morning. She hadn't mentioned not going and he hadn't expected her to.

Making love never stopped the world from turning, but when the time was right, it was only that way for brief moments of time. It had seemed that way for him tonight.

CASSIE SEARCHED for ten minutes and finally found a space near the back of the third level of the airport parking garage. Airlines were still recommending checking in two hours early for a flight, but she seldom did. However, today she was there two and a half hours before the scheduled departure time. She'd never known her mother not to be exceedingly early for a flight.

Cassie had reconfirmed last night. Her mother's name was still on the passenger list for flight 622, departing for Houston at 3:25 p.m. Her seat was assigned. Everything was in place except that there was no return flight booked from abroad and New Orleans would not have been a connecting airport for Houston even if Rhonda Havelin had been returning from Greece.

At this point, Cassie no longer cared where her mother had been or why. She just needed her to be at the airport today. If she wasn't… No. She was booked on the flight. She'd be here.

Cassie stopped at the gift shop and picked up copies of *Vogue* and *The New Yorker,* then stopped at the coffee stand for a large, iced caramel latte. She was eager to get to the gate, yet hesitant. Once she was there, the time would drag until she saw her mother walking down the corridor.

A brown-haired woman in a black, two-piece warmup who had the same build as Rhonda was standing by the door to the women's restroom. Cassie's heart jumped to her throat and she hurried toward the woman, only to have her spirits crash to her toes when the woman turned around. Two hours of this was going to be murder.

Any other day, Cassie would have had trouble thinking of anything but last night and making love with John. Today, the night of being deliciously aroused and totally fulfilled had to take a back seat to the building apprehension that her mother might not appear.

Once at the gate, Cassie found a seat where she could see all the approaching passengers. She took a sip of the coffee, then opened the *Vogue,* though she never moved past the first advertisement. She was far too intent on watching people show up at Gate 10.

The first hour dragged by with Cassie's anxiety intensifying with each click of the airport clock. Arriving a mere hour before flight time wasn't her mother's style, but then her mother was clearly changing her style, so maybe this was part of the new Rhonda Havelin.

Twenty minutes later, her anxiety had reached the panic stage. If her mother wasn't on this flight, then no one had any idea where she was or what she was doing—or who she was doing it with.

"In just a few minutes, we'll start boarding those people traveling with small children or needing extra assistance. Those holding first-class tickets or who have platinum memberships are also welcome to board then or at any time during the boarding process."

Cassie jumped up and went to stand near the crowds who were pushing toward the loading ramp. Her mother was here somewhere. She'd missed her somehow, but she was here. She had to be.

Cassie walked to the desk. "I'm traveling with my mother, but I haven't seen her yet. Can you tell me if Rhonda Havelin has checked in?"

"Spell that last name for me."

She spelled it, scanning the crowd as she waited.

"She hasn't checked in, but if she only has carry-on luggage, she could be here and waiting to board."

No way she was carrying six weeks of luggage. "Could you page her for me?"

"If you'll give me a minute. I need to give the next boarding call, but I'll page her right after that."

"Thank you."

Cassie walked away from the desk. She had her ticket, but she wasn't boarding unless she located her mother. She scanned the crowd again, making sure she missed no one.

The page was made requesting that Rhonda Havelin report to the check-in desk at Gate 10. Cassie watched the desk. Her mother did not respond to the call.

The first group of coach travelers were boarding now. Rhonda would never be this late unless... Maybe she was caught in traffic.

Cassie dropped into a chair by the boarding area and watched every person who walked by. Once the plane was loaded, the airline sent another page, this time for Rhonda Havelin and Cassie Pierson. Cassie went up and told them she wouldn't be flying since her mother had not shown up for her flight.

"Excuse me. Are you Rhonda Havelin's daughter?"

She turned and stared at the man who'd spoken. He was in his mid-forties, slim with sandy-colored hair and deep blue eyes. Nothing about him made him seem suspicious, but Cassie was rattled all the same. "I'm Rhonda's daughter. Who are you?"

"Brady Cates. I'm a detective. Your dad hired me to look for your mother."

Cassie exhaled slowly. "Then I guess you know she's a no-show for her flight back to Houston."

He nodded. "Mind if I sit down with you a minute?"

"Please do."

"I'm sure you're upset about this," he said.

"I'm a little more than upset. No one's heard from my mother in six weeks except for postcards that she probably didn't send. And pretty much everything she told us about the trip she's on was a lie."

"She may have had her reasons for leaving."

"Tell me, Mr. Cates. Do women her age do this often—just make up a bunch of lies and walk away without telling their own children where they're going?"

"Not often, but it happens."

"For what reasons?"

"All kinds of reasons, just like there are all kinds of reasons people stay. A bad marriage. Mental problems. Another man—or woman. She took fifty-thousand dollars with her so she must have planned to be gone awhile."

"I can understand her leaving. Well, actually I can't, but I could deal with that if she'd told us how to get in touch with her. But if something had happened to my dad or to me, we—"

The words stuck in Cassie's throat and echoed in her mind. She'd been shot at the other night and the bullet had barely missed her head. If she'd been killed or was lying in the hospital dying, her mother wouldn't be there. She wouldn't even know.

The dread came to life, something that had seeped into the lining of Cassie's chest and was twisting itself into painful knots, and for the first time she felt as if she might never see her mother again.

"Are you okay, Miss Pierson? You look pale."

"What do we do now?"

"I keep on trying to find Rhonda Havelin. If she's in the New Orleans area, I'll find a lead."

"What if she's been kidnapped or—I don't know.

Shouldn't we contact the police and fill out a missing person's report?''

"That's an option. You and Mr. Havelin have to decide that. I wouldn't expect much help from the cops with this, though, since your mother basically cleaned out her checking account and told you she was leaving the country. That doesn't add up to kidnapping.''

"The six weeks are up.''

"Not quite.''

"This was the day she said she was returning.''

"She still might. It's not that far from New Orleans to Houston. She may have decided to rent a car and drive home. She has money and credit, she may have bought a car.'' Brady lay a hand on her shoulder. "I know this is tough, but hang in there. Your mother left of her own accord and she'll likely come back the same way.''

"I'll keep that in mind.'' But the dread didn't evaporate. It held on and dug in.

Cassie called her father's office on the way to her car. This time Dottie put her straight through.

"Mom didn't show.''

"I know. I heard from the detective a few minutes before takeoff.''

"I met him.''

"What did you think of him?''

"He's nice enough. I don't know anything about his credentials.''

"He came highly recommended.''

"I want to file a missing person's report with the NOPD.''

"That's a little extreme.''

"I don't think so, Dad. We don't know where she is and we haven't heard from her except through fake postcards. She *is* missing.''

"The postcards aren't fake. They have Greek postmarks. For all we know your mother's in Greece and flying back today just like she said. The airlines get things screwed up all the time."

"If she's been in Greece, it wasn't with Patsy David."

"It could be Patsy someone else. Or some Greek guy she met and went traipsing halfway around the world with to look for excitement and fulfillment."

"Mother? C'mon, Dad. At least be realistic." And not so exasperating.

"Let's give it another day or two, Cassie. Then, if Brady Cates doesn't have any leads or she hasn't shown up, we'll talk about this again. Why don't you fly home for the weekend?"

"I am home, Dad, but you can fly here if you want."

"I'll think about it."

"Call me if you decide to."

"Will you be in New Orleans or in Beau Pierre this weekend?"

"I'm not sure, but if you fly to New Orleans, I'll make it a point to be here."

"Thanks, Cassie."

But right now, she'd give anything to be in John's arms. Not to make love or to thrill to his kisses. She just needed strong arms around her to help hold back the fear. Logical or not, she was certain now that her mother was in serious trouble. Or else...

She couldn't form the word, not even in her thoughts, but it loomed there all the same. By the time she reached her car, she was crying.

BUTCH WALKED INTO the house at 5:10 in the afternoon. He had a million things to take care of at the office, but he couldn't concentrate, so he had left about forty-five minutes after talking to Cassie. He vacillated between worry and downright anger that Rhonda could have pulled this kind of ridiculous stunt at this time in their lives.

If she'd wanted out, she could have just said so. If she'd found someone new, he could have lived with that, too. But if she'd found out about him and Babs and was doing this to punish him, she'd gone too far.

If she didn't care what this was doing to him and his ability to stay on task at work, she should at least think of their daughter. Cassie was sick with worry, wanting to call the police in on this.

The company would love having their CEO involved in a police investigation for a wife who'd disappeared and gone to all this trouble to hide her tracks.

He guessed Rhonda would be happy then. Instead of spending his evenings in the city, he'd spend them hanging around here being bored out of his skull.

He pulled his cell phone from his shirt pocket and held it for a couple of minutes, not dialing, just cradling it in his hand as if the vibrations of past conversations with Babs were still hanging around and could give him some kind of comfort.

He'd promised himself he wouldn't call her until this mess with Rhonda was settled. If they did have to go to the police and anything about his affair with Babs came out, there would really be hell to pay with Conner-Marsh.

But he didn't really see how one phone call would change any of that. He hit the fast-dial key for her cell phone. If nothing else he could hear her voice. She was always upbeat, always supportive. He could use that to-night.

"Hi, Butch," she answered, obviously having checked her caller ID before answering. "I didn't expect to hear from you tonight."

"I hadn't planned to call."

"You sound down. What happened?"

"Nothing. Rhonda wasn't on the flight."

"Oh, no. This isn't good, Butch."

"Tell me about it."

"Cassie must be frantic."

"She is. She wants to go to the police and report Rhonda as missing."

"You have to, Butch. The circumstances surrounding the trip are too bizarre. They're giving me cold chills and I barely know Rhonda."

He exhaled sharply. This was not what he needed from Babs. "Rhonda said she was going to Greece for six weeks. I have postcards that say she's been there all this time. Now I'm supposed to go to the police and tell them she's missing because she's a day late returning. And that's based on what Cassie remembers. We don't even have an itinerary."

"I still think you should talk to the police."

"I hired a detective. They're far more effective at finding people than the New Orleans Police Department."

"I guess."

She sounded as down as he felt and just as upset. He shouldn't have called her tonight. It wasn't fair to pull her into his problems. "I miss you," he said, not able to keep the words off his lips.

"Miss you, too, Butch, but you have to take care of this and it's probably not smart for us to be seen together now."

"Do you have plans tonight?"

"I'm going to dinner with friends. You?"

"I'll stick around here."

"Take care, Butch, and give some more thought to reporting this to the authorities."

"I will. Sweet dreams, but have them alone." He hated that he'd added that last. It sounded juvenile and possessive. He was neither, at least not under normal circumstances.

He broke the connection but took the phone with him and walked out to the backyard pool. The day was still warm and Butch shed his clothes and tossed them onto a lounge chair. He'd put up a privacy fence when Cassie had left for college, just so he and Rhonda could swim their evening laps in the nude.

Rhonda never had. She'd said that someone might still shinny up a tree and see over the fence. As if anyone young and agile enough to shinny up a tree was interested in seeing people their age in their wrinkled altogether.

He dived in and swam laps until his body was as weary as his mind, then climbed from the pool and grabbed a beach towel from the basket by the door. He felt a little more like tackling the Rhonda issue now.

Rhonda never did anything spontaneous. If she'd gone to Greece, she'd made plans. If she'd done something else, she'd still have made plans, and there had to be some sign of them somewhere in the house.

It might take him a while, but he'd have to locate those plans. He tied the towel around his waist and went to the bedroom to begin the search, one drawer at a time.

Two hours later, he struck gold in the bottom drawer of a cabinet in her sewing room. The treasure was in the form of a blue journal that had been meticulously kept since January 12, two years ago.

He carried the journal to the family room and tossed it on the sofa. He'd make a ham-and-egg sandwich and a drink—a double—and then he'd find out what had been going on in his wife's head.

CASSIE TOOK the elevator to her condo. She'd driven by the lakefront before she'd come home. She'd walked the jogging path and shed a few tears, but mostly she'd searched her brain for some logical explanation for her mother's lies and disappearance.

She was as clueless now as she'd been when she first realized that Patsy David did not exist. She felt exhausted, like she'd run a marathon instead of sitting in the airport for hours and taking a slow walk, and still she dreaded going into the empty condo and spending the rest of the night alone.

She'd hoped John would volunteer to come into town and spend the night with her tonight, but he hadn't, and she hadn't asked.

The elevator door opened and she stepped off, then stopped. There was someone sitting on the floor slumped against her door.

John. He was sound asleep, even snoring a little.

It was an omen. There could be no more bad news tonight. She didn't really believe that, but it was a nice thought, she decided as she collapsed beside John right there in the hall floor.

"Am I dreaming or did some gorgeous sex goddess just kiss me?" he asked, opening his eyes and slipping his arm around her shoulder.

"It was a gorgeous sex goddess."

"I see that now." He cradled her in his arms. "How did it go?"

"Mom was a no-show."

"I'm sorry. Anything I can do to help?"

"Hold me. Hold me tight and for a long time."

"Will all night do?"

"For a start."

It felt terrific to just sit there in his arms, but still the dread returned, crept right back in and clutched at her stomach like a buzzard's claws.

She'd run out of optimism and halfway logical explanations. Her mother had disappeared, and whether she'd done it by choice or through no control of her own, neither Cassie or her father had any idea how to find her.

She'd simply vanished without a trace.

CHAPTER SIXTEEN

BUTCH SKIMMED the first few pages of Rhonda's journal. Entries were sporadic. At times she wrote almost daily. At other times, she went weeks without penning a word. The topics ranged from an outline of her day to details surrounding a specific event, but for the most part, they dealt with how things affected her emotionally.

Butch didn't give much time to thinking about feelings. He liked things he could tackle, needed tangible results for his efforts. But apparently Rhonda spent an excessive amount of time examining her emotional state.

He was mentioned a few times in the journal, though not so often as he'd expected. She'd been irritated when he'd missed a church picnic, liked the way he looked in blue, and thought he should involve himself more in charitable projects. The jewelry he'd splurged on her last birthday had been a big hit—a necklace that Babs had helped him pick out in the Atlanta airport during a long layover.

Her forty-fifth high school reunion had earned several journal pages. The late Patsy David got a half page. Apparently the reunion committee had put together a special memorial for the homecoming queen who'd never lived to collect her diploma. Butch guessed that's where Rhonda had come up with the idea to reincarnate Patsy as part of her fabricated trip to Greece.

The rest of the reunion entries concerned women who'd married real jerks, or those who'd married well. Someone named Betty who'd been mousy in high school had married a Georgia senator. Mary Louise had had a face-lift and looked fab and Evelyn had gotten smashed and told somebody off. Good old Evelyn. Butch liked her without even meeting her.

He searched for men's names, a hint that Rhonda might have reconnected with someone at the reunion, but he didn't see anything that vaguely resembled a romantic tryst. Truth was there was little mention of any men except him and the gardener who didn't weed to suit her and a couple of male movie stars. She still had the hots for Robert Redford and Sean Connery.

After a half hour of reading running commentary that had no plot and little action, Butch skipped to the back of the journal. The last entry was dated April 20, approximately three weeks before Rhonda had left on her so-called vacation and about the time she'd started talking about the trip.

A name jumped out at him as if it had been written in bold caps. Babs Michaels.

Bingo. This is where he should have started reading. He stopped skimming and read every word.

Yesterday started out like any other, but before it was over it ranked as the worst day of my life. Butch called just after lunch and said he'd have to work late and would be staying in his apartment in town— *again.* I actually felt sorry for him—gullible me—and decided to surprise him with my company.

I took advantage of being in the city to do some shopping at the Galleria before driving to the apartment about eight. I didn't realize until I took the keys from the ignition that the apartment key I usually kept on my key ring was missing.

I waited in the car, trying to call Butch approximately every fifteen minutes. There was no answer at the office or on his cell phone. After an hour of waiting, I decided the surprise was a bad idea and was ready to drive home. Butch picked that precise moment to make his appearance—with Babs Michaels.

They were in her car, and she parked beneath the security light, making it easy for me to catch the full show. They were laughing and she was hanging all over him, both of them slightly tipsy. Butch kissed Babs on the mouth before they reached the door. I expected her to get back in her car and drive away, but she went inside with him.

I became physically ill and threw up at the edge of the parking lot. I spent the rest of the night driving aimlessly around Houston. I kept seeing Butch and Babs, as they looked walking into the apartment building, laughing and enjoying each other. I tried to remember how long it had been since Butch and I had been that loving and happy together.

The truth was undeniable though I tried at first. Butch and I had never been like that, not even in the very beginning. He had never had that much fun or been that happy with me. And I had never been that happy with him.

But I want to be. One time before I die, I want to feel that way about a man who feels that way about me. I plan to do what I can to make that happen. I only hope it doesn't hurt Cassie too much.

Butch read that last line, then went to the bar and fixed himself a very dry martini. Rhonda had known about him and Babs for three weeks before she left, but she hadn't said a word about it to him. She'd just made her plans down to the most minute detail, packed her bags and left.

He thumbed through the stack of mail that had accumulated while he was in London. When he came to that last postcard, he pulled it from the stack and studied the handwriting. It was the same as the writing in the journal.

He didn't understand why Rhonda had lied about her traveling companion or why Cassie had gotten the phone call requesting her to meet someone in Cocodrie, but if Rhonda had sent these postcards from Greece written in her own hand, she had to have been there. No matter what flight the airlines showed Rhonda booked on, she had to be in Greece unless…

Unless she'd written the cards here, mailed them to Greece in bulk and had someone there mail them back at various intervals and from different locations.

Damn.

That was it. That's why he'd found the Greek postcard in the brown envelope. She had someone mailing her postcards so that she could write her lying messages.

Having them mailed from Greece would be no big deal. For a fee, a Greek tourist agency would have taken care of that for her. For the right fee, you can get anything done.

And now that he'd read the journal, he knew exactly what was going on. Rhonda was going to divorce him, and she'd have all the details meticulously worked out before she told him and Cassie of her plans. This way there would be no complications and everything would go her way.

This was so like her, so absolutely like her. She'd give them a lot of hogwash about how she'd come to this decision after much soul searching—Rhonda was big on soul searching. No one would ever know she'd been hurt and humiliated by his affair with a co-worker. Of course, she hadn't expected him to go rummaging through the cabinets in her sewing room. Before this, he probably hadn't even stepped into the room in years.

Butch tossed the postcard back to the desk, then walked outside. He was upset, sure, but not as much as he'd have expected to be. He'd never meant to hurt Rhonda, and was really sorry about that. He'd never planned to divorce her, but he was pretty damn sure that's what she was planning now.

All's out come in free.

Funny that should pop in his mind now. They'd yelled that when he was a kid playing hide-and-seek. It meant you were ready to give up the hunt. He was ready to do just that.

So come in free, Rhonda, and we'll work this out together—one way or another.

CASSIE WOKE with her legs tangled in the sheets. She stretched and tried to get out of bed quietly so as not to wake John, but he opened his eyes before her feet hit the floor.

"Stay in bed," he said. "I'll make the coffee."

"You're spoiling me."

"No, just afraid of what you might do to the kitchen after the way you kicked me around all night."

"Was I that restless?"

"About like sleeping with a puppy on speed."

He gave her a kiss, then pulled the jeans he'd worn last night over his terrific, bare butt.

"Where do I find the coffee and filters?"

"The coffee's in the short canister next to the coffee-maker and the filters are on the bottom shelf of the cabinet just above it."

"Sounds simple enough."

Cassie fluffed her pillow and checked the clock. It was

already after eight. She hadn't slept this late in a long time, but then, she'd lain awake until after three, unable to get her mother off her mind.

She snuggled under the wrinkled sheet that held John's scent. They hadn't talked all that much last night, other than her filling him in on the details of her conversations with Brady Cates and with her father, but just having him there had made things easier.

John Robicheaux of the dark, piercing eyes and sexy Cajun accent. Somehow she'd imagined he'd be out of his element here in her apartment, but he fit in her world far better than she fit in Beau Pierre.

He'd had his own place in the city once, worn suits and ties, argued in courts of law and worked in an office instead of on a fishing boat. He'd had the notoriety and success lots of struggling attorneys would give an arm for, but John had given it all up and walked away. If he missed it at all, he showed no signs.

John returned a few minutes later with the coffee. He handed her a cup then climbed back in bed with his, propping his pillows against the headboard and sitting upright with his legs stretched over the sheets.

"Do you feel any better about the situation with your mother this morning?" he asked. John did have a way of cutting to the chase.

"I'm calmer. I know she left of her own free will and that there's no real reason to think she's in danger, but it would sure help if any of this made sense."

"It must have made sense to your mother, unless she was mentally unstable when she made those decisions."

"She always sounded fine when I talked to her on the phone, and Dad's never indicated she was having any emotional, health or mental problems. Actually, I can understand her need to do her own thing better than I can accept that she lied to Dad and me.''

"So what's your next move?"

"Going to the police and filing a missing person's report would be my first choice, but I'll hold off awhile longer on that since Dad is so insistent that we not involve them yet. I know I overreact sometimes, but he swings too far toward the conservative stance. I think he's in denial.''

"And maybe a little worried about the publicity this will garner if you bring the police in,'' John said.

"Publicity would be good. That would get Mom's name and picture out there and have people looking for her. But I doubt we'd get much media coverage. Flanders and Guilliot have the stranglehold on that.''

"If the wife of a CEO of a Fortune 500 company is listed as missing, you'll get publicity.''

"I hadn't thought of that angle. I guess it could cause some problems for Dad, but it's not as if he's responsible for her disappearance.''

"People will still talk.''

"And he won't like that. Don't get the wrong idea about him. He was a terrific father and a good provider, but he's a workaholic and his career is pretty much his life. Today's his sixty-second birthday. He probably doesn't even know it. He never does until either Mom or I wish him happy birthday.''

"You should call him.''

"I will later.'' She drank her coffee, but the issues of the birthday and phone calls stayed on her mind. "I guess that's the thing that really makes this so strange. Mom normally calls two or three times a week, and always has, even when she's been out of the country with Dad.''

John linked his right arm with hers. "I predict she will

make a birthday call to your father, maybe even show up with cake and ice cream.''

"I hope you're right.''

They had their second cup of coffee on the balcony. "You have a nice view,'' John said, "for a city dwelling.''

"It was the main reason I chose this condo, but it's also convenient to my office—not that I'm in the office all that much. I need to go in for a while today, though.''

"The work must go on.''

"What about your work, John? I'd think this would be your busiest time of the year.''

"It is. I canceled this week, but I'll have to be back at it starting Monday. I have a group of six guys coming in from Dallas for a week of deep-sea fishing in the Gulf.''

"Not in your pirogue, I hope.''

"Not a chance. My fishing rig is docked at Grand Isle. It's not a huge boat, but I can take twelve fishermen at a time along with my two-man crew. We provide the bait, equipment and food for the charters. All the fishermen have to do is show up with money.''

His fishing guide business was more ambitious than she'd realized. That surprised her. Lots of things about John Robicheaux had surprised her over the last few days.

"Let's take a walk,'' she said, suddenly restless. "We can cut through the French Quarter and have beignets at Café du Monde.''

"Sounds good.''

As good as anything would until she located her mother and knew she was safe. Cassie started to get up and go inside, then lingered. "I'm not sure I said this last night, but I really appreciate your being here.''

He put his elbows on his knees and leaned closer to her deck chair. "I'm here because I knew you'd need someone if your mother wasn't on that flight, but don't read anything more into this, Cassie.''

''I'm not reading anything into it. All I said was I appreciate your being here.''

He nodded, but didn't comment.

''Will you stay the weekend?'' she asked, not wanting to push, but not wanting him to go, either.

''I'm not sure I can.''

''Do you miss Beau Pierre that much?''

He stood and tugged her to her feet, holding her hands and staring at her with that smoky gaze that she could never read. ''It's not missing Beau Pierre that's the problem, Cassie. It's…this. All of this. Going to bed with you. Waking up with you. Making love with you.''

''Are those things so terrible?''

''You know the answer to that. I wouldn't be here if they were terrible. But you'll start thinking I could do those things forever. I might even start thinking it. And then when we realize I can't, we'll both be hurt. Neither of us needs that right now.''

''Are you so sure we couldn't make it work?''

''Would you be happy living in a trapper's shack in Beau Pierre.''

''Are you?''

''Happy enough.''

''And you don't miss the life you had as an attorney at all?''

''I never said that.''

''If you miss it, come back. Give it another try.''

''I can't.''

''Because you made one mistake? Because you defended a man you thought was innocent and found out later was a fiendish child molester?''

"Let it go, Cassie." The words had a finality to them, and he stood and walked to the edge of the balcony.

He was withdrawing again, climbing back into his shell and if she pushed, she was almost certain he'd drive right back to Beau Pierre, and she wasn't ready to risk that right now.

The phone rang and she went inside to answer it. It was likely her father making sure she was all right, or Olson wanting her to cover some event this weekend.

She was wrong on both counts. The caller was Brady Cates, already on the job.

"I tried your father's office, but they said he's speaking at some kind of business breakfast and won't be in until after ten. He doesn't answer his cell phone."

"Is there something I can help you with?"

"I had some news for him, but I guess I can give it to you."

"Good news, I hope."

"Looks like it. In fact, could be real good. I think I may have located your mother."

CHAPTER SEVENTEEN

JOHN WAITED on the balcony while Cassie took the phone call. For her sake, he hoped it was good news. For his sake, too. If things were okay with her mother, she wouldn't need him around and he could leave before he let things go too far between them—not that he hadn't already.

"That was Brady Cates," she said rejoining him on the deck.

"Good news?"

"News, anyway. He's located a transportation service that sent a car and driver to pick up a woman named Rhonda Havelin at the New Orleans airport at 3:45 p.m. on May ninth."

"The date and time fit. Is there a record of where they took her?"

"Yes. Are you ready for this?"

He nodded.

"The driver took her to the Magnolia Plantation Restorative and Therapeutic Center in Beau Pierre, Louisiana."

"Sonofabitch!"

"That pretty much sums it up."

"Did they ever go back and pick her up?"

"No. It's conceivable that my mother's been there the whole time. No one at Magnolia told me, but then there's no reason to suspect they'd know that a patient named Rhonda Havelin was my mother.''

"Is Cates certain this was actually your mother?"

"He hasn't talked to the driver yet. He's trying to find him now. When he connects, he'll show him Mom's picture and see if he recognizes her.''

"You don't seem overjoyed with the news."

"Going to Dr. Guilliot's surgery-slash-indulgent spa in the bayou is a far cry from vacationing with a friend in Greece.''

"Maybe she wanted the surgery to be a surprise."

"I hope that's all there is to this, but I have this scary feeling that I'm going to get to Beau Pierre and be sucked into some new complication.''

"I'm not surprised after all you've been dealing with this week.''

"I guess that's it. Dennis's murder. The cemetery sniping incident. My cabin vandalized and my laptop and notes stolen. And now I find out my mother may have been in the midst of all that, and no one even knew, except…''

"Except what?''

"Dennis mentioned my name in a phone call the night he died.''

John's muscles tensed, but he didn't interrupt as she told him what Celeste had said. This was way too bizarre to be believable. "Why didn't you tell me this before?"

"I'm not sure. Do you have any idea what it means?"

"No." Hell, no, but he didn't see a way in the world it could be good. "Is there anything else you haven't bothered to tell me, Cassie?''

"I did get this one strange phone call that ended up in a wasted trip to Cocodrie. I'll tell you about it on our walk. We'll take the cell phone with us, just in case Brady tries to call, though he said he may not be able to get in touch

with the driver until he shows up for his shift this afternoon.''

"Can't he go to the driver's house?''

"He would, but the guy drove up to Baton Rouge this
morning to visit his mother who's in the hospital, so we
have no choice but to wait it out.''

"Then let's take that walk.''

By THE TIME Brady Cates called back at 2:45 p.m., Cassie
was a total mass of frayed nerves.

"I showed the driver the picture,'' Brady said.

"And?''

"He says it's definitely the woman he drove to Beau
Pierre that day.''

"Did he say anything else?''

"Said she was a nice lady, but that she seemed nervous.''

"Did you give the news to Dad?''

"I did. I actually got through to him this time. I told
him the reason his wife hadn't called might be that he's
too hard to reach.''

"I'd love for that to be the only reason.''

"I asked your dad if he wanted me to go to Beau Pierre
and see if Rhonda's still at Magnolia Plantation. He said
to check with you first, that you might want to do it yourself.''

"He's absolutely right. I'll take care of it from here.''

"Good luck, and let me know how it comes out. If she's
not still there, I'll keep looking until I find her.''

Cassie went to find John after the call. He was on the
balcony thumbing through old copies of the *Crescent Connection.*

"That was Brady. The driver positively identified Mom

as the woman he took to the plastic surgery center. Are you up for a trip to Beau Pierre?''

"Sure. Home sweet home."

"I have serious doubts about the *sweet* part, John. Very serious doubts, but I'm going to Magnolia R and T and demand to see my mother. And if she's not there, I expect to find out when she left the premises and how long she's been gone."

"Then we'd better hurry. The business office probably closes by five, and I doubt you'll find out anything from the night crew."

"That's okay. I know where Dr. Guilliot lives and I'll camp on his doorstep if it takes that."

John had a strong suspicion that it might.

CASSIE OPTED to ride back with John in his truck rather than take her own car and fight the Friday afternoon traffic herself. She'd taken just long enough to pack a few essentials, but it was already five-thirty, and they were still about five miles north of Magnolia Plantation.

"Mom withdrew fifty thousand from her bank account when she left Houston," Cassie said, still racking her brain to make sense of the newest information. "Do you think that's Dr. Guilliot's fee for a face-lift and six weeks of recuperating in his *Gone With The Wind* setup?"

John gave a low whistle. "Rhett Butler could have done a lot with that kind of dough. Might not cover the sticker price on the Porsche Guilliot drives or pay Annabeth's charge accounts for a month, though."

Annabeth. With all that was going on, Cassie had forgotten abut her and the fact that she was carrying Dennis's baby. Cassie was certain John hadn't forgotten, no more than he'd gotten over Dennis's death or lost his zeal to find the person responsible.

And still he'd been there for her these past two days in a way she'd never expected of him. Not as a brooding loser who'd given up on life, and not solely as a lover. He'd been there as a friend. She'd have made it without him, but not nearly as well.

They drove past the road that led to the cemetery and an involuntary shudder slithered up her spine. The night of the sniper and the snake would live in infamy in her mind and no doubt lead to an article somewhere down the line. Right now it was just freaky.

"Do you think Annabeth left the white roses for Dennis?" she asked.

"No."

"You sound sure about that."

"Annabeth's too extravagant to be sentimental. If she'd left roses, she'd have made it at least two dozen and a card so she'd get credit for them."

"You took her into your house, but you don't seem to like her very much."

"It's the Cajun way. We never turn out a friend, especially one who claims to be pregnant with our dead brother's child."

"But if it isn't Annabeth who leaves the roses, then who?"

"Could be half the single women in the parish and a good number of the married ones. All Dennis had to do was smile and they were fighting to get in his pants. He didn't turn too many of them down."

"My boss suggested it might have been the killer who left the roses, that the death could have been the result of a lover's quarrel."

John grimaced. "I thought about that. Or a woman scorned. I tried to catch the person in the act. That's how

I ended up at the cemetery the night you were so intimately engaged with the snake.''

''Hooray for the white roses. They probably saved my life.''

''The white roses and *me*. The gate to Magnolia Plantation is just ahead,'' John said. ''Are you ready?''

''I'm ready to find out Mom's there. I'm not ready to deal with anything else.'' But ready or not, the newest moment of truth was upon them.

John stopped the truck, lowered his window and pushed the call button. A few seconds later, a woman with only a trace of Cajun accent responded.

''May I help you?''

''Yes,'' Cassie said, leaning over John to be closer to the speaker. ''I'm here to see my mother, Rhonda Havelin. She's a post-surgery guest.''

''Could you give me the name again?''

''Rhonda Havelin.'' Cassie spelled out the last name so there would be no confusion.

''I don't find that name on the list. What was the date of her surgery?''

''Approximately six weeks ago.''

''No. I'm quite sure we haven't had anyone by that name registered as an extended-stay guest.''

''I know she was here on the ninth of May.''

''If she was in for a simple procedure, Dr. Guilliot may have seen her as an outpatient. I don't have a record of those names.''

''Who does?''

''The business office, but they've already left and won't be back until Monday.''

''Please, just check your records again? Rhonda Havelin or possibly Mrs. Butch Havelin.''

''Could she have used her maiden name?'' John asked.

"Try Rhonda Clarkson," Cassie said, reminding herself that her mother could have used any friggin' name she wanted since she'd obviously paid cash for this.

"I'm sorry. We don't have a guest by any of those names. Perhaps if you call back Monday between nine and five someone in the business office can give you more information."

"What about the surgery staff?" Cassie asked. "Are any of them still available? Dr. Guilliot? Angela Dubuisson? Fred Powell? Susan Dalton?"

"No. They're all gone for the day."

"Let it go," John whispered. "Let's get out of here."

Cassie scooted back to her side of the seat while John thanked the woman for her trouble and gunned the engine.

"Do you think she was lying?" Cassie asked as John threw the car in reverse, then turned around in the driveway.

"I doubt it."

"But Mom *was* here. This is where the driver dropped her off."

"I don't know what the hell is going on, but you're not going to get any answers from that woman. So, buckle your seat belt, *chère*. It's time to pay a visit to the surgeon."

CASSIE JUMPED OUT of the black pickup truck the second John stopped in front of the Guilliot home. She could deal with problems, but not situations that were so bizarre as to defy reason. She'd finally obtained what she thought was an answer to her mother's whereabouts only to be given the runaround by the keeper of the gate.

She was really starting to hate this town.

"Stay calm," John said, reaching around her to push

the doorbell. "Give Guilliot a chance to talk. I'd like to hear his side of this."

"I am calm."

"About as calm as a trout caught on a fishhook."

Norman answered the door. He stared at both of them, clearly not pleased to see them. "Can I help you?"

"I'm looking for my mother," Cassie said, unable to stop herself from blurting out everything. "Her name is Rhonda Havelin and she came to you for an operation on May ninth."

"Excuse me?"

"I'm looking for my mother, Rhonda Havelin. And don't start with the confidentiality policy. It's urgent that I speak with her at once."

"I've got to hand it you, Cassie. You do try some unusual angles to get a story. Unfortunately, you're wasting my time."

"This has nothing to do with my being a reporter. I know that my mother is either at Magnolia Plantation now or was there recently, so just level with me."

"You're talking nonsense, and I don't appreciate your attitude."

"My mother, Rhonda Havelin."

Guilliot shook his head. "Never heard of her, and I think you both know that. So what is the real reason you're here? Never mind. I don't even want to know. I'd just like for you to leave."

He started to close the door.

"No, please," Cassie pleaded, desperation stealing the accusatory edge from her tone. "Just look at this." Cassie's hands shook as she took the photo of her mother from her handbag and stuck it in front of Dr. Guilliot's face. "She may have used another name, but this is her picture."

He stared at the photo for a minute, then shrugged his shoulders. "I've never seen that woman before."

"I have proof she was dropped off at Magnolia Plantation on May ninth."

"She may have come to pick up a friend or to visit a friend who was recovering, but she wasn't my patient."

Annabeth appeared at the door behind Guilliot. Her eyes were red and swollen as if she'd been crying. Guilliot turned and put his arm around his wife's shoulders.

"Please go now and leave us alone. As you can see, my wife isn't feeling well."

He closed the door in their faces.

John took Cassie's arm as they left.

"There's something evil in this town," she said when they reached the car. "It may look like a peaceful bayou setting, but it's inherently evil."

"It's not the town, Cassie."

"Then why do I feel as if I'm being dragged into the depths of something debased and perverse?"

He didn't answer. There was no answer. This time when Cassie collapsed into the passenger seat of the truck, she didn't try to stop the tears.

NORMAN GUILLIOT was lying. The signs were all there; body language that John had learned to read as a defense attorney. The shifty eyes, the flexed muscles, the rattling keys, the way he'd tried to turn everything back to Cassie's being a reporter.

The guy was definitely hiding something. That was no surprise, but John couldn't comprehend how Cassie's mother fit into this. Surely her being in Beau Pierre and her disappearance weren't related to Ginny Flanders's death.

John drove toward his house, thinking of the strange

turn of events and how complicated his own life had become. Two weeks ago he'd been a simple fishing guide, taking tourists into the choppy waters of the Gulf to fish for tuna, amberjack, wahoo and whatever else they might sink a hook into. Now his boat lay idle and he was caught in a mystery that had more twists and turns than the Mississippi.

Worse, he was being dragged back into a situation that was far too similar to the ones he'd dealt with as a defense attorney. Deception. Lies. Murder. The images crept into his mind the way they always did when something lured his thoughts into the past. He saw Toni Crenshaw's tortured body. The tiny arms and legs twisted and broken. The smashed-in skull.

He took a deep breath and willed the images to recede to the dark corners of his mind where they hid but never vanished. When this was over, he could go back into the miserable existence he'd lived before and try to convince himself it was a life, but first he had to make sure his brother could rest in peace. The killer was going to pay. One way or another he was going to pay.

And as for Cassie... As for Cassie, she'd see him for what he was soon enough. But she couldn't see it now, and there was no way he could walk away from her as long as she needed him. He'd already let her crawl under his skin, stir him back to life, make him remember what it was like to experience emotions that didn't begin and end with regret.

She sniffed into a tissue and turned to face him. "What now, John? What do I do now?"

"I think it's time you pay a visit to the cops. File a missing person's report and see what comes from it, but don't file it in Beau Pierre."

"Why not? This is where Mom was last seen."

"I don't trust Babineaux any more than I trust Guilliot, which is about as far as I can spit."

"I guess even Dad will be ready to take the next step now."

"You have to call him."

"I know. I dread it. I just gave him the good news. Now I have to hit him with this."

"He's her husband. He has a right to know."

"To know that his wife has disappeared without a trace from the sleepy bayou town of Beau Pierre. A town where... Oh, God!"

He knew what was coming because the same terrifying possibility had already crossed his mind. "Don't jump to conclusions, Cassie."

But she'd already jumped.

"That could have been part of Mom's body that was found along the bayou." Her voice trembled and she turned deathly pale.

John reached across the seat and took her hand in his. "Don't start thinking like that."

"How can I help it? Mom was here. Now she's no-where. I can't go on like this, John. I have to know where she is. I have to know the truth."

The truth. Whatever that might be. The truth about Dennis. The truth about Cassie's mother. The truth about Dr. Norman Guilliot.

He only hoped the truth was not as bad as he feared. But then he always expected the worst. That way life seldom surprised him.

"I'M OUT OF HERE," Norman said.

"Where are you going?"

"To find someone I can be with who hasn't betrayed me."

Annabeth stared at him with that pouting, pleading look that used to get her anything she wanted. ''I wish you'd stay in tonight.''

He turned away and yanked his keys from the hook by the back door.

''What do you want from me, Norman? I've told you I'm sorry. Dennis meant nothing to me.''

Cheating on him meant nothing to her. Maybe it had meant nothing to Dennis, either, but it was killing Norman. He'd trusted both Dennis and Annabeth completely, and both had betrayed him. They'd cheated on him with each other. Above all, he hated them for that. And now there was Cassie Pierson to deal with, the jagged blade in the two-edged sword that was slicing his life apart.

He couldn't go on this way much longer.

Once he'd cleared the driveway, he dialed Susan's number. They hadn't scheduled surgery today and both Susan and Angela had taken the day off, which had been great. Norman couldn't take much more of the constant bickering between them. Angela didn't trust Susan. Susan didn't trust Angela. A ridiculous situation, considering that they were both in this too deep to walk away.

Susan's answering machine clicked on and Norman broke the connection without leaving a message. He turned at the next corner and headed toward Angela's house. She wasn't sexy like Annabeth or fun like Susan, but she worshiped the ground Norman walked on and had for twenty years.

Sometimes a man needed that.

WHERE IN THE HELL ARE YOU, Rhonda?

The question echoed in Butch Havelin's mind as he turned the steak he'd started grilling before the call from Cassie had burst his mood and spoiled his celebration dinner. He was supposed to be meeting with and entertaining Cabot Drilling's executive officers this weekend. Now he'd be flying to New Orleans to go with Cassie to talk to the cops.

As for the mixup with the records at that bayou clinic, what more could you expect if you went to some quack who was accused of letting another patient die on the operating table? Rhonda had probably gotten there and backed out.

He took the steak off the grill and plopped it onto a plate. It was rare, barely hot through and through, the way he liked it. Carrying the plate in one hand and a drink in the other, he settled at the outdoor table next to the pool. He took a few bites, then tossed his fork to the table. The damn steak tasted like glue, or else he'd lost his appetite.

He was basically a nice guy but this had gone on long enough. He wanted his life back. He wanted his damn life back the way it was.

Was that too much to ask?

CHAPTER EIGHTEEN

SERGEANT BOSCO RYAN walked into his supervisor's office at the NOPD and dropped the latest missing person's file on his desk. "You gotta take a look at this. It's the weirdest damn case I've ever seen."

"Weirder than that transvestite with the three breasts?"

"Different kind of weird. The husband of the missing woman is Butch Havelin, the CEO of Conner-Marsh. The man's got to be pulling down some major money, but he's got a doozy of a wife—that is if he can find her."

"A certified nut?"

"I don't know yet. Rhonda Havelin is either a few raisins short of a fruitcake or one really smart cookie. She concocted some bizarre tale about a trip to Greece with a dead friend, even had postcards sent from there in her own handwriting, but according to airline records, she never left the country."

"The plot thickens."

"Gets thick as cold grits. The guy who was along with them for moral support and who I'd guess is banging the daughter, is the brother of Dennis Robicheaux."

"Guilliot's anesthetist, the guy who killed himself?"

"You got it. John Robicheaux, the illustrious *ex*-defense attorney."

"The media is going to have a field day when this leaks out. So what's the deal on the missing woman? Do they suspect foul play?"

"The daughter's worried that it could be. The husband's harder to figure. He didn't say much for one of those corporate honcho types, but he seemed a little nervous."

"Do you think he's behind the disappearance?"

"That would have been my guess if the woman hadn't told them all she was leaving, then withdrew fifty-thousand dollars from her personal bank account when she left town."

"And they have no idea where she went?"

"That's the real kicker in this. Butch Havelin hired a detective who located a driver who claims he picked Mrs. Havelin up at the New Orleans airport on May 9 and drove her and her luggage to the Magnolia Plantation Restorative and Therapeutic Center in Beau Pierre. The company he works for has records that verify that."

"It should be simple enough to find out if she had plastic surgery in Beau Pierre."

"Dr. Guilliot claims he's never laid eyes on the woman and that she's never had an appointment with him."

"So she went to Beau Pierre and that's the last anyone's seen or heard of her?"

"Except for the postcards that she may or may not have mailed herself."

"What about that body part they found along the bayou the other day? Have they matched that with anyone?"

"No, and this is where this case gets really interesting. The missing woman's daughter, Cassie Pierson, works for *Crescent Connection* and was down south researching a story on Dennis Robicheaux's death the day that partial hand was discovered. Get this. She happened to be driving by at the very time the troopers were there investigating."

"And, of course, she stopped."

"Of course."

"Hope you're writing this down, Bosco? You can sell this to Hollywood."

"Guess that all depends on the ending. If we get a DNA match on that body part and Rhonda Havelin, this thing is going to blow sky high."

"Do you have DNA on the missing woman?"

"I'm sure we can get the Houston police to dig some up at her house if we have to. Hairs from her brush, that sort of thing, but we'll know before that. Cassie Pierson volunteered to provide a sample of her DNA, and if the match comes back positive, we've got ourselves one hell of a case."

"*Someone* has one hell of a case," the boss said, looking over the notes. "The FBI could come in on this since the woman lived in Texas, flew to New Orleans and was last seen in Beau Pierre."

Bosco nodded, his thoughts already switching back to Cassie Pierson. She was a nice-looking woman, smart, too, and she was really worried about her mother. Bosco figured she had a reason to be, but he sure hoped he was wrong.

Odds were, he wasn't.

CASSIE AND JOHN dropped Butch at the airport after the meeting with the NOPD and started the drive back to Beau Pierre.

"Your father was quieter than I'd expected him to be," John said.

"I don't understand how he remains so calm about all of this."

"He handles things differently than you, but I'm sure he's worried."

"I don't know. I think he still thinks this is no big deal,

that Mom's going to appear at any minute with a logical explanation.''

"That's not such a far-fetched scenario when you look at the facts. Your mother told both of you she was leaving and she took enough cash to live on so there's no necessity for her to use credit cards.''

"Why lie? Why leave at all if she wasn't going to Greece with a friend?''

"Women leave all the time, Cassie, for lots of reasons. It could be the marriage isn't what she wants and she decided to see if living alone worked for her before she talked about divorce.''

"After thirty years?''

"Five, ten, thirty, what's the difference? If something is over, it's over. You let it go. Maybe your mother was at that point, or thought she might be.''

"How would that explain her visit to Magnolia Plantation?''

"That does throw a couple of kinks into the mix, but she might have been thinking about plastic surgery so she'd feel younger and more attractive in her new life.''

"Dr. Guilliot claims he never saw her. Give it up, John. You don't believe any more than I do that there's a logical excuse for my mother's disappearance. There are too many inconsistencies, too many lies.''

This time John didn't argue the point. He just stared straight ahead, with a look of deep concentration on his face, likely lost in his own worries.

So here they were, both struggling to find answers. Him with his grief, her with a dread that at times all but consumed her, and the only thing they had to hold on to was each other.

But what she felt for John was a lot more than gratitude for broad shoulders to lean on and a pair of strong arms to hold her. She liked him a lot, probably too much, might even be falling in love with him. When this was over, she'd have to deal with all of that and might have her heart broken in the process.

For now, she was just glad to have him in her life.

"ALMOST TO BEAU PIERRE," John said, finally breaking the silence that had existed most of the trip.

Cassie glanced out the window. "Let's make a stop at the cemetery before we go to your place. The road's just ahead."

"It's almost dark. The mosquitoes will be out."

"I have some spray repellent in my handbag, and we won't stay but a minute."

He slowed, but she could tell he didn't want to do this and now she felt bad for asking. "We don't have to stop if you'd rather not."

"It's okay. Maybe I need a visual reminder that all that's left of Dennis is rotting in that old mausoleum since I haven't found his killer yet."

Now she was really sorry she'd suggested stopping. It was silly for her to want to go back to the grave site again anyway, but she just kept thinking that whoever left those roses held the key. She had no idea what the key would open.

John pulled to the side of the road in front of the cemetery. Cassie stepped out of the car and was hit with the eerie reminder that this was the same time of day she'd gotten shot at and chased into the swamp.

They both sprayed the repellent liberally before starting across the maze of family mausoleums.

"Looks like we have company," John said.

Apprehension hit in a heartbeat. "Where?"

"Right in front of the Robicheaux crypt."

Cassie hurried to get past a tall stone structure that blocked her view. Once past it she saw Annabeth, standing in the shadow of the cross holding one white rose.

Annabeth spotted them and waved. "I didn't expect to see anyone else out here this late," she said, dropping the rose to the grass.

"Neither did we," John said. "I didn't see your car when we drove up."

"I parked it around the curve, where the road dead-ends. I'd rather Norman not know I'm out here."

"Did you tell him the baby is Dennis's?" John asked.

"I had to. He kept pressuring me."

Finding out that your wife had been impregnated by the anesthetist on your surgery team must have been a shock, Cassie decided, unless Norman had already known about the affair.

Adultery. Motive to kill. Cassie shuddered at the thought.

"But you're back with him," John said, "all lovey dovey from the way it looked when Cassie and I saw you last night."

"Norman's still upset, but things will get better."

"Guess that means you're staying with him?"

"I know you don't care for Norman. Dennis told me that the two of you had some kind of clash years ago, but he's not all bad, John, and he is my husband."

"If you stay with him, he'll be raising my nephew."

"I won't let him hurt my child. You surely know that."

"No, Annabeth. I don't know a damn thing these days except that Dennis is dead and still getting screwed over."

Cassie stooped and picked up the rose. This time half the petals were missing, all on one side, as if someone had peeled them away. "I wondered who was bringing these," Cassie said. "I thought it might be you."

"I didn't bring the rose. It was lying in the grass when I got here. This is the first time I've been to the cemetery since the burial service."

Cassie wasn't sure she believed her, especially when Annabeth kept looking around as if she expected a ghost to spring from one of the mausoleums or someone to jump from behind one.

"I should get home," Annabeth said.

"Before your loving husband finds you here?"

"Be fair, John. It's Dennis and I who did wrong by having the affair. Not Norman."

They started back to the road. Annabeth matched her pace with Cassie's. "Norman said your visit last night had to do with your mother. He said you thought she'd come to him for surgery."

Cassie considered her answer before she spoke, not sure how much she should reveal to Annabeth. It was clear the woman's loyalties lay with Guilliot, but Cassie desperately needed a friend on the inside, and Annabeth might unwittingly turn out to be that friend.

"My mother was driven to Magnolia Plantation on May ninth."

"If she was there, she didn't see Norman. Perhaps she had a consultation with Fred."

Cassie hadn't even thought of that. Fred was doing a fellowship with Guilliot, but he was a fully licensed plastic surgeon, certainly qualified to do a patient consultation to consider surgery. This conversation was paying off already.

They reached the car a few minutes later. John walked Annabeth to hers, but Cassie said her goodbyes, got in the car and pulled out her notebook. The first word she wrote was *motive*. The second was Fred Powell.

"ANNABETH LOOKS SO SAD," Cassie said.

"Not sad enough that she'll walk away from the money and the lifestyle Guilliot offers. I don't care what she does, but I hate to think Dennis's child will grow up with Annabeth and Norman Guilliot for parents. It's a rotten legacy to leave a kid."

"Annabeth mentioned a clash between you and Norman. What was that about?"

"A typical Guilliot stunt. He and a contractor friend from Florida wanted to build a golf course on some land he owns near my place. They were going to haul in a lot of dirt and make it into a high-priced resort. My grandfather got wind of it and started a petition to keep him from doing it."

"Why?"

"Didn't want a bunch of yuppies around. Bottom line, Guilliot stormed over to my grandfather's place and threatened him with everything from mayhem to getting him kicked off his own land. Puh-paw took his shotgun and fired a few shots into whatever expensive vehicle Guilliot was driving at the time, and Guilliot smacked him with a lawsuit."

"What happened?"

"Guilliot finally dropped the suit and things settled down."

"There's no golf course."

"The state declared the whole area under wetland protection right after that."

"And you wouldn't have had anything to do with that?"

John smiled. She'd forgotten how great one looked on him. "Perhaps a bit," he admitted.

Or perhaps a lot. "Obviously Guilliot's anger didn't extend to Dennis."

"Who knows what goes on in Guilliot's mind?"

"Do you think he suspected that Dennis and Annabeth were having an affair?"

"No."

"Why not? That would have been motive for the murder you seem so certain happened."

"If Guilliot had known, he'd have come to Annabeth with the accusations, not waited until she told him she was pregnant to explode."

"Then you still think this has to do with Ginny Flanders's death?"

"Yeah, I do. Hopefully I'll find some proof of that soon."

"Are you still thinking of breaking into the clinic?"

"I'm past the thinking stage. I'm going in tomorrow night, late, after the residents are asleep and the night staff has settled down."

"How will you get through the gate?"

"I won't. I'll go the back way, by water. It will be a moonless night, pitch-dark in the swamps. No one will see me slip my pirogue into the bayou just north of the plantation. No one will see me when I dock a few yards behind the house."

Just the thought of the pitch-dark swamp made Cassie's skin crawl. "There's no guarantee you'll find anything," she said, wishing he'd change his mind.

"There are no guarantees of anything."

"If you get caught, you could go to jail."

"I won't get caught."

There was no use arguing with him. His mind was made up and she didn't want to think of dark bayou waters right now. But the thoughts were already planted in her mind. Slow-moving, murky water. Alligators.

Body parts.

John stretched his arm along the back of the seat and rested it on her shoulder. "Are you okay?"

"No. Not until I find Mom."

"We should stop at the grocers," he said, no doubt trying to get her mind off the fears that must shadow her face the way they shadowed her soul. "What are you hungry for tonight?"

"Nothing. I just want a quiet evening with you."

He massaged her shoulder, but didn't answer.

A few minutes later they stopped in front of Dubois Super Mart. Apparently John needed food.

JOHN FOLLOWED Cassie into the store. "I put some filets in the refrigerator to defrost, so all we need is the fixings for a green salad and a loaf of French bread—unless you don't like steak."

"Ordinarily, I love a good steak," Cassie said. "I'm not sure I can do one justice tonight, but I'll try."

They stopped at the produce section first. The choices were limited in the small family-owned establishment. The only two kinds of lettuce were iceberg and Romaine. Cassie put a head of each in the basket John had picked up at the door.

What Dubois Super Mart lacked in lettuce varieties, it made up for by having vine-ripened creole tomatoes grown in the rich soil of the Mississippi Delta region. There were no better in the world, and Cassie searched through the bin to select the best.

"Hello, Cassie."

Cassie looked up to see Fred Powell standing a few feet away. Every muscle in her body tightened. He might well be the only link she had to finding her mother. The produce section isle of the grocery store wasn't where she'd planned to confront him, but it would have to do. She murmured a hello while she strived to get her thoughts together.

A stunning young woman walked up and took a possessive hold of Fred's arm. She was tall and thin with long, straight black hair that was so shiny it glistened even under the artificial store lighting. They went through the introduction, and even her voice was seductive, low and breathy.

"So what brings you two to Beau Pierre on a Saturday night?" John asked.

"The doc met with his attorney again this afternoon," Fred explained. "Jacobbi sent some questions back with him that he wants me to look over before Monday so Gina and I drove over to pick them up." Fred rested his basket of groceries on top of a stack of apples and turned his attention to Cassie. "How's the article coming?"

"The one that mentions you is finished and will be on the shelves next Friday."

"I'll be sure and pick up a copy. It might be my only fifteen minutes of fame. Will you be covering the trial?"

"Most likely."

"I'm sure I'll see you around the courthouse then."

"I thought you might be spared the hassle of the trial," John said, "since you were out of town the day of Mrs. Flanders's surgery."

"I'm not named in the suit, but Clayton Jacobbi thinks it will look better if I'm in court every day with the others, and he wants me to take the stand. Mostly he wants me to reinforce the fact that we take all reasonable precautions to avoid problems once the patient is under the knife."

"Sounds like the court proceedings aren't going to leave much time for operating on patients," John said.

"There's no surgery at all scheduled for the next two weeks. We'll take turns checking in on the patients staying at Magnolia, and Dr. Guilliot will be available if he's needed."

"Sounds as if you have it all covered."

"Dr. Guilliot makes sure everything is covered."

"Do you live in Houma, too?" Cassie asked, directing her question to Gina.

"For now."

"Gina's my fiancée," Fred said. "We live together."

Cassie glanced at Gina's hand, the ring was a very impressive Marque diamond, at least a couple of carats surrounded by rubies.

"We better go and let you two finish shopping," Fred said.

But Cassie had no intention of letting him walk away just yet. "I need to ask you something first."

"Sure, as long as it's not about Ginny Lynn Flanders or anything to do with the trial."

"It's not about Ginny Lynn. It's about another patient, Rhonda Havelin."

Fred's expression didn't change, but he took a quick glance over his shoulder before answering. "I don't know a Rhonda Havelin."

He picked up his basket and hooked it over his arm, but Cassie wasn't ready to give up yet. She pulled out her mother's picture and handed it to him. "She may have gone by another name, but I know she was at Magnolia and I think she had some type of surgical procedure performed."

Fred looked at the photograph, then shrugged his shoulders and handed it back to Cassie. "I've never seen her. Did you ask Dr. Guilliot about her?"

"Yes, but he claims he's never seen her, either."

"Then I guess you must be mistaken about her having had surgery at Magnolia. See you around."

"No, wait!" She worked to keep the panic from her voice. "I know she was there. If you know anything at all about this, please tell me."

"Of course, I would tell you. Why wouldn't I? Who is she anyway?"

"My mother."

His eyes narrowed. "I don't understand. If you're wondering if your mother came to the clinic, why don't you just ask her?"

"It's a long story." And one that hurt so much right now Cassie was having to bite back the pain and frustration just so she could maintain a reasonable semblance of control. "Thanks anyway, Fred."

Cassie stood there and watched him walk away with his arm around Gina.

John put a hand on Cassie's shoulder.

"I'm sorry, really sorry. But hang in there. We're going to find your mother. Things like this just take time."

"But what if we don't, John? What if we don't?"

John led the way down the short grocery aisle. "Did you notice the size of that rock on Gina's finger?"

"Yeah. Pretty impressive."

"The guy must be in hock to his eyeballs."

"Trying to keep up with Dr. Guilliot, I guess."

John grabbed a loaf of French bread and a bottle of dishwashing liquid, then walked to the one check-out counter where Mrs. Dubois was busy ringing up the groceries for an elderly woman who liberally mixed her Cajun French with her English.

"C'est pas de ta faute."

"Bien, merci."

"You heard about the nurse?"

"What nurse?"

"The *jolie* blonde who works for Dr. Guilliot?" Mrs. Dubois said as she weighed the woman's bananas.

Cassie stepped closer to hear the conversation better.

"Don' told me dere's more bad news."

Mrs. Dubois nodded. "*Pas trop bien.* Heard it from Sheriff Babineaux himself. Poor Angela she found the body. Looked like the nurse choked to death on a bite of chicken."

"*Mon Dieu.*"

"*Mais,* yeah."

Cassie looked at John, then back to Mrs. Dubois. "Did you say Susan Dalton is dead?"

Mrs. Dubois nodded. "The sheriff himself, stood right here and told me."

"I'm going to look for Fred," Cassie told John. "Someone should let him know."

"You stay here, I'll check."

John was back and shaking his head just as the woman in front of them left with her groceries. "No sign of him. I guess he checked out while we were getting the bread."

"*Comment ça va,* John," Mrs. Dubois said.

He pushed the basket within her reach. "I'm making it."

"I told you how sorry I am about Dennis?" Mrs. Dubois said as she rung up the bread the old-fashioned way, sans scanner.

"You told me and I appreciate it," John said.

Cassie walked to the door and looked outside for Fred and Gina. She didn't spot them, but stepped outside anyway. She needed a breath of fresh air, but only found more suffocating heat and humidity.

And more dread. Yet another death. Choked on a bite of chicken. Cassie didn't buy that for a second.

Cassie looked up as the first hint of a breeze stirred her hair. The sky was rolling with thick, dark clouds.

"Why wait until Sunday?" she said, when John joined her.

"What are you talking about?"

"Why wait until Sunday to look for answers at Magnolia Plantation? What's wrong with tonight?"

"Are you trying to get rid of me?"

"No. I want to go with you, but I want to go now."

CHAPTER NINETEEN

THE NIGHT was not only pitch black but threatening rain as John slid the pirogue from the bed of his truck into the still, dark water of the bayou that flowed behind Magnolia Plantation. Cassie stood near the truck, thinking how her life had changed since the day she'd called and asked her father for the itinerary.

Then, the Flanders v. Guilliot case had been just a job. Dennis Robicheaux had been a name she'd typed in an article as part of the infamous surgery team. Beau Pierre had been a dot on the map. Her mother had been vacationing in Greece. And Cassie had never even heard of the man with whom she was about to commit her first criminal act.

"Are you ready?" John asked.

"As ready as I'll ever be." She took his hand, stepped over a cluster of cypress knees and into the boat. Careful not to lose her balance, she moved to the other end and sat gingerly on the plank of wood that served as a seat.

John got in after her and pushed them from the bank with the end of the long oar. The waterway was deeper than the one behind his house and more or less clear of vegetation, allowing him to paddle rather than pole the small boat through the water.

Cassie barely noticed the noises that had seemed so loud and unfamiliar on her first ride in John's pirogue. But some noises still gave her the creeps, like the throaty, bellowing roar of an alligator or anything that sounded like a hiss.

"What makes that grunting noise? Listen, you can hear it now and I heard it the day I was running through the swamp."

"That's a mother gator talking to her babies. You want to stay away from a mother gator. Like most other creatures, they're fiercely protective of their young."

"We're not far away from them now."

"No, but we don't pose any threat as long as we're not in the water with them. Like I've told you, it's rare for an adult to get attacked by a gator. Gators are smart enough to make certain they have the advantage before they strike."

"What do they normally eat?"

"Fish, crabs, turtles, snakes, nutria, pretty much anything they can handle."

Which occasionally included humans. She swallowed hard, finding it even more difficult to talk about this now that she'd actually had her mouth swabbed for the DNA testing. "The state trooper said the partially decomposed hand they found looked as if the person it belonged to had been eaten by alligators."

"Probably had been, but the person was likely already dead when the gators found and fed on the body."

"Beau Pierre has more than its share of people showing up dead," she said, her mind going back to Susan Dalton. Murder or suicide? If the question applied to Dennis, it surely applied to Susan Dalton, as well.

"How did Beau Pierre get its name?" she asked, not caring, but needing the sound of John's voice to quell her fears.

"It was named after Jean Pierre Joubert. He was the town founder, him and his passel of kids and relatives. At least that's what Puh-paw said, and he knew pretty much everything about the history of this area.''

"Were you always close to your grandparents?'' Cassie asked when John had been silent too long.

"Yeah, even before we moved in with them, the old shack seemed more like home than anywhere else I lived.''

"You always refer to it as a shack, but it's not falling in or anything. I mean it's dry and you have all the necessities, even a television and your computer.''

"*C'est* a shack, because trappers had shacks on the edge of the swamp and Puh-paw was a trapper. Muh-maw made him fix it up a bit when he got the shrimp boat and started bringing in more cash, but it was never fancy. Wouldn't seem right if it were, though Dennis had always craved a little more luxury.''

"How much older are you than Dennis?''

"Dennis was thirty. I'm an old man of forty-two. I was his big brother, watched his back for him, kept him out of trouble—when I wasn't getting him into it.''

The big brother type. It figured. John had those caretaking ways about him, and that's what he was doing with her. Taking care of her, a trait he no doubt had inherited from his grandparents.

"Your grandparents must have been very proud of you when you earned your law degree.''

John didn't respond to the comment. Mention law degree or anything about his life as an attorney and he shut down just as literally as if someone had reached inside him and pushed a button. She wondered if he'd done that with Dennis and with his grandparents when they'd tried to talk to him about why he'd given up and run home after one mistake.

If so, they must have felt shut off from that part of his life the way she did. He let her get just so close, and no closer. But if they were ever to have a relationship beyond what they shared now, he'd have to trust her enough to let the barriers fall. She wasn't at all sure that he could.

"The plantation's just ahead," John said. "We'll tie up and stay hidden until we see the guard make his rounds to the back of the house. Once he's gone back to the front, we'll sneak inside."

"The place surely has an alarm system."

"It has one. I just happen to know the code—unless it's been changed in the last few days."

"No way. How would you?"

"I've been working on this since the day Dennis was killed. I finally found the right man to buy beers for, one of the cleaning crew who works nights."

"You asked him and he told you?"

"No. I tampered with his truck so it wouldn't start. Like the good guy I am, I offered to drive him to work, then asked to go in with him so I could use the bathroom."

"And you memorized the code when he went in."

"Where there's a will, there's a way."

"You never mentioned that."

"You didn't want any part of the break-in."

"What do we do once we're inside?" Cassie asked, growing more nervous by the second.

"Hold our breaths and take the service elevator to Guilliot's private office on the third floor."

"How do you know about that office? I don't remember mentioning it to you."

"Annabeth told me."

"You told her you were breaking into the clinic?"

"*Mais, non.* I just listened while she vented about Guilliot's getting so irate at her indiscretions with Dennis when she's certain he's bonking Susan Dalton and maybe Angela, as well."

"How does she know he's been with Susan?"

"She's caught the two of them in Guilliot's office with the doors closed and locked on several occasions when she's come up the back way unannounced."

"Do you think her affair with Dennis was to get back at her husband?"

"Who knows. I'm fairly sure it wasn't based on love."

"Did Dennis tell you he was having an affair with his boss's wife?"

"No, and I didn't see that one coming."

Cassie clutched the seat as John rowed to the bank. He stepped out into the muck and pulled the small boat onto the shore next to another pirogue, one that apparently belonged to the center. Ready or not, she was in for her taste of crime. "I hope you're good at picking locks," she whispered as John helped her up the bank.

"I thought you might take care of that."

"Think again."

"Then we'll see if my crash course in locksmithing pays off."

CASSIE WAS AT LEAST sixty pounds lighter than John, but he was far stealthier, opening the door with the help of a thin metal tool and moving without sound across the carpeted floor. The service elevator was at the back of the house just as John had said. There was no bell, and the doors slid open almost silently, much quieter than the pounding of Cassie's heart. No wonder it had been easy for Annabeth to make surprise visits even during the day.

Cassie barely dared breathe until they reached the third floor. If John was nervous at all, it was indiscernible. Once they'd exited the elevator, Cassie led the way to Dr. Guilliot's office using the beam of one small flashlight to illuminate the hallway.

"This is it," she whispered, grimacing at the creak of the door as it opened. "Where do we start?"

"Log on to the computer and check for financial records. See if any payments were received from Rhonda Havelin in the days and weeks preceding May ninth and anytime since. I'll search the file cabinet for anything that looks helpful."

Cassie logged on easily. Either no password was needed to access the files, or Dr. Guilliot had set his system up to bypass that step. Financial information was given in several formats. Cassie chose the file that reported daily receipts of payments by check, credit card and cash along with the name of the payee.

She skimmed the material quickly, sure her mother's name would stand out if it was there. If she didn't find anything by skimming, she'd go back and examine each item more closely. There was no Rhonda Havelin or Rhonda Clarkson listed.

Cassie went back for a closer look at dates around May 9. She was deep in concentration but still aware when John pulled several folders from the file cabinet and set them on the back corner of Dr. Guilliot's desk.

"Surgery notes," he whispered, "apparently copied from the patients' charts and filed by month."

"I'd have thought those would be kept in the business office."

"The originals probably are. The copies more likely serve as a quick reference when he gets a phone call from a patient. That way he can always sound as if he remembers them and their surgery."

"The all-knowing, caring surgeon," she said. "Part of his charisma. Do the records go through May?"

"They're current through this past Thursday."

Their voices were low murmurs, but they seemed blaring to Cassie, though she knew there was no one on the third floor to hear them.

"Are you having any luck?" John asked.

"I found an interesting entry, but it's not in Mom's name."

John stepped closer and looked over her shoulder as she highlighted a cash payment of $42,000 on Sunday, May 9.

"The date correlates with Mom's arrival," she whispered, "and the amount is fairly consistent with the fifty-thousand dollars she withdrew from her bank account."

"Paid in cash, too," John said.

"I'd think that more significant if there weren't so many other cash payments."

"Cash leaves no money trail."

"No money trail or any other kind of trail if you happen to use a fake name when you come here," Cassie said.

No money trail. No name. No way to track a person down. Cassie's hand slipped from the keypad. "A person could die on the operating table, John, just the way Ginny Lynn did, and if no one knew she was here and all she'd given was a fake name, her family and friends would never know what happened to her."

John placed his hands on her shoulders. "I know what you're thinking, but no one's died here since Ginny Flanders. If they had, the media would have gotten hold of that by now and made a big issue of it."

"I suppose," she admitted, but the fear didn't fully recede. John moved to the desk to examine the surgery notes. Cassie closed the file on payments and pulled up one labeled Admitting and Discharge. This time she went immediately to May 9.

One person had been admitted that day for face, brow and eyelid surgery scheduled for May 10. Mary Jones, age

59, married. Her weight was listed as 160 pounds, the height as five-six. No health problems. Full medical checkup within the year. Allergies: None. Previous surgeries: a hysterectomy, gall bladder surgery and a breast biopsy.

Mary Jones could have been Rhonda Havelin. The age, the weight, the marital status, even the medical history matched—except for the allergies. Cassie couldn't recall exactly which anesthetic her mother had been allergic to, but her mother would have known and as close as she'd come to death having a simple biopsy performed, she'd never have failed to make everyone aware before she was administered any type of drug.

"Take a look at this," John said, setting one of the files he'd been perusing next to the computer and shining a beam of light on the center of the page.

It was a copy of the surgery notes from the day Ginny Flanders died. Cassie read the notes. There were three pages of them, most written by Dennis, explaining what had gone wrong and the steps he'd taken. It was bone-chilling, but there was nothing there to indicate malpractice.

"Everything seems to back up Guilliot's claim that the death wasn't their fault," Cassie said.

"Exactly, but take a careful look at Dennis's handwriting."

"What's wrong with it?"

"It's shaky. Guilliot's notes for that day are shaky, as well. Now look at these entries." John thumbed through the surgery notes, stopping at several and in every case, Dennis's writing was incredibly neat and the letters perfectly formed.

John picked up a second file, this time pulling out the page for May 10. Again the handwriting of both Dr. Guilliot and Dennis was so shaky that some of the words were difficult to decipher. Only this time, the notes indicated that the surgery performed on Mary Jones was successful with no complications.

"Now look at this," John said, flipping to the next page. "Ordinarily Fred Powell makes notations on the surgery notes, as well, but he didn't on those two days."

"That's because he wasn't at work the day Ginny Flanders died.'

John went back to the previous day's notes. "And it looks as if he wasn't at work on May tenth, either."

"Oh, John, maybe Norman Guilliot is as incompetent as Reverend Flanders claims. Maybe that's why he always has a fellowship assistant." The thought of it gave her the creeps.

"Kill the monitor," John whispered. "Someone's in the hall."

Cassie switched it off as the footsteps in the hallway grew closer. John grabbed the files and pulled her behind the desk. They crouched and waited, expecting the door to open. It didn't. The footsteps faded.

"Stay quiet," John whispered. "It's likely the guard is making routine rounds. He'll leave soon."

A few minutes later, she heard the footsteps again, only this time they stopped outside the office door. The door creaked open and the beam from a flashlight swept across the room.

Cassie could hear her own breathing and she was certain the guard could hear it as well, but a second later she heard the door slam shut. They stayed crouched in the darkness until they heard the clang of the front elevator.

"Dodged that bullet," John whispered, standing and tugging her to her feet and into the circle of his arms. "Guess dodging bullets is old hat for you, though."

She pressed John's hand to her chest. "Does that heart-beat sound as if this is routine for me?"

"No, and I got a little adrenaline rush there myself. You never know when you'll get a nervous, trigger-happy guard, especially when he's probably never run into an intruder in his career."

"Thanks for sharing that with me." Her nerves were not nearly as nonchalant as her comment. "I think we should get out of here, John. I've seen enough to know my mother's name is not on any of the surgical records and there's no indication at all of Ginny Flanders's death being different than the way Dr. Guilliot's reported it."

John nodded. "We'll give the guard a few more minutes to clear the area, then we'll sneak back to the pirogue and hopefully make it back to the truck before the rain sets in."

Back into the swamps on a dark, moonless night, and a trip along a bayou that might hold the only real clue to whatever horror stalked the town of Beau Pierre. Someone had been left as food for the hundreds of alligators that slithered through the murky waters and built nests in the muddy mire.

And Cassie was faced with the burgeoning fear that the unidentified female could be her mother. She put her arms around John and held on tight.

"Hang in there, baby," he whispered, as his fingers stroked her back.

"I'll be okay."

"I know you will, Cassie Pierson. You're too strong not to see this through, but everyone needs someone to hold on to sometimes."

"Even you, John?"

He was silent for a long time, and when he finally answered, it was as if he were frightened to whisper the words.

"Even me, Cassie. Even me."

JOHN HAD HATED to leave Cassie alone on Monday, and yet he was grateful to be back out in the Gulf where locating fish for a group of boisterous Texans claimed his energy.

Cassie continued to claim far too many of his thoughts, the way she had since he'd encountered her on that first Sunday outside the gate at Magnolia Plantation. He'd followed her there just as she'd accused him of doing, partly to intimidate her, mostly to manipulate her. Strange that those skills he'd honed to such perfection while he was a defense attorney were still razor sharp.

But Cassie had turned the tables on him. She was too honest, too straightforward, and he'd been far too attracted to her. Timing, he guessed, and chemistry or whatever mental or emotional stimulant it was that made two people connect in the second it took for their eyes to meet.

He'd encouraged her to fly to Houston yesterday, take some time off, far away from the mess in Beau Pierre. But Cassie had other ideas. She'd had him drive her to New Orleans to pick up her car, then had followed him back to Beau Pierre. She planned to stay until she found out what had happened to her mother after she'd arrived at Magnolia Plantation.

So they'd made love again last night. It was as good as it got, but making love didn't touch the surface of what she was doing to him. She had him second-guessing his life, wondering if he could go back to the world he'd run from. Had him thinking of the future—and that scared him.

The opportunities were out there. He never went more than six months without hearing from someone wanting

him to take a case or join their law firm. The last offer
had come from New Orleans's newly elected D.A., an old
law school buddy.

Every offer was tempting, but then the haunting memories would return. Memories so strong they would almost
drive him mad.

John knew who he really was, and if he couldn't stand
that man, how could he expect someone like Cassie to?
That was why he couldn't move beyond the here and now.
And that was why, when this was over, he'd let Cassie go.

"You are living every man's dream life! I'd change
places with you in a minute," one of the fishermen said
to John as he let out his line after hooking a big yellow-
fin tuna.

"Yeah," John said. "I've got it all."

IT WAS TEN PAST FIVE when Butch stood in his doorway
watching the two policemen walk back to their unmarked
car, thankful he'd had them meet him at home rather than
the office. This was the moment he'd hoped would never
come. He'd almost lied to them, but it wouldn't have mattered. They'd done their homework before they'd asked
him to answer a few questions for them.

He hadn't wanted to go to the police, but Cassie
wouldn't have it any other way. Now there was nothing
to do but face the truth—at work—and with his daughter.
He only hoped Cassie wouldn't hate him as much as he
hated himself right now.

He hated the lies and deceptions. Hated that he'd held
on to a marriage when there was nothing left but tattered
remnants of a love that had grown cold years before.

The only thing he didn't hate in all of this was Babs.
How could he? She was the one really right thing in his

life. He'd likely lose her for good now, the way he was losing everything else.

THE MUSCLES in John's neck and shoulders relaxed a little as he turned down the dirt road to the old trapper's shack. The fishing trip had gone well and the fishermen from Dallas were excited about the day's catch and eager for the next day's trip.

John was just ready to catch a quick shower—or maybe not so quick if he had company—and hopefully to have a night without a new round of bad news.

He parked his car behind Cassie's. She was standing on the porch waiting for him, wearing a pair of black running shorts and a white pullover shirt that showed off her breasts to perfection. Her hair was down for a change, hanging past her shoulders, shiny and wet as if she'd just stepped from the shower. She looked absolutely terrific, but she did not look happy.

So much for his hopes for a night without bad news.

"MY DAD IS HAVING AN AFFAIR."

The words were more an eruption than a sentence, exploding in the hot, humid air before John had reached the porch.

"How do you know that?"

"He just called and told me. He's been seeing a much younger co-worker for over a year. Apparently Mom found out about it six weeks before her so-called Greece trip."

"What prompted that confession?"

"A visit from a couple of Houston cops. Come inside, and I'll fill you in on the details."

John followed her in, then poured them both a glass of wine while she spun a story that didn't surprise him nearly as much as it had her. In fact, it explained a lot about why

Butch had been so hesitant to go to the cops in the first place. Cops had a way of digging out those nettlesome details like *giving* at the office.

Evidently the NOPD had called for a little assistance from the Houston police department, which also didn't surprise John. The husband is always the first suspect in a wife's disappearance. It was a rule of thumb that turned out right way too many times not to give it a shot.

"I'm so angry," Cassie said. "Angry and hurt, about the lies as much as anything else. If either one of them had leveled with me, I might have had a better handle on this."

"I'm sure they were trying to spare you from being hurt by the situation."

"I'm a grown woman. I could have handled the truth. Now I don't know what to think. Is Mom off building a new life? Or is she in trouble or…" Cassie threw up her hands in exasperation. "I might be able to convince myself things were all right if there weren't so many questions surrounding her visit to Beau Pierre."

John wished he could genuinely offer some encouraging words, but he'd become increasingly concerned about the mystery surrounding Rhonda Havelin's visit to Magnolia Plantation. Butch's affair was going to make for a major scandal and give the cops a new angle to work, but John wasn't convinced it was related to the disappearance, other than that it may have spurred Cassie's mother into wanting plastic surgery.

He'd just have to offer consolation the Robicheaux way. "Get your boots on, Cassie. Let's go fishing."

ANGELA DUBUISSON walked through the cemetery in the long shadows of a deepening twilight carrying one perfect white rose clutched between two fingers. It would be her ast visit to Dennis's grave site. It would be her last visit anywhere.

The secret was eating at her like a merciless cancer that wouldn't quit until it destroyed her. She'd thought she could go through with this, had thought she could do anything for Norman Guilliot, but she'd been wrong.

Some acts were so evil that they couldn't be forgiven in this life and maybe not even in the one beyond the grave. She prayed theirs would be. Prayed that for all their sakes, but especially for hers and for Norman Guilliot's.

She'd loved him for twenty years. She loved him still.

Angela stopped in front of the Robicheaux mausoleum and dropped the flower in the grass in front of the door. "We were friends, Dennis. I understood why you took your own life. But I won't be bringing any more roses from *Maman*'s garden. I'll be on the other side with you."

Reaching into her pocket, she pulled out the silver knife. She'd never have had the nerve to pull a trigger, but she could slice her wrists, one a time, then lie down in the grass and wait to die.

She wondered if Norman would shed a tear when he heard.

THERE WAS ONLY a sliver of a moon, but still enough light to see the group of nutria a few feet in front of them foraging for food along the banks of the bayou. She and John had been out almost an hour and while she'd talked little, she'd done a lot of thinking, mainly about relationships and what happened to them over the years.

With Drake and her, the marriage had never had a chance, but her parents had stayed together for thirty years. They must have loved each other in their own way, though looking back she didn't remember ever thinking of them as being particularly close. Their interests were different.

They seldom touched or cuddled, but then neither of them was a touchy-feely sort of person.

"Were your grandparents in love, John? I don't mean in the beginning. I mean at the end."

"*Mais,* yeah. Very much in love."

"How do you know?"

"It showed, not so much in big ways, but in little ways."

"Like what?"

"She cooked to please him. Kept her hair long even when it was gray and so thin you could see her scalp through it because Puh-Paw liked it long. And when I'd go off fishing or trapping with Puh-Paw, he'd tell stories about when they met and how she was the most beautiful girl he'd ever seen. You could tell the way his eyes shone when he talked about it that he still saw her that way.

"And on Saturday nights when Puh-paw grew tired of playing the fiddle, he'd have me play and he would waltz Muh-maw around the room as if they were young and courting again."

"You may not have been wealthy growing up," Cassie said, "but you had a lot."

"I know. Thanks to my grandparents, we always belonged somewhere. They made Dennis and me feel we were special. Of course, we also had them on us to excel.

"You go out dere, make your Muh-Maw some proud, huh? You don' got to make yourself rich, just do your best," John said, mimicking his grandfather in an exaggerated Cajun accent.

"And have you, John?"

Even in the deep purple of dusk she could see his muscles grow taut.

"What's the matter, Cassie? Are you embarrassed that your lover is only a fishing guide?"

"I just asked a question."

"Well, don't. Don't ask questions that you don't really want answered."

"But I do want it answered."

"I'm what I am. If that doesn't suit you, go back to town and find yourself another Drake Pierson."

"I'm not looking for anyone else. I wasn't looking when I found you."

He didn't comment, just continued to pole them through the thick, half-clogged waterway beneath a canopy of Spanish moss and moonlight. He was ready to drop the subject, but she wasn't ready to let it go. She'd had enough lies from everyone else in her life. She needed the truth from John, needed to understand what he was running from.

"Why did you give up your law practice?"

"Don't play games with me, Cassie. You're too good a reporter not to have done all your homework."

"I know about the Gregory Benson case, but you were a defense attorney. Your job was to defend him, and you did it."

"Doing my job let a child molester back on the streets. Doing my job put a ten-year-old girl through hell before she was brutally murdered."

"But you didn't create that hell. Gregory Benson did. You didn't know he was guilty or that he'd do the horrible things he did to Toni Crenshaw."

"Let it go, Cassie."

"If we let it go, what happens to us, John? What kind of relationship can we build if there are always things we can't talk about or parts of your life that are off-limits?"

"There's nothing to build on with me. Can't you see that? We're good as long as we're good and then you'll move on."

"That's a cop-out, John. Your grandfather would be the first to tell you so."

He exhaled sharply, then lifted the long pole from the water and slid it to the floor beneath the seats. "You want the truth, Cassie? You want to know the real John Robicheaux? Then let me tell you and see how much interest you have in a relationship then."

CHAPTER TWENTY

CASSIE STARED at John, shocked at the change that came over him. It was as if everything warm and human inside him had fossilized and left only an impenetrable layer of stone.

He propped his elbows on his knees and leaned toward her. "I didn't make a mistake, Cassie. I knew what Gregory Benson was the day he walked into my office. I always knew, with all my clients, the same way I read what jurors were thinking. The same way I know Dennis was troubled that last night but not about to kill himself.

"I have a natural talent for reading people, but I honed the skill to perfection when I became a defense attorney. Body language is a lot of it, but the real clue to what a person's thinking almost always lies in the eyes. Anger, hurt, fear, guilt. They're all there unless you're dealing with a total psychopath."

"If anyone's a true psychopath, I'd think Gregory Benson would qualify."

"No, he was a very sick and perverted man who should have never been left free to walk the streets, but he wasn't a psychopath. His anguish and inner demons were sticking right out there, as easy to read as Dr. Seuss. I still fought just as hard to win that case as I did every other case I handled. It wasn't about right or wrong or innocent or guilty with me. It was about winning and being the best damn defense attorney in the state.

"That changed the night I went to the morgue and saw Toni Crenshaw's little body after she had been tortured and sexually molested for days and then dumped into the river. That image was seared into my brain and I live with it day after day, night after night. So don't preach to me about getting over my *mistake* and going on with my life, Cassie. I live in hell, and that's not nearly punishment enough for my sins."

Cassie shivered in spite of the summer heat. She'd known John harbored guilt but she hadn't realized the depth of it or the extent to which it tormented him. She tried to think of something to say, but words seemed so trite when John had just bared his soul.

Besides, what was there to say? That she was willing to share his hell for the rest of her life? That they could build a relationship on top of the sickening images that haunted him day and night?

The sounds of the bayou seemed deafening as John poled them along the shallow waterway back toward his dock. Her father was having an affair. Her mother had vanished. The man who held her heart lived in a private hell with no doors leading out.

In thirty-two years of living, she'd never felt so hopeless and alone.

ANNABETH STAGGERED to the phone, still reeling from the drugs and the abortion. The baby was gone. It had been growing inside her this morning and now it was gone.

Norman had handed her the small white pill and a glass of water and ordered her to take it before leading her to the car early this morning and shoving her into the passenger seat. She didn't remember much after that. But now it was over. She'd given up everything for Norman. Everything.

It didn't matter that the baby wasn't his. *She* was his, and she would have never even been with another man if Norman hadn't demoralized her so with his tawdry affairs. But it was Norman she loved. She'd sold her soul to the devil for him and the kind of life he'd promised her. What were a few stolen hours in another man's bed compared to that?

She cradled her barren stomach in her hands as tears rolled down her cheeks. She was tired, so very, very tired, but she had to be strong. Everyone thought Norman was the strong one, but it had always been her. Norman played the role of brilliant surgeon to perfection, charmed every woman he met, impressed every man. He was Dr. Norman Guilliot, the famed plastic surgeon to the rich and famous. He was the legend.

And that's the way it would stay.

She picked up the phone. One more death and they were home scot-free.

JOHN HAD DROPPED Cassie at the dock without a word. She'd walked to the cabin by herself, her emotions raw and confused, not sure if she ached more for John or for herself.

She understood his guilt now, but she didn't want to lose him to it. She wanted him to fight for himself the same way he'd fought to win cases before he'd left it all behind. She wanted him to fight for her and for a chance at a relationship for the two of them.

She wanted him to fight because she didn't want to lose him. Oh, God, she so didn't want to lose him.

Her phone rang. She'd like to ignore it, but didn't dare. It could be someone calling with news of her mother.

"Hello."

"Cassie?"

"Yes. Who's calling?"

"It's Annabeth Guilliot, Norman's wife, but don't say my name out loud. I don't want John to know I've called you."

"He won't. He's not here."

"Good."

"Is something wrong? You sound upset." Or drunk. Her words were slightly slurred, but then it might just be that she'd been crying again.

"I have some information about your mother."

Cassie held her breath, afraid to hope for good news, more afraid to consider bad. "Was she a patient of your husband's?"

"I'd rather not talk about this over the phone. Can you meet me at Magnolia?"

"When?"

"As soon as possible. I'm sitting in Norman's office now, but I need you to come alone. There are things John shouldn't have to hear."

"Things about Dennis?"

"Yes. Dennis. That's it."

"I can be there in twenty minutes."

"Don't bother to buzz the intercom when you arrive. I'll be watching for your car through the security camera and I'll have the gate open for you. Drive to the back and park next to my car. It's a light blue BMW convertible. You can let yourself in the back door, then take the service elevator to the third floor."

"Is Dr. Guilliot there with you?"

"No. He's staying in New Orleans tonight for a meeting with his attorney. I'm quite alone."

Cassie grabbed her handbag and dashed for the door. She had no idea what she'd learn from Annabeth, but whatever it was, good or bad, she wanted to know. Only...

She couldn't just walk away without leaving John a note, and she wouldn't lie to him. Not about Dennis. Not about Annabeth. Not about anything. She'd had all the lies she could bear.

THE GATE at Magnolia opened as Cassie drove up. She parked the car, then took the back door and the service elevator just as she and John had two nights ago. Even her heart hammered in the same erratic pattern.

Annabeth was standing at the elevator door when it opened. Her face was a pasty white and her eyes were rimmed in black circles as if she hadn't slept in days.

"What's happened, Annabeth? What's wrong?"

"Everything."

Cassie's apprehension level shot skyward. "What do you know about my mother?"

Annabeth took Cassie's hand and squeezed it. "I don't know how to tell you this."

"Just say it, Annabeth. Please. Just say it."

Annabeth stared at the floor for what seemed like an eternity, then took a deep breath and met Cassie's gaze. "Your mother is dead."

Dead. The word hung in the air. Cassie waited for the finality to hit her, expected to scream, or cry, or crumble. Instead she felt her muscles tense for a fight. She wanted to beat her fists into the wall or shove someone out the damn third floor window. If Dr. Guilliot was behind this...

"How do you know?" she asked, though the question felt empty. The word had been said now. Dead wasn't a word you could pull back.

"Come with me, Cassie. I'll tell you everything. You deserve to know the truth."

The hallway seemed a hundred miles long, each step a struggle as Cassie followed Annabeth toward the double doors emblazoned with the words Do Not Enter. Ginny Flanders had entered anyway, and she hadn't come out alive. Cassie visualized the gurney being wheeled out the doors with a sheet pulled over Ginny Flanders's head. Only it wasn't Ginny. It was Cassie's mother. The hurt seeped past the anger now, and tears burned at the back of Cassie's eyes.

Annabeth pushed through the swinging doors, then waited for Cassie to follow. Cassie was a step behind her, but she stopped at the door, hit with the crazy feeling that if she entered those doors she wouldn't come out again. Go in healthy. Come out dead. Do Not Enter.

"Please, just tell me what happened to my mother, Annabeth."

"It was an accident."

"No. I don't believe you."

"It's true. Your mother had a reaction to a drug. Drug allergies can be very dangerous."

"What do you know about my mother's allergies? What do you know, Annabeth?"

"Rhonda Havelin came here for surgery."

"Your husband said he'd never seen her."

"Norman lies, Cassie. He's my husband, but he lies. Susan, Angela, Dennis. They were all in on the secret, all part of the lie."

"What secret?"

"Come with me," Annabeth said, motioning Cassie to follow. "I'll show you the file with Rhonda Havelin's name on it." Annabeth switched on the bright lights above the operating table and adjusted the controls on the air conditioner so that icy air flowed from every vent, as if she were preparing to perform surgery herself. Then she crossed the room and stood beside a metal cart that held an array of surgical tools and a manila folder.

Cassie's body had gone numb, but her mind fought to understand. Her mother had been in this room. She'd been on the operating table. And she'd died. Oh, God, this hurt so much!

Annabeth picked up the file and held it so that Cassie could see the name Rhonda Havelin written in bold black letters. "Read this," she said, holding the folder out to Cassie. "Read it before the secret destroys all of us."

Cassie's hands shook as she took the file from Annabeth.

She opened it and the truth stared back at her. Rhonda had died May 10 of complications during a face, eye and brow lift. The primary contributing factor had been an allergic reaction to propofol.

"The death was no one's fault, Cassie, the same way Ginny Flanders's death was no one's fault."

"That's not true. Mom knew about the allergy. She'd have never had any kind of surgery performed without making sure everyone knew of her history."

"That's not what the notes in the file indicate."

"I don't care what the files say, Annabeth. My mother would have made the doctor aware. And if my mother died on the operating table, why wasn't the death reported?"

"That's the reason for the ugly secret, Cassie. It was an accident, but it wouldn't have been good to have another death with all the fuss over Ginny Lynn. It wouldn't have looked good for Norman at all."

Annabeth moved to Cassie's side and put an arm around her shoulder. Cassie jerked away. She didn't need Annabeth's comfort. All she needed was the truth.

"Dr. Guilliot screwed up. Say it, Annabeth. Just say it."

The elevator bell rang. Someone was coming.

Cassie clutched the file to her chest, ready to rush past whoever was getting off the elevator and get the hell out of here before someone tried to stop her. That's when she saw the needle in Annabeth's hand. A breath later she felt the prick and the burn as Annabeth plunged the injection through the flesh of Cassie's left arm.

Cassie shoved Annabeth, knocking her to the floor, but not before some of the drugs had reached her bloodstream. Cassie fell against the cart, sending the instruments flying as the door to the operating room swung open and Norman Guilliot stepped inside.

"Norman!" It was Annabeth's voice, though it seemed to be coming from the glaring lights above the operating table and to be bouncing off the walls.

"Surprised to see me, Annabeth?"

Cassie didn't hear the answer. She was floating, up toward the lights, but someone turned them off, and everything went black.

THE BAYOU held no comfort for John tonight, no escape from the pain. He'd left himself wide open for this the first time he'd made love to Cassie. No matter how good they were together, no matter that she slid into his arms and into his heart as if she were meant to be there, the relationship had never had a chance of making it beyond a few weeks in Beau Pierre.

A summer to remember because there wasn't a snowball's chance in hell he could forget.

But the bayou wasn't the answer, and though he was a lot of things, he wasn't a coward. So he'd go back to the old shack and if Cassie was still around, he'd tell her goodbye.

"Sorry Puh-paw and Muh-maw, sorry I let you down. You'd have loved Cassie." But then, how could anyone not?

The house was dark except for the glow of his desk

lamp. He walked to the bar and took down the bottle of whiskey. He hadn't had a drink of hard liquor since the night Cassie had come here and found him drunk and reeling from Dennis's death.

But tonight he needed a drink, needed it bad.

He poured the amber liquid and swirled it in the glass, taking it with him to the desk. There was a slip of paper stuck under the corner of the lamp. A note from Cassie. Dear John. Just the kind of note he needed to make the night complete.

For two cents, he'd wad it and toss it into the garbage. No one offered two cents.

CASSIE LOST her balance and toppled forward. Someone caught her and held her upright as she faded in and out. From light to darkness. From silence to voices that came from all around her and back to the knowledge that she was being dragged along between two people.

"We can't kill her, Annabeth. I'm a doctor. I took an oath."

"We have to do this, Norman. There's no other way."

Norman and Annabeth. Fragments of reality stole into Cassie's mind on a hit and miss basis. Her mother was dead. Now they were talking of killing *her*.

"We'll need to put her to sleep, Norman. The drugs I gave her will wear off soon."

"Then what do we do with her?"

"Drive her to Grand Isle and dump her in the Gulf. That way we won't have any new body parts washing up here. And you won't have to kill her. You can simply leave her to drown."

"No. This has gone too far. It has to stop, Annabeth. I can't take any more of this. It has to stop."

"It will stop, Norman. Once Cassie's gone, it's over.

The secret will only exist between you, me and Angela, and Angela will never tell.''

"No. I can't.''

"You have no choice. You shouldn't have operated without Fred. You forget to write everything down when you talk to the patients and you didn't check Fred's notes. Now you'll have to pay for your mistake.''

"They'll find Cassie's body.''

"Not for weeks or even months. Maybe not ever if you take her out far enough. I'll help you, but we have to act quickly.''

Cassie heard the words, but they jumped about in her head, coming together slowly. They were going to kill her. She tried to scream, but her tongue was stuck to the top of her mouth and she choked instead.

A blast of hot, humid air hit her in the face and her feet were scraping now instead of sliding. They were outside, behind the old plantation house, in the dark.

Cassie tried to scream again, then realized something was stuffed into her mouth to keep her quiet.

"Put her in the car, Norman.''

No. She couldn't let them take her away from here. She'd left John a message. If she stayed here, there was a chance he'd find her in time, but if they took her away...

"I can't do this, Annabeth. I can't. I'm a doctor. I took an oath.'' His arm fell from around Cassie and he collapsed to the ground, put his head in his hands and started to sob.

Cassie heard the purr of a car engine and the squeal of brakes, though she couldn't see the vehicle. *John. Please let it be John.*

She tried to break away, but Annabeth's fingers dug into her arm and she shoved Cassie to the ground.

Norman reached up and grabbed the gag from Cassie's mouth.

"Tell whoever it is that she passed out, Annabeth. Tell them she fainted from the heat."

Cassie sucked in a breath and tried to regain her equilibrium. She had to stay conscious, had to let whoever was coming know that she needed help.

The car door slammed and Cassie saw the figure moving toward them, not recognizable in the dark until he was mere feet away. Fred Powell.

"Help me!" she begged, knowing there was little chance he would.

Her voice was little more than a squeaky shudder, but Fred ran toward her and grabbed her arm, pulling her toward him. "Don't worry, Cassie. I've got you now."

"Trying…to kill…me."

Cassie relaxed against Fred as the world started fading out. When she opened her eyes again, he was setting her into one of the pirogues tied behind the plantation. She tried to grab hold of a spindly cypress tree. Her hands didn't move. They were tied behind her. Her feet were tied as well, and someone had stuffed the gag back in her mouth.

She'd wanted to join her mother in Greece. Now she'd join her in death.

A ONE-YEAR FELLOWSHIP under the tutelage of Dr. Norman Guilliot will change your life.

And so it had, though not in ways the professor who'd told Fred that would ever have imagined. He'd learned a lot about fame and wealth and what it could get you. He'd learned that the rules changed the closer you got to the top. Mostly he'd learned that beautiful women like Annabeth and Gina could be bought as long as you had the price. And that legends like Norman Guilliot were all too human.

Cassie sat deathly still in the opposite end of the boat. She'd quit swaying back and forth and her pupils had returned to near normal. She was regaining full consciousness. How unfortunate for her.

EVERY SOUND, every smell, every movement seemed magnified a hundred times over as they floated down the bayou. An owl screeched. A fish splashed in the water, sending ripples cascading to the shore. A mosquito buzzed around her face.

The same swamp, the same bayou, the same hot, stifling air as when she'd been here with John, and yet everything was different. She choked on the gag and Fred reached over and pulled it from her mouth. They were too deep in the swamp for anyone to hear her even if she screamed.

"Why are you doing this, Fred?"

"For the money, of course. Why do people do anything? Money or passion. That's all there really is. And Annabeth pays very well to keep her and Norman's secrets hidden."

"What secret does Annabeth have? Her affair with Dennis Robicheaux?"

"Annabeth and Dennis. Never happened, though she'd have liked for it to. She came on to him often enough, but Dennis would never have betrayed his boss."

"Then why was he murdered?"

"Annabeth didn't trust him to keep the secret, especially after I told her Dennis was leaving here and taking a job in L.A."

Words tumbled about in Cassie's head and she struggled to make some sense of what she'd learned tonight.

"Whose fault was it that my mother died?"

"The good surgeon, of course. Had it been anyone

else's mistake, they'd have just had to face the music. But a man like Guilliot shouldn't have to pay for forgetting to note a drug allergy on a patient's surgery chart—not when the price of that mistake was going to be so high. Another death on top of Ginny Lynn's would have ended the Guilliot dynasty and his loyal surgery team couldn't let that happen."

"So you threw my mother to the alligators?"

"You make it sound so much worse than it was. She was dead. Nothing was going to bring her back to life. And if you hadn't come snooping, no one would have ever known. She told us herself. Her family thought she was in Greece. No paper trail. No trail at all."

"Will I be dead when you dump me, Fred?"

"No. Think of it this way, Cassie, I'm giving you a fighting chance. Of course, you won't likely make it to the bank with your hands and feet tied."

Cassie watched in horror as two gators swam a few feet from the boat. Fred would throw her overboard and she'd sink slowly to the bottom while the air left her lungs. But she might not die fast enough. She might still be alive when the first sharp teeth bit into her flesh. Might feel her body being literally torn apart in the strong jaws of the alligators. She'd see her bloody flesh floating away from her in the dark, turbid waters.

There was no way to stop Fred. The most she could do was kick him and perhaps turn the pirogue over so that he'd fall into the water with her.

A person's life was supposed to pass in front of them at a time like this. All Cassie reviewed was the last few days. She saw herself in John's arms. That was the image she'd carry with her to her death.

"It's time, Cassie. If you thought John Robicheaux was going to save you, you're all out of luck." Fred reached for her. She screamed and kicked at him as hard as she could. Fred fell backward, cursing as he did, but somehow he managed not to sink the small boat. He picked up the oar and swung it. It hit a glancing blow to her head and before she could regain her balance, he'd rolled her over the edge of the boat.

She heard the splash, felt the water as it slid over her and sucked her under. John would find her. She knew that he would. But he would be too late.

She kicked frantically, buying seconds of time, fighting to keep from sinking to the muddy bottom. Beau Pierre. God, she hated this town.

JOHN HEARD the scream and the splash. It was close by, maybe yards in front of him, around the next bend—or two. He poled with frantic, hurried strokes the way he'd been doing ever since he'd lifted his pirogue from the bed of his truck and slid it into the bayou.

Surely Cassie was still at the plantation with Annabeth. He'd be there in under ten minutes. He'd find her safe, but the scream…and the splash.

He saw the boat when he made the bend in the bayou and spied Fred Powell staring over the edge and into the water. The picture was clear. It had been Cassie who'd screamed, and she was nowhere in sight.

John zeroed in on the bubbles floating to the surface, then dived into the water and swam toward them. It would be too dark to see beneath the murky surface. He'd have to go by feel and pray for a miracle. When he reached the bubbles, he looked up and saw the silver pistol in Fred's hand, pointed at his head.

With one fell swoop, John tipped the boat over and ducked beneath the surface as Fred spilled into the water with him. Fred kicked and sputtered and one of his boots caught John's groin. He doubled over in pain, but didn't surface. The water was only about six feet deep, but darker than ever with Fred stirring up the mud. Finally, John's foot hit on something bulky, and he went down for it with the last bit of breath in his burning lungs.

He caught hold of Cassie's hair, then found her shoulders and tugged her to the surface. He half swam, half waded to the bank, slipping and falling with her onto the muddy bank. He didn't notice Fred until he felt the heel of Fred's boot cracking against his ribs.

"Nice show, John. Too bad it was for nothing."

Cassie coughed, choking on the water expelled from her lungs. John rolled her to her side, but kept his eyes on the pistol in Fred's hand.

"Make one move and I shoot the reporter first," Fred warned.

"The way you shot Dennis?"

"Yeah, but he was luckier than you. He never saw it coming, not until he turned around and watched me pull the trigger."

John reeled from the anger that ripped through him, then felt as if something had exploded inside his head. He dived toward Fred, tackling him around the ankles and knocking him to the ground. The gun went off, and the bullet grazed John's leg. He felt the pain, but it was no match for the driving anger and the knowledge that if he didn't stop Fred, he'd kill Cassie.

They wrestled for the gun. It went off again, but this time, it was Fred who took the bullet. Blood gushed from his stomach and the gun fell from his grasp.

John rolled away, grabbing the gun as he did. He didn't know if Fred was dying or not, but Cassie was lying face down in the mud, deathly still.

Panic burned in his lungs.

He fell to the ground beside her, rolled her over and started CPR. Seconds later she opened her eyes and started coughing again. He pulled her into his arms and buried his face in her wet hair. Relief had never felt so good.

"Where's Fred?" Cassie asked, between watery coughs.

"Over there." He nodded to the lifeless body. "Dead I think, but I'll go check now that you're breathing again."

John walked over and felt for a pulse. There was none and from the looks of the stomach wound, it was probably best for Fred that he'd died almost instantly. He walked back to Cassie, limping a little and still bleeding.

"You're hurt," she said.

"A flesh wound. No worse than getting snagged by a fish hook. You okay?"

He held her close, thankful that for once in his life he hadn't failed someone he loved. At least he hadn't failed her yet. "Let's get out of here, Cassie." He lifted her in his arms and carried her to the pirogue.

"I owe you my life," she whispered.

"No problem. I'm just glad I could make the party."

"Me, too. Stay around for the cake and ice cream?"

"I'll try, Cassie. I'll try."

It was a promise he'd never expected to make.

EPILOGUE

Six weeks later

CASSIE SAT on the edge of the dock at the trapper's shack at dusk and swung her legs over the water. An old gator half-hidden in the high grass didn't even give her a rise. They seldom did anymore unless she started thinking about the night she'd almost swam with them. But even then it was Fred Powell who gave her the creeps instead of the spiny reptiles.

John sat next to her, sipping a glass of wine and staring at the unopened present she'd brought him. "It's not my birthday."

"Birthdays aren't the only time people get presents."

"It's the only time we ever got them. That and Christmas, and you're much too thin and pretty to be Santa Claus."

"Wait until I show you a little of my ho, ho, ho-ing later."

"You could ho for me now and we could open the present later, or wait until I have one for you."

"No. Actually, I got a present of sorts today myself."

"From whom?"

"Dad. He's resigned from Conner-Marsh. It was either that or get fired, but he seems okay with it."

"Is he still seeing Babs Michaels?"

"No. She's taken another job with a company in Boston. He wants to sell the family house. He asked if I minded."

"Do you?"

"No. I want to always remember the good things about Mom, but I don't need the house for that."

"What will your father do?"

"Learn to relax, he says, but I don't believe that for a minute. He's taking some time off, but he's already been contacted by a London firm. I think he'll probably take their offer. I don't mind. I think getting away from Houston will be good for him."

"Is his moving to London the present you mentioned?"

"No, but his moving on with his life is. A person has to move past the pain and the mistakes or life is wasted. It's too short as it is and too precious to squander on regrets."

"I'm sure Annabeth, Norman and Fred would agree with that, especially since they'll be spending the next twenty years or so in prison. Angela will face charges, too, as soon as she's deemed ready by her psychiatrist after that failed suicide attempt."

"The secret destroyed all their lives," Cassie said.

"Not surprising," John said. "A conscience can only take so much."

"All that hype over the Flanders's lawsuit, and it never happened. The fact that Guilliot settled out of court practically went unnoticed when the much bigger story broke." Cassie experienced the same chill that always hit when she thought of her mother's death and the inhumane way it was handled. The DNA testing had come back positive. The hand found at the edge of the bayou had belonged to Rhonda.

"Knocked your ex right out of the limelight," John said,

swatting at a mosquito buzzing about his ear. "The next trial won't end with a settlement. You can count on that. Even Babineaux's acting like a real lawman now that the FBI is on the case, scrambling around to hide the way he shrugged off the murders and the attempt on your life."

"I'm glad, but I'd have never guessed Annabeth and Fred were behind the murders," Cassie said. "She seems so sweet when you meet her."

"I'm just thankful she only claimed it was Dennis's child she was carrying, to get back at her husband."

"And that she admitted everything," Cassie said, "since Fred didn't live to talk."

"She wouldn't have if she wasn't going for a temporary insanity plea. The latest according to the six o'clock news is that Fred had been blackmailing her to keep quiet about an affair she was having with a used car salesman in Houma. Then when she learned through her eavesdropping what had happened on May tenth, she'd paid him extremely well to help her make sure the secret wasn't leaked. She had him kill Dennis and Susan and he was supposed to get rid of you after she broke into your cabin and decided you were a threat. Luckily, Fred decided it was too risky to kill you that day in Cocodrie and then his shot at the cemetery missed its mark."

"And that you poled your pirogue to my rescue before I became food for the alligators."

"The once renowned Magnolia Plantation Restorative and Therapeutic Center destroyed by diabolical secrets, lies and greed."

"Annabeth claims she did it for love," Cassie reminded him.

"Then it was a very sick love." John set his glass on the dock. "Guess I should open the present."

"I think you're afraid of it."

"A little." He pulled the tape and paper from the package, wadded it into a ball and tossed it behind him. Finally, he lifted the top from the box. The nameplate stared back at him.

John Robicheaux, Attorney at Law

"For your new office," she said, leaning close and trailing his arm with a couple of fingers.

"I start day after tomorrow."

"Right there in the New Orleans's D.A.'s office, just a few blocks from my office."

"I'm giving it a try, Cassie. Not just for you. For me, too. But I can't promise anything."

"I know, John. And I'm not pushing. Lawyer. Fishing Guide. Burger flipper. I don't care. I just need you to work at us, to work at a future instead of being buried in the hell that used to claim your soul."

"There may be days I slip back into the old nightmare."

She nodded and scooted closer. Things weren't perfect yet for either of them. She still missed her mother, some days so much she walked around in a blue funk that she couldn't shake. He not only had his own past to deal with but the fact that Dennis had gotten involved in such an abhorrent conspiracy. At times John pulled away and crawled so far back inside himself she couldn't reach him.

But they were making progress. The sexual attraction was as strong as ever and the love just kept growing. John put his arm about her shoulders and kissed her, a long, wet, sensual kiss that thrilled her to her toes.

There were no guarantees, but she had John Robicheaux at her side, a lazy bayou at her feet and a sliver of a moon already climbing in the sky.

She'd take her today and hold the promise of tomorrow in her heart.

Forrester Square

LEGACIES . LIES . LOVE .

Secrets and romance unfold at Forrester Square...
the elegant home of Seattle's most famous families
where mystery and passion are guaranteed!

Coming in June...

BEST-LAID PLANS
by
DEBBI RAWLINS

Determined to find a new dad,
six-year-old Corey Fletcher
takes advantage of carpenter
Sean Everett's temporary
amnesia and tells Sean that
he's married to his mom,
Alana. Sean can't believe
he'd ever forget such an
amazing woman...but more
than anything, he wants
Corey to be right!

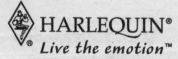

HARLEQUIN®
Live the emotion™

If you enjoyed what you just read,
then we've got an offer you can't resist!

Take 2 bestselling
love stories FREE!
Plus get a FREE surprise gift!

Beneath tropical skies, no woman can hide from danger or love in these two novels of steamy, suspenseful passion!

UNDERCOVER SUMMER

USA TODAY
bestselling author

ANNE STUART

BOBBY HUTCHINSON

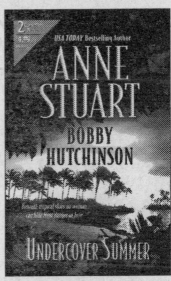

Two page-turning novels in which romance heats up the lives of two women, who each find romance with a sexy, mysterious undercover agent.

Coming to a bookstore near you in June 2004.

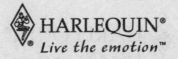

HARLEQUIN®
Live the emotion™

Visit us at www.eHarlequin.com

BR2US

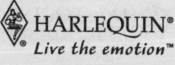